RED JACARANDA LEAVES

THE RIGHTS OF PASSAGE SERIES

Book One

CURTIS SAGWETE

For my dad.

CHAPTER 1

It was the dead of night and the only light that shone was that of the Sangoma's red eyes glaring through the cracks of his large mask. He carried a raggedy satchel with an assortment of rare plants he had picked on his excursion. On the other side, a large, dark and shiny horn with slick smooth curves hung on his hip. He resembled death with his pale ghostly skin, as dry as the northern desert. His long black nails cut through the shrub as he slid along the narrow pathway toward his little hut, deep in the depths of the Forest of Abominations. It was a dark and menacing place where the dominant sound came from crickets and lizards slithering in the bush. He could also hear the low growls of stalking predators, and if he listened very carefully, the quiet mischief of the evil spirited tokoloshe that roamed the deepest, darkest and most haunted regions of the forest.

"Hello," the Sangoma greeted, as he took a break from his strides by a tree. "How do I find you today?" There was no response from the skeleton that lay on the foot of the old and rotting tree in a pitiful pile with its mouth ajar. "The same? Oh good, I'm doing well myself. Thank you for asking. Still alive! Anyway, I have to be on my way. Hope to see you again soon . . . don't go anywhere," he grinned. "Goodbye." This was just one of the countless carcasses the Sangoma had discovered in the forest. Each had their own story, some more gruesome than others. This skeleton, he called Magoo. "Do not worry, I will find your arms and legs . . ." he reassured. "And then you can be at peace." He had scoured the area, but nothing had turned up. He would take his search to an unexplored zone, deep in the darkest and most perfidious parts of the forest. Maybe he would find them there.

Here in this detestable forest is where he lived amongst the giant thirty-foot crocodiles and venomous snakes. Sure, most of the fruit was poisoned and fetching water from the river was dangerous, but he had made the forest his home. The Sangoma had dedicated his life to the ancestors, thus *why* he asked, was he here.

When he arrived at his little hut, he reached into his bag to produce a boar leg and cast it to the porch. A hyena pounced on it enthusiastically, snapping the bone with one bite. *Take your sweet time Reza, gnaw on that juicy bone as long as you like so master can do the ancestor's work in peace.* The hyena looked up to see if its master had more treats. "I know, I know, Reza. The ancestors cast me here and didn't even give me death. I know what you are thinking, but their work must be done nonetheless."

He walked up the porch-steps, pushed the vines to the side and entered the hut. He had left a gigantic pot slowly simmering on a pile of logs, in the middle of the round room. He grabbed a large spoon, dipped it into the cauldron, lifted it and sniffed his amalgamated concoction. He wrinkled his nose, and cast the brew back into the pot. *Just a little longer.*

On the walls hang an array of vases and clay jars he kept his herbs and potions in. He had been called everything except brave and he was the first to admit it. Conversely, he had no qualms grabbing a venomous snake by the neck and pumping its deadly venom into his containers. He laid down his horn and took off his mask, revealing large protruding eyeballs. Pasty saliva sat on the edges of his thick red lips, which flapped as he turned to observe Reza trotting in, sniffing at the sack the Sangoma had brought home. The hyena's bushy black tail flapped wildly as the witchdoctor gave her a good stroke, and chunky beads of saliva fell from her mouth. He reached into the bag and took out a batch of leaves. Some green, some dark with luminous burgundy veins. He placed them on the cutting board and diced them into small particles, expeditiously. When he was done, he looked around perplexed. "My muddler, where did I put that thing?" Before he finished his sentence up came Reza with the wooden crusher between its teeth. "Thank you . . . dog." The hyena giggled and returned its attention to the bone.

After the leaves had become a mound about the size of his open wiry palm, he discerned a rumble in the bush outside. He peeked out the window and saw . . . *nothing.* As he sighed in disappointment he sensed another bustle. "It might be your lucky day Reza. More meat!" He grabbed his bow and arrow and darted out as the hyena gnawed at the bone. "Stay here. I would bring you along, but you are likely to scare the prey away, as ugly as you are." The Sangoma shook his head, disappointed. "You truly are useless. Be good for once and stay out of trouble. I won't be long."

When he returned empty handed, his red eyes widened. "I can't leave you for a mere moment without you making a nuisance of yourself, can I?" Reza had toppled some of the Sangoma's jars and vases over the cutting board and across the floor. "What have you done, dog?" He shook his head. "Why even bother anymore?" He picked a piece of the broken jar and placed it on a table nearby. "I'll clean this mess later. I am too tired." He grabbed a horn lying nearby and inserted a tuft of dream-root, using a small twig to pump it in and lit it aflame. *This is strange,* he thought between puffs. *Perhaps I left the root out for too long.* He coughed a little and then lit it again. He took another drag as he held the horn with both hands, exhaled, and then slumped into his chair, finally relaxed. Before he nodded off, he remembered he had to take in the hides he had left to dry outside behind the hut. He tried to get up, but something compelled him to stay where he was. His mouth became dry, so he wrestled to his feet and dragged them toward a wooden bucket. *What's happening to me?* He reached in and brought up the water over his face. It ran down his neck and crept down the cracks of his meatless back. He peered in and stared at the reflection. It reciprocated, its obscenely large round eyes protruding, as red as a tomato. He screeched in horror and tears followed shortly. He looked at the table where he had set his dream-root, then at the hyena. "What have you done to me, dog?"

Reza looked on discombobulated as the Sangoma paced around the room like a man afflicted. She giggled and whined, but the fallen priest took no notice. Suddenly, he began gurgling, then froze and collapsed headfirst. Reza ran to her master's side, sniffing and licking the mage's motionless body.

When the Sangoma came to, he was ascending a giant mountain, reddish copper. The mountain was so great the top of it was hidden behind violet and luminous clouds. Reza, surprisingly, stood in his midst. "What are you doing here? Okay then, since you're already here, let's go." Reza just stared. The Sangoma shook his head in annoyance and pointed into the distance, beyond a great river of molten rock.

Reza followed at his heels, moving up the mountain as his master gnashed his teeth. A boulder came rushing from the clouds, but the Sangoma was nimble of foot, hopping away to safety. He followed the footpath up the mountain until he got to a thin pathway with no barriers. He stopped and looked down. The fires burned violently as the acid fumes huffed creating mushroom-like clouds. He hurried along with both hands extended outward, struggling to stay balanced.

As he approached the end of the trail, he heard chanting up ahead. It started faintly, but as he moved closer and closer, it became clearer. It sounded like thousands, if not millions, chanting in unison. He found a small crack in the mountain and crawled into it, making his way through the narrow duct only big enough for a child. When he emerged, he was on the other side of the mountain looking down into a pit.

A host of thousands chanted, like a colony of bloodthirsty ants looking for flesh to sink in their mandibles. The Sangoma had never seen so much nakedness. It reminded him of the mortuaries he would frequent when he lived amongst man. A spirit emerged, levitating above the horde as they wrestled amongst themselves. The tussling was fierce and savage, like a pack of wild dogs all vying for a juicy bone the alpha had left them. The spirit wore a light red robe, with streaks bright and golden. It caught sense of the Sangoma and met his eyes . . . *Holy ancestors,* the fallen priest muttered as his bowels unleashed a smell so hideous even Reza disapproved. *He has seen me. I am a dead man,* the Sangoma fretted, as he trembled on the warm rock he lay on. The little priest looked to make an escape, but the ghoul's mercurial eyes pierced him again, not unlike a skillful hunter's arrow hitting the mark.

Behind the phantom emerged a giant creature, hideous in its nature and frightful to behold. Its long scaled neck shone a bright color, and smoke flared from its eyes. The monster dipped its head as it hovered over the wraith, now with its arms raised, with fire glowing from its fists. The monster snarled and lashed its teeth but it did not hurt the spirit. Instead, the leviathan cowered as the earth shook and a red object zipped through the skies faster than any animal the wizard had come across, even swifter than the strike of the black-mamba. It left a trail of smoke following behind like a shadowy fiend. Red and violet eyes flickered in the cloud of smoke, sending the Sangoma ducking. He tried to stay calm, but the craven in him wouldn't allow it. His teeth crackled and hands shook uncontrollably as he defecated on himself again and there stood Reza with that dumb look, with a vine of saliva dangling from the side of her chin.

The creature shrieked, like the many women the Sangoma had tended to during the gift of labor and other blood ceremonies he had performed. The sky flashed as the spirit sent bolts toward the creature until it began to shake irrepressibly as it grew bigger and even larger than it had once been before. Its breast vibrated as its claws slashed at the hot air. Another bolt shot, this time hitting the creature's forehead and then its eye.

Now he found himself in a swamp, and his body that was once covered in an assortment of animal hides, was now naked. The creature looked down at him in all its reptilian horror. *This is how the ant must feel, evading the giant footsteps of man!* The phantom was now hovering before him, left and right, in and around his arms and legs, through his mouth until it engulfed him before he exhaled, letting it out. There in front of him the wraith made an ear ringing screech and cast a finger at the cowering mystic. The mob turned and began to drag toward him. He wanted to defecate on himself a third time but managed to control himself. He turned and began to waddle away. His heart rate accelerated. They were gaining on him and the brackish water was rising by the second. He jumped and tried to swim, but he looked more like a swan in mortal terror, trapped in a crocodile's jaw. The forest dweller could now feel it caress his nose and then eventually, he felt it tickling his eyelashes. He closed his eyes as a certain halcyon overwhelmed him, and his feet left the earth. He was sinking slowly, and could see the light that once shone from the spirits bright robes slowly darken until he was kissing the lips of a dark abyss.

Although the Sangoma's body had transformed into a numb and pleasant state, he could barely make out a hand floating above him. He was now blissful in the underworld, but the hand felt so welcoming. It was soft and smooth, like milk, but sturdy all the same, helping him up until he feasted on the breath of life, and then almost instantaneously, the murk was gone as was the nakedness and the leviathan. All that was left was Reza's rough and smelly tongue licking his side, as his pet snake slithered over his legs.

He squelched as he raised his eyebrow up and down, with a look Reza had never seen before. The hyena giggled alarmingly and bared its thick yellow teeth. "Finally, I know what I must do." He tried to lift the hyena, but it was too heavy for the Sangoma's lithe arms. "Whatever you did while I was away was magnificent." He had embarked on several white-paths in his time, but none quite like this. He wiped the sweat that had settled on his forehead as Reza looked on, skeptically. "The ancestors have spoken to me and they are very angry." He grabbed his long-crooked staff and threw on whatever he found over his shoulders. He gave the hyena a resentful gaze. *You are useless. You don't have anything, or do anything . . . well, except this time.* He shook his head. "What is it? Oh, you are asking, what about the hieroglyphics in the caves we discovered the other day? That must wait Reza. We have more important business to take off. Our expedition deep into the forest must wait. It is time I finally returned home."

Reza stared mockingly, as thick saliva balanced unsteadily from the side of her snout.

CHAPTER 2

"Nia," a mildly irritated voice hollered. "You naughty girl, where are you? It's time we returned to the palace. Must it be like this every time?"

The little princess popped her head out of the vegetation and with great reluctance moved toward the motherly voice, plucking out the twigs and weeds that had made a home on her head. It had been just a few hours, but to her it felt like they had been there for eternity. She felt miserable every day she had to follow her mother into the woods picking flowers, guava and berries. She loathed the girlish chatter and the sweetly harmonized singing that went about as they filled their bowls with fresh water from the river that ran nearby. She found chatter about boys the most annoying of all. That was problematic because amongst her peers, it was that time in a girl's life that these things started taking precedence. She could care less how handsome and brave they thought this chief's son was, or how this general's son was in line to inherit a ranch worth a thousand cows.

Every afternoon she would steal away and borrow her uncle Machupa's spear whilst he snored under the shade of an umbrella tree. She would creep up slowly on her tip toes like a cat, and grab the spear by her uncle's side, doing well to dodge incoming bird droppings. Sometimes she would discover him with bird feces all over his face and once almost got caught when he woke up suddenly, and droppings flew into his open mouth.

It became a little game in the end, testing how fast and quietly she could 'borrow' the spear whilst his snores revealed a thick tuft of nostril hairs. At the back of the servant's quarters she practiced, reciting the graceful spear work her older brothers exhibited, and the back flips and somersaults they performed.

When her brothers happened upon her stabbing and swinging her borrowed spear in the air, fighting an imaginary winged lizard, they all laughed. Her youngest sibling, Alinafe had found it so amusing he laughed until a pasty white liquid came sniffling out of his nose. "Put down that spear dear sister." Atakachi, the oldest and heir to the Piripiri throne had told her. "You have well enough brothers to protect you. Besides, if you were facing a kongamato, a spear would be of no use. Hand it over."

"Step away or I'll hit you," she warned.

Atakachi chuckled nonchalantly. "That is like the moth challenging the flame, little one. You know I can't let you keep that. Whom did you steal it from?"

That secret would never break her lips, and not only for selfish reasons. Sure telling would ruin her daily access to a spear, the way her uncle Machupa drank, but also, she didn't want to get him into trouble as a man his rank was expected to carry his blade at all times. "How can a man expect to protect one's family from robbers without a spear," she once overheard, as her father, King Maghedzi, reprimanded his younger brother. "What do you think our enemies think when they see this? How is a king supposed to protect his tribesmen from invaders when he suffers one of his generals constantly misplacing his weapon?" The Piripiri took this very seriously and had Machupa not been the last of the king's brothers, he might have been a dead man.

"Come on Nia, cough it up," Atakachi insisted. "I don't have time for this you bony stack of elephant feces. Give me that . . ." He reached out to grab it, but Nia dropped a shoulder, sending Atakachi one direction and darted the other. The prince tripped and crashed into a comedic heap. The others laughed as he did his best to maintain the little dignity he had left.

Laughter greeted the queen, Zandile, Nia and their entourage as they were ushered into the Pyre Fortress gates, the heartbeat of the Kingdom of the Piripiri. Alinafe rolled around in the grass with the new batch of puppies Ata the bitch had begot. Nia's favorite was the one her brothers had named Ginger because of its reddish-brown tint around her snout. She adored its furry paws and the faint mustard-golden tuft of hair it had on its brisket. She begged her mother for one, but no matter how she flattered, behaved, or batted her eyes the answer was always the same. She felt forsaken by the ancestors and dare she say it, the fire gods themselves. She felt the guilt of blasphemy immediately, promising to light a locust the next day for forgiveness - and also for a puppy. The boys stopped their activities and waved. Queen Zandile, and her entourage waved back but Nia screwed her face in protest. Crimson covered the queen's dark copper hair. All the fiercest warriors and most skillful hunters from the deepest valleys in the Akuwa region to the highest canopies in the Uche Jungles longed for her. Only the bravest of men could stand to gaze into her almond eyes, but here her only daughter stood, with little prospects. Not with her un-kept hair and dusty cheeks.

Court was busier than usual, arousing Nia's curiosity. She liked to know things, however, sadly, she was ignorant. *No one tells me anything. Well maybe not everyone.* Her playmate Wafula would tell her things, but ordinarily, Nia had to rely on sleuthing for any information that didn't involve princes, babies or a recipe. A passel of strangers atop great zebras arrived shortly after. Some of them wore long robes with opaque patterns and similar colored hats. Others were bare-chested with large feathery headdresses.

Nia arrived as her father introduced the visitors to the rest of the family one by one as they stood in line. "This is my first wife, Zandile, Queen of the Piripiri." Zandile bowed obsequiously and clapped her hands. "This one here is Alinafe, the littlest from my Zandile. This one is Mukina and the young man there, is Atakachi."

Feathered headdresses bopped back and forth as they stooped their heads. "And who might this be?" one of them asked as Nia arrived.

"Oh, this one is Nia, my daughter."

"Hello," Nia greeted, suspiciously. "Who are you? Why are you here?"

The men chuckled, seemingly amused by the young girl's abrasive manner. The one with the lion claw necklace replied: "We are your father's friends, from far away lands. We have business with the eternal flame."

Nia noticed most of the men were carrying spears, and others, war clubs, very different to the ones she was accustomed to. Whilst the Piripiri spears were made of the shiny obsidian rocks from the slopes of Mount Pyyros, these men's were made of steel, blade and shaft. "May I see your spear?"

Maghedzi tightened his jaw irritably. Gesturing toward the queen to get Nia to shut up. It was unbecoming of a girl, a young one at that, to be asking such men of title, questions. "You must forgive us, esteemed guests. She is still young and yet to learn her place."

"No offence taken at all," one of them replied. "In our lands, it is not uncommon for a woman to have a voice."

The king looked at him strangely, like the man had recited a cerebral parable - Surely the man was just being polite, he decided. "Anyway, if you will, follow me to somewhere more private. We have a lot to discuss." Maghedzi led the way as the enigmatic visitors followed, leaving Nia alone on the thoroughfare.

"Nia, Nia. Look what I got!" Her friend Wafula trotted in, with two light brown kites made of sun dried goat intestines held together by a light wooden crucifix. "Look at the thread. It's so long. They're going to fly really high, just you wait," the boy smiled.

"That's childish," she snapped, dismissing him with the wave of her hand. The boy looked crushed as his eyes swelled. "I have a better idea. Lets go the Fire Caves."

"We can't. We're not allowed."

"Says who?"

"Says your father, the king."

"We won't get caught. I promise. You're just scared."

Wafula vehemently denied the accusations. "Fine, I will join you on one condition."

Dark berry juice flowed down Wafula's chin. It had taken some heartfelt apologies, promises and the luscious fruit to get him to follow her into the Fire Caves. It did not stop him though from protesting nonstop along the way as they meandered through a labyrinth of narrow pathways, chambers and cobwebs. Finally they found themselves in an oval chamber with beautiful paintings lined around the room. Nia lifted her torch. "The Ifirit," she gasped, "and why that is, the flaming spear," she and Wafula exclaimed in unison. "I think this painting here, is telling the story of the first men."

"I thought it was just a bedtime story my mother used to tell me when I was a lot younger."

"You're such a big fat liar. She told you that tale last night." She paused. If she didn't need her tongue, she would cut it off.

"You were spying on me?" Wafula's face flashed with the little anger his baby face could muster.

"I wasn't spying . . . I just overheard when I was passing by."

"So you were eaves dropping?"

"What? No, I wasn't doing that either. I can't just shut off my ears at will, you know?"

The boy shook his head in disbelief. "You are a strange one, princess Nia."

"And you smell like a hippopotamus," she slammed back, uniting the bridge over her eyes.

On the side was a wooden vase with a flame and spear carvings. She tried to open the lid, but it wouldn't budge. Wafula gave it a try, but he wasn't strong enough. "Give me that." She grabbed it back. Wafula did not like the look she bore as she stared intensely at the vase and felt uncomfortable the way she caressed it like it had cast a spell over her. Suddenly, a bolt of pain cut through the princess' stomach. She looked down and there on the dusty, stone floor between her legs was a small red puddle. She froze. *I can't let Wafula see me like this.* She had to do something, anything. "Here, you take this." She handed him the vase reluctantly. "I have to urinate. I'll go round the corner. Don't peek or I'll put a curse on you," she warned. "I will have a witchdoctor turn you into a toad."

Wafula screwed his face and covered his eyes. "Are you done yet?" There was no response, only his light echo. "You can't peepee and talk at the same time? Is it different for girls? Whenever I'm urinating with my friends around, I just keep talking, like normal." It was a while before he realized he was talking to no one.

The air was filled with music when Nia emerged from the Fire Caves. The feast for the foreign dignitaries had begun whilst they were away. Usually, she was enthralled by the smiles on people's faces and the sight of the drummers drenched in sweat from their enthusiastic drumming; however, now, all she saw was a maze of hellacious images.

Queen Zandile was leading the singing, magnificent as usual in her crimson headband with precious stones and golden studs embroidered into the sols silk cloth. Nia wished she could teleport herself on to her mother's lap, alas she couldn't go there. She tossed her torch to the side and disappeared into the night.

Hours later Zandile came bursting through the door raging. "What do you have to say for yourself young lady? Your father had to send a dozen of his best men around looking for you." The girl shrugged her shoulders. "Don't be sulky with me. What in the ancestors would make you run off in the night?"

Tears began to fall from the little princess's cheeks.

Zandile paused and studied her daughter's face. Then she sat herself next to where Nia trembled. She glanced at her feet, saw the cause of her daughter's fears, lifted her skirt and there revealed a stream of dried blood, crusted onto the young girl's thighs and down her legs and over her feet where the queen had first spied the girl's problem. She pulled the skirt back over, kissed her daughter on the forehead and hugged her tight.

CHAPTER 3

Comrade Chengetaii of the Amakazi was a wide-shouldered man with skin as dark as midnight and a nose that flared like a hippopotamus. He sported a thinly cropped beard and a shiny bald head with a silver tuft of hair on the crown. He was a familiar presence at court as the commander of the elite warrior group, Amakazi, sworn to protect the king and breed the next generation of Akuwa warriors. "You are late," he snarled as his nephew, the king's bastard, Xolani and a couple of other boys strolled in with bags under their eyes. Chengetaii's staff raised and before Xolani could make his excuse, the wood crashed hard on his upper arm.

The boy winced in pain. *Why me, why not the others too?* he wanted to ask. *I wasn't the only one late.* His mouth began to open until he caught sight of the commander's whites.

"Today juniors, we are going to practice spear and shield." He could hear the relief from the young hippos. Chengetaii had put them on a hard training regime for the last moon, focusing on endurance, with endless runs up and down the Akuwa Kingdom landscape. He whistled as he pointed his staff at Xolani. "Today you spar with me." He flung a blunt spear toward the boy, which Xolani caught with a fumble. The rest of the cadets spread out, Khaya the Glut paired with Xolani's cousin, Thokozani, Matata paired with Gumisa, and Batanai with Korokoro the Squirrel.

Chengetaii stood a few paces away from his nephew, but even so, Xolani felt like an ant at the mercy of man's footsteps. "I see you seem to think you are still lying on your mat? Perhaps this will wake you up." Chengetaii unleashed a quick jab, but this time Xolani was up to it, parrying it away. "Protective stance," he commanded. The boy did as tasked, shuffling his feet steadily into the earth. "Your positioning is wrong. Angle your feet boy. How many times have we been through this? We are not leaving here until you get it. Protective stance." This time Xolani's heel sank even deeper. "Better." The commander began twirling his staff with one hand, then as it got faster, his other hand joined in, creating a gust of wind that blew Xolani's cow tails backward, like he was walking toward a gale. "I've been watching you boy. Your level is unacceptable. You can barely hold your shield, let alone your spear right." Chengetaii whistled and soon thereafter, a boy came running with Dread, handing the war club to the veteran. The head was smooth and shiny, and on its shaft, ornate carvings of the ancient water dragon, nyaminyami.

Master and student took to their starting positions. "Higher," he snarled. "You want your knuckles level with your eyes." Xolani adjusted his grip and made some progress in getting the spear in line. Chengetaii swung Dread. The boy winced. "Loosen your grip on the shield. That way it will absorb more of the force." He twirled the club between his fingers before striking again. "You think you will go to the rites of passage at this rate? You are wrong. You do not deserve to even look at a spear." The commander came again. "Much better. Now attack me." Xolani kept his shield close to his body and stabbed low. Chengetaii flipped around his club and parried the strike with the tilt, and in a flash had the cold head of his wooden club resting on Xolani's ribs. "Now you are dead." This went on for hours. The commander was determined to take everything the young hippos had. They were a pathetic bunch in his estimation, but he meant to change that.

When he was certain he had taken the boys' bodies as well as spirits, in came a boy with a basket full of oranges. "We meet tomorrow at the same time." He pointed at Xolani. "This time, don't be late. You are a hippo, not a tortoise. Remember that. Dismissed!" Some of the boys started laughing. "And you, Matata, are no snail." That shut him up and the rest that hovered around him like flies.

He felt his stomach grumble and looked up into the sky. It was time he visited Chipo, who had promised him lunch. Unfortunately, he could not avoid passing the queen's royal compound where Queen Sibongile of the Akuwa Kingdom was scolding one of her servants. He hobbled faster, hoping she wouldn't spot him but alas, luck deserted him.

"Captain," she hollered.

Chengetaii gritted his teeth and stopped in his tracks. "How has your day been?"

He shouted back, "Very well, thank you."

"Please come in."

The commander could not turn down a queen's request. Sibongile clicked her fingers, and up came a servant with a tall wooden chair. Hippos, crocodiles and fish eagles were carved into its backrest and on the seat, smooth leopard skin. "Please sit, commander."

"I really can't, I have an appointment." He did not want to say. "I'm on my way to pay Chipo a visit."

"You visit Chipo, a mere concubine, yet you cannot visit your queen. What is that?" Sibongile smiled thinly, unctuously. "You and I are brother and sister. Once we were very close. If anything were to happen to our lord, you will become my husband. Is that not so?"

"My type does not deserve a woman such as you."

"You are too humble, Chengetaii. That has always been your problem. You are a prince, the brother of the king. Sometimes you should act like it. Like your half-brother, Munyaradzi, he takes what he wants." He hadn't been there for more than   five minutes, but it felt like five minutes too long. "Please stay for lunch." There was a loud screech and in swooped Koko, whom settled on the commander's shoulder, the swarthy color of burnt amber. "Your bird can stay too. We have fresh peanuts, boiled and cooled."

"Thank you, mom, but I promised Chipo I would eat at her hut today."

"That small hut? Why go there? Do you want diarrhea, Chenge? Who is to protect us if you fall ill?" she joked. Today she was simple by her usual standards with a hippopotamus imprinted blue dyed cloth wrapped over her shoulders with one of her teats pointing menacingly at the commander. She smiled and ordered a girl to bring some *umqombothi*. When the wench finally came, the queen screwed her face. "Did you go all the way to the Turkana to get the beer?" The servant looked at her flummoxed. Sibongile shook her head and cursed as her fingers snapped. "You would think as queen I would have the best servants, but that is not true." The queen was notoriously fastidious.

Chengetaii held the calabash with both hands, turned it upside and washed it all down, wiped his mouth and rose.

"Off so soon?"

"Yes, like I said, I have an appointment. Thank you for the *umqombothi*."

"Please come and see me again soon and send my regards to Chipo."

He nodded and hobbled off making his way through countless rows of huts until he found himself at the back ends of the Stone Houses. Compared to where the king's compound lay, as well as the queen's and other high-ranking members of court, Chipo's compound was comfortably unostentatious, with little huts tightly stacked around a great fireplace. Chipo smiled and waved as she stopped pounding the sorghum grains in the large wooden bowl. She wiped the effort off her forehead then set the large wooden rod by the smooth curved walls of her hut. She looked him up and down as she washed her hands until the white they had become, returned to a shiny burnt umber. "Look at you, you are becoming skinny. We need to put some food in your belly."

He tucked his head low and walked into the hut. He sat himself on a stool as a young girl came with a bowl and cloth for him to wash his hands. Before long the water had turned an ashen brown. He performed a silent prayer then stuck his fingers into the orange calabash.

Chipo shook her head. "That boy, Xolani. Lately, he does not even come home for lunch. He goes off somewhere, on that zebra of his. We should have never given him one. He is not ready."

"What's he doing? Has he found a girl?"

"I don't think so. It doesn't seem like it. A mother would know such things." She poured water into his cup. "Any news on the rites of passage? Have the elders made their decision?"

"I don't know," the commander replied as he chewed.

"What do you mean you do not know? Are you not on the council?"

"Yes, but the boy has to want it."

"The boy does. It is all he talks about when he is home." She meant to say it was all she spoke about.

"Maybe so, but he has to show it on the training grounds. Furthermore, he is often late. If the boy doesn't learn, he might sleep through a war."

"You are right brother. I will talk to the boy. I must apologize, you must be tired, and here I am, pestering you . . . mothers, it is our job to be worried for our children." He nodded as he scooped up a thicket of vegetables from the side bowl. "Any word from my brother, Batusai?"

"Nothing I'm afraid. He and the Green Rangers could be anywhere at the present moment, but I'm sure he is well." That was a lie. Being assigned to the Green Rangers was no better than a death sentence. The bush was dangerous, and often these rangers died by the hand of the animals they had been deployed to protect.

"Anyway, how is Farakaii? He has not visited me for ages. Could you send him a message? Tell him I love him." Chengetaii looked at her and tried to smile as he licked his fingers. "Has he asked about Xolani? Do you not think it's time he acknowledged him like a true son?"

"You know these things are complicated Chipo. He loves the boy, it is apparent to see when he talks about him. His time will come. Just have faith." He licked his fingers and stood up to make his leave with a swollen belly. "Of all the times you have made me pumpkin, this is the best."

"Oh, Chengetaii, you say that all the time."

"I cannot help it keeps getting better. Thank you for the food." He grabbed Dread and crept through the door. "I will relate your message to Farakaii."

"That is all I ask." She smiled heartily and off the commander went.

After his spirit walk, meditating in the quiet of the wilderness, Chengetaii thought to see how his older brother was holding up at court. It wasn't something he was particularly fond of. He was more accustomed to war strategy and the way of the spear. He left politics to the likes of Mutasa, Moyo, Shato and Sibongile. He grabbed his club and walked toward the king's shed, arriving as King Farakaii waved his hand, signaling the end of the meeting.

"What about the grievances of my people?" Everyone turned curious to find a young man with a thicket of creamy white and golden cow tails hanging from his neck down to his belly. "Heathens continue to defile the Crescent, fishing in lands that belong to my clan whilst my people have to make do with shallow streams and lackluster fishing routes. I cannot, won't allow this to continue. The other day, their men came, beat our boys and stole the fishing they had done for the day. They said it belonged to them. My son, my only son almost died in the struggle. Today he lies in his hut under his mother's care. How is she to allow me to enter her chambers, knowing her son's perpetrators have escaped justice? My boy has scarcely lived more than two fists."

"I advise you lower your tone and be reminded whom you are addressing. A tongue is a most valuable instrument," threatened Ganizani, the king's youthful personal bodyguard, considered by many the future captain of the Amakazi.

The king raised his hand but was as calm as the lull before a storm. "Lower your weapon Ganizani." The Amakazi grudgingly did as he was told. "You are that man Mudzamiri are you not? You are Akinukwa's boy. The tiger fish is your clan's totem."

"So then you would have heard of our sharp spikes."

Farakaii chuckled as he took a pause from his silver-bush laced pipe and studied this Mudzamiri, as licorice-laced smoke rose above him and into the air, seemingly amused by the liberality of his speech. "Why has your father not come himself, if this is such a grave matter?"

"Because he has passed," Mudzamiri answered, with dead-faced hostility.

That surprised the king, as it did the congregation. "Our condolences. When did this happen?"

"Not a fortnight ago."

"That is too bad, your father . . ."

"No disrespect, but save us the trouble."

The king took some time to study Mudzamiri. "Why do you come to me with this? Why haven't you gone to your local chief with this matter? The Salt-Fish Merchant, I believe. He presides over matters in those areas."

"My quarrel is with the Salt-Fish Merchant. Our people . . . my father, suffered him for too long, but I won't. He is fishing on waters that do not belong to him. They belong to my people, and have for generations. Ask anyone. Ask Sekuru Rwizi, he ought to remember." The ancient was considered by many to be the oldest man in the kingdom and beyond.

This matter was now proving trickier than the king had anticipated. "Very well, Mudzamiri. We have heard your grievances, and we shall look into this matter. Return in a fortnight."

That was not good enough for the man. "We have come a long way and might I add, not the first time. I demand satisfaction. Are my men supposed to sit and wait to fish in the waters their ancestors gave them whilst you . . ." Luckily enough for Mudzamiri, he managed to collect himself and remembered he was talking to the mighty hippo. His moustache shone as his lips quivered. His thick eyebrows were united, and his nose crunched, barely masking his boiled up fury. "Very well *mambo*, may your reign remain long and prosperous." With that, he bowed and slid backward, crouched, as his palms touched, and his white and golden skins brushed the stone floor. When he got to the exit, he turned, spat and walked off contemptuously. Chengetaii gritted his teeth, narrowed his eyes and began darting toward Mudzamiri with his club raised.

"Let him be," Farakaii commanded. Chief Akinukwa was an honest and upright man. For his father's sake, do not harm him."

Chengetaii looked on in disbelief. Many influential men of the region were in attendance: Shato, Mutasa, Moyo, and visiting chiefs from neighboring villages, land owners, merchants and men of title. It did not look good, the king being insulted in person with no ramifications, but he had made his disposition clear. "As you say," Chengetaii conceded grudgingly.

The king raised himself. "I am finished here. It is time I pray. Comrade Chengetaii, walk me to my chambers."

When they were alone, finally Farakaii and Chengetaii could be brothers. "I am worried about you," said Chengetaii. "You need more men around your hut. There was a harsh wind last night, did you hear it?"

"No, I slept well."

"That might be your undoing. I advise against it."

"One day you will come to me advising me against breathing the air."

"Jest all you want Farakaii. There was something strange about that wind, like it was carrying spirits of the wicked."

"What were you doing up in the middle of the night? Are you still having troubles sleeping?"

"Don't worry about me, we have other concerns."

"Nothing is more important than family."

"There will be no family if you keep this up. I warn you brother."

"Enough of this talk. I always found it frustrating your dedication to silence, but sometimes when you do open your mouth, I see why it is for the better." Farakaii took off his headdress, an assortment of sunstone, black pearl and serpentine feathers. "I will do as you say. Meanwhile . . ." The king pulled

Chengetaii close and whispered in his ear. Chengetaii nodded. "Tell Ganizani to not allow anyone in. I need to pray. No one shall disturb me under any circumstance."

"So be it." Chengetaii exited the king's chambers and relayed the message to Ganizani, posted outside the king's door.

"With my life, I swear upon it, commander. I swear it upon my ancestors." He was young and still eager to please, ambitious too, and protecting the king was a good way of picking up titles.

"Swear to whatever you will, just do as I have commanded."

Chengetaii's ear tweaked as he locked his sack onto the back of his great zebra and prepared to set out on the king's errand. The temperature chilled and a gust of wind similar to the one that had visited Hippo Valley the night before came howling in. He frantically rummaged in his sack, emptying the entrails onto the red earth. *Where is it?* the commander fretted. *I had it. I had it at the king's audience shed.* He was pressed for time, but he had no choice but to make the climb back up the winding footpath up to the top of the Akuwa hill where the sprawling stone civilization sat. "Wait here," he commanded one of his lieutenants.

When he reached the stone stairs at the foot of the large ominous gate and giant stone nostrils that welcomed newcomers, a golden bolt flashed in between the gloomy clouds that sailed by. Finally, he arrived outside his brother's chambers, Ganizani stood where he had left him, his dark blue Amakazi cloak wrapped around his shoulders.

"I didn't expect you to return so soon, commander."

"Nor did I." Oddly enough for Chengetaii, the boy did not make way. "Excuse me young man, but I need to go in."

"Sorry commander, but I cannot let you do that." The boy retained an air of inexorable equanimity that betrayed his meager years. "You commanded it yourself. You said no one is to disturb the king, under any circumstance. I made an oath. You are a fearsome warrior commander, but I fear the ancestors more!"

Meanwhile inside the comfort of his hut, King Farakaii set his pipe to the side, fell to his knees, and combined his palms. He was happy to get some peace finally. It had been a long day attending his people, from poor farmers to disgruntled landowners. He tried his best to be just on all his judgments, but sometimes it was hard, so he turned to the ancestors for guidance. Although there was a fire in his chambers, the air became cold creating goose bumps over the king's bare-chested body. He felt so small in the commodiously built room, like a spec in emptiness. He raised himself, but as he did, a blade zipped past his ear, taking a chunk with it. Frantic, the king turned to find two masked men, each brandishing deadly weapons. Out from the shadows emerged two more, masks more gothic than the first set. They seemed to be smiling behind their wooden canvases, but their eyes did not. A blade flew toward the king, but he turned his face imperceptibly, allowing the projectile to fly past him and into a pursuing assassin.

Meanwhile outside the king's confinements, Chengetaii's patience was running thin. He tried to negotiate as best as he could, but the young man stood by his vow. He had molded Ganizani himself into a fine warrior, and shared a similar preference for the club; however, he was no match for his experience and the boy had never seen true battle. Another bolt of lightning illuminated the sky, this time as ice-cold beads tapped on the commander's back. He snapped his teeth like a wild beast being challenged for the right to mate. He slowly paced forward, brandishing his war club, a club that had tasted Piripiri blood, Shumba blood and even some Uche blood. To the comrade's regret, it had also tasted hippo blood, and for that, he was sure the ancestors would never forgive. "Out of my way, junior, I have no time for your childish games."

As the commander threatened, a wail aroused both men's attention and then another one. The two men looked at each other, and then turned swiftly, kicking down the wooden door.

28

CHAPTER 4

Xolani was charged with the honor of slaughtering an ox in homage to the ancestors and the river gods that presided over the Akuwa Kingdom. Veterans idly sat on their stools as they exchanged sips of their fermented milk, whilst mothers gossiped as their infants dangled on their backs, strapped in tight maternal knots. "Look at that boy," one woman said to another, covering her mouth. "He is a little too spindly to be Farakaii's son."

"What you say is forbidden, but I see your point. Farakaii is fearsome and thick boned. This one here by Chipo, one cannot say the same. Simba and Themba though, they are true Akuwa."

"They say Farakaii favors her."

"Who, that Chipo? The hippo's concubine?" The woman shook her head. "Men sometimes. They cannot tell the difference between cow and dog manure."

When the local clairvoyant, a dwarf of a man covered in layers of hides had finished pleading to the ancestors the drum rang. The diviner walked up to Xolani with a maniacal grin on his face, and dipped a cow tail into his calabash. He looked deep at Xolani, clucked like a chicken, and waved the liquid onto his face. Xolani squinted his eyes irritably as he wiped it off, screwing his face from the foul taste that had found its way onto his lips. He collected himself and stood before the ox, his concave chest heaving back and forth. He tried to appear brave, but he was afraid on the inside. Despite that, he found enough composure to grab one of the ox's horns and lift his spear in preparation. Laughter erupted from a small section led by his half-brother Prince Themba, as it appeared Xolani's spear was too blunt for use. His other half-brother Simba, the heir to the Akuwa Kingdom, who stood cross-armed nearby tossed him his. "Good thing the ox can't fight back, isn't it little brother?"

Xolani ignored that. He was too enthralled by what lay in his little sweaty palms. *Now this is a proper spear,* he enthused. Everything about it was right, from the balance to the fine woodwork and embroidery. He was shaky at the start, but a smile from his mother, Chipo, helped him remain resolute. He wished his father was present, but he could not dwell on that. He counted all the ancestors he could think of and called upon them all, eager to demonstrate that a seed did not fall far from its tree, born out of wedlock or not. Simba's blade was so sharp Xolani barely applied any effort. *Masimbi* steel they called it. He kept his eyes open throughout the whole ordeal until he felt the warm, sticky, wetness engulf his hand.

After the honor, or rather, the trial, he needed a break from the congestion and noise that had settled around court so he tied his bag around his shoulder, whistled for his zebra, Shiri, and headed toward the banks of the River Khumalo. There he could hone his spear work in peace. He rode through the King's Gate, down the spiraling stone pathway and past the Hippo Valley market square until he was on the plains.

The wind bristled and the sweat scent of the Khumalo tickled his nose as he arrived by the riverbank. He found himself a good stone, took off his bag and raised his spear high above his head into the late sun and inspected it, cursing his luck. It was nothing like Simba's spear. If he were to make it to the rites of passage, he would need a new one. The dark ashen metal was dull and jagged from the rust growing at the base and the wooden shaft was so fragile, it was likely to crack from one fall.

After a few drills and exercises, he jumped on top of Shiri and began to leave, but the zebra wanted to go another way. He tugged hard at the reigns but Shiri's will was resolute. He caressed her by the breast and allowed her to lead him into the bush. They came upon several bodies lying in a canvas of blood. Some still had their eyes open and the gruesomeness of their deaths was apparent by their twisted faces. "Help me," someone, *or something* whimpered.

Xolani followed the voice until he was standing in front of a large bush, staring at two blood orange eyes. He displayed his spear and commanded it out. His voice broke into a high pitch, so he coughed and tried again, this time deeper. He was afraid, but he could see in the creature's guileless eyes, it was more afraid of him. It did as told, shuffling out slowly, revealing a shiny, serpentine body, a combination of grey and azure scales. It had an elongated snout with two large nostrils and sharp rows of ivory colored teeth. Two slick horns sat above its eyes and a row of spikes down its spinal cord. On its back were two small wings, folded like a bat and under it, four webbed talons. He had seen all the creatures in his father's dominion, but this one, he did not know. Xolani put his hand over his mouth and gasped. "What are you? Are you a . . ."

The creature nodded. "Yes, I am what you people call a nyaminyami. "But we refer to ourselves as water dragons."

"But," Xolani stammered. "You're small . . ." He realized it was better a small nyaminyami, than a large one. "You understand my speech?"

"You understand mine," the creature replied, similarly bemused.

"I grew up hearing stories about you . . . water dragons. But we were told you no longer existed, not since . . ." He didn't want to say, *Not since Goromonzi slew the last nyaminyami.* "What happened here to these men?" Some of them were women, he noticed as he looked around more closely.

"I was taking a swim when a fish appeared in the waters. I pursued it, but when I had my teeth wrapped around it, a net grabbed me and took me up. I tried to wriggle myself free, but I wasn't strong enough." The creature looked down embarrassed. "Then they carried me off. I don't know where they were taking me, but wild beasts appeared and killed them. They speared me. Here, could you pull it out of me?"

It hissed as Xolani pulled out the harpoon from its side. Smoke sailed from the wound. Xolani went into his bag and pulled out some herbs and cleaned the lesion. "This should keep away any infection."

Rather than the slimy moist he imagined, its scales were smooth like silk, but not slippery, and he could tell that under its scales was thick pulsating muscle. When he was done, he helped the creature back into the river. Its long tail, which comprised of about two-thirds of its length, went in last, creating a big splash that fell all over Xolani and Shiri. The water around the dragon turned a bright reddish maroon. "What's your name?"

"I don't have one," it replied, somewhat confused by the question.

"Everyone has a name," Xolani replied, slightly amused. "Very well, I shall give you one. From now on your name is Aku." The dragon repeated the name a few times until the side of its lips rose. "You are named after a great Akuwa warrior."

"What's your name?"

Xolani erected himself, put one fist on his heart and declared: "I am Xolani of the Akuwa tribe. My father is King Farakaii of the Akuwa . . ." His shoulders slouched when he came to the realization. "But, I am a bastard. That means my mother and father were out of wedlock when I arrived on earth."

"Your father is a king?" Aku was rather confused.

"Yes."

"So, you are a prince." The creature's eyes became sad.

"Have I said something wrong?"

The dragon did not reply. "I should return. Thank you for cleaning my wound, and all your help. If you need me, come to the river bank and hum this tune." The creatures black tongue lashed then began.

Xolani recited the song, but he couldn't get it right. He tried again and again until he could just make the first part. It took some time before he made it through to the end. Aku, laughed throughout the whole ordeal. "You are mean, laughing at me like that. You don't know how difficult this is."

"I'm so sorry for making fun of you, Prince Xolani."

That took Xolani aback. No one but his mother in private moments referred to him by that – *A prince*.

"It's just that, you look so funny trying to sing it. You should see your face. You look like a bloated fish."

Xolani waved his fist at the creature and tried again, this time making a better effort.

"Like I told you, you need to use your stomach. It comes from within. Yes, like that." Peculiarly, Xolani felt like a choir had descended from the heavens and joined him as the song became richer by the accompaniment of soprano, alto, tenor and bass. When the song was done, the ancestors ascended into the clouds and now Shiri's yip was all that was left. "Hum this tune whenever you need me, and I will be there." Xolani jumped onto the zebra and prepared to leave. "Can you promise me one thing? Please say nothing of this."

Who would I tell? Who would believe he had befriended a nyaminyami? Let alone one that could understand his speech? Xolani made a solemn vow, nudged Shiri with his heel and off they went.

He arrived last for dinner to the sweet aroma of goat stew and boiled pumpkin. Despite that, the home cooked brew could not mask the stench on Xolani's hands. His mother, Chipo, wrinkled her nose and looked at Xolani with an eyebrow raised. "What's that smell?"

Xolani took a sniff of his hands. "What smell?" He was a bad liar.

"What have you been up to young man?"

He wanted to tell the truth, but he remembered the creature's words. "I think Shiri ate something bad. She vomited. I had to clean it up."

Chipo was not satisfied, but decided to let this one go.

Her hut was brightly lit from the flaring lamps mounted on the walls that hang around the circular, compact room. The walls were dark and smooth and a fireplace sat in the middle of the space as wood crackled under the heat. Xolani, unlike his brothers was not in the succession line, for he was born a bastard, but he could join the Amakazi, the elite warrior unit his uncle, Chengetaii captained. That was easier said than done. One had to first prove their worth at the rites of passage. He was so tense about the prospect he sulked every time his mother brought it up. "Don't look at me that way son. I have not jinxed it. I have seen it," she reassured.

"You went to that witchdoctor of yours, didn't you?"

"Yes, his magic is strong. He saw it in the liquid. He showed it to me."

"And how much did it cost you this time, for these 'visions', another five chickens?" There was some light laughter in the room.

He was the rooster, one would say, amongst a group of hens, but he felt anything like.

"Mock me all you want but you cannot mock the ancestors. One day you will see, child. Come let us pray." Chipo raised her hands and began. "Oh ancestors, protect us all, protect us from our enemies and those who seek us harm. Bring us plentiful rains and ward off the locusts, drought, illness and most of all, the tsetse fly. Keep us safe from the serpent's fangs, and the beasts that prey on our people. Help us find a wife for Xolani and lastly, grant him acceptance to the rite of passage. Praise! Let us eat." Chipo handed Xolani a bowl, and his head sank until the wooden container was scraped clean, only to ask for more as he licked his fingers.

"So, how was your day young man?" Aunt Rabia inquired, dipping a large wooden spoon into the large cauldron and refilling Xolani's calabash. "How was it slaughtering your first ox?"

"It was okay," the boy replied, seemingly unfazed.

"Only okay? Was it not scary? Or exciting?" Xolani did not reply. "Very well young man. Anything else happen today? Nothing out of the usual?"

"No, not really. Trained spear in the morning, that's about it."

Chipo could not help but notice the bruises all over his thighs and side. She shook her head. "Is that what it takes to become a great warrior? Does Chengetaii have to drill you boys so hard? You look like you have been to war with the Piripiri!"

"He says we must suffer to become stronger."

"Your uncle is a good man and wise. You would do good to pay him heed. Why did you not perform your chores? We were expecting you. I ask you to help around, but all you do is go on your rides."

"Every time I come to visit," Aunt Rabia cut in. "Instead of spending time with your great aunt, you always go off. What is it you do on these rides of yours? You are just like your cousin. No sense!"

"Listen to your great aunt, she is right. You spend too much time in the wilderness, lazing around idly. Half the village is beginning to think you are mad. You are almost a man grown."

"Indeed, I was at your relatives the Sibanda's a few moons ago, and they have a very beautiful daughter. She is about your age."

Xolani raised his head momentarily, before it sunk again. If he revealed he had been talking to a nyaminyami it was likely they would take him to visit a necromancer. "Did I tell you how beautiful you are today mother?"

"Why thank you son. I acquired a new paste for my face, it works wonders . . . wait." Her eyes narrowed in suspicion.

"This boy is clever. Just like his father," Aunt Rabia laughed.

"If this boy keeps it up, he will be nothing like his father. You are mad if you think my sweet baby will be the laughing stock of the village. We need to start discussing possible arrangements. Your cousin Thokozani has just been betrothed to a lovely girl, and your uncle Rufaro, not much older than you, the other day married the Kastande's second daughter. Is that not wonderful?" She smacked him lightly on the back of his head.

"A fine young lady," Aunt Rabia concurred. "I was there at the bedding ceremony." She smiled revealing the small gap between her front teeth. "What were you telling me earlier Chipo? About the Piripiri girl?"

Xolani almost emptied the half chewed goat onto the smooth shiny floor. "A Piripiri? Never."

Chipo gave her sister the eye. She had wanted to reveal the possibility at a better time. Rabia could be a handful, but she always meant well. "Enough of that."

"Nonsense. Xolani is soon to be an adult. Soon he must remove his head from the sand. Speaking of that, I visited a very powerful witchdoctor the other day. He warned us to be braced for uncertainty." Rabia's harkening words were interrupted by a knock on the door. "Who would disturb us at such a time?"

"People these days," Chipo exclaimed. "No respect for the hour." She rose and walked to the door where she was greeted by beady eyes, one alert, the other half closed and sleepy. "Good evening Tariro, how do you do?"

"I'm afraid not too well, your grace."

"Oh my, what is it? Please enter, get yourself out of the rain." All he had was a leather pelt to protect him from the elements.

"The king, your grace."

CHAPTER 5

Gamu and his family had been walking ponderously for days, unshielded from the harsh rays of the unrelenting sun. Their throats were as dry as the sands they tottered and their soles throbbed mercilessly from the blistering heat. They could have done with a donkey to help carry their niggardly possessions, however, they didn't even have that. They were on their last legs and also on their last goat. When he looked at his wife's swollen belly he would smile, but when he heard his stomach grumbling, dread would fill his heart. What business did he have making children when he didn't have a home or security? He already had three and one was on the way. He wanted to instill honesty and hard work into his children, but that was proving difficult. How could he remain honest and upright when he could barely afford a few seeds? There was no point in being morbid though. They had been in this situation for almost a year now, and they had made it thus far. What he needed to do was dwell on the blessing the ancestors had laid in his wife, Tanaka's belly. *Is it going to be a son or daughter?* Gamu did not care. He loved all his children equally . . . even the one he had not sired himself.

They were fortunate they hadn't run into any bandits along the way. It was a great risk travelling between villages in a small group armed with the small hammers and picks Gamu used in his trade. He was tall and broad of shoulder, though hunger and the rigors of travelling had burnt away the fat from his body, exposing his piercing cheekbones and broad jaw structure. His eyes sunk into his skeletal sockets, and below them were dark shadows, like thick clouds announcing the coming rain. His oldest son bore a sturdy skeletal structure too and much like his father, most of his fat had eroded away. Despite that, with a pregnant woman, a young girl and an awkward, sickly boy, two men could not hope to protect them against well-armed robbers.

It was moments like these though, when they took a rest and the children played that he cherished the most. It made him sad, knowing it had to end, that soon they had to continue on their mission for food, shelter and work. He whistled and beckoned his eldest to help set up a fire. Before the night took over the day, the inferno was up and the aroma of the rabbit crackling over the flame would quench their hunger for now. "You have gotten much better at making a campfire, Chiiko," Gamu praised, crouched behind his son.

"Thank you, father. Your friend Yago really helped me. He told me what I was doing wrong and showed me how to make the flame last longer."

"That was very kind of him." Gamu was mildly startled.

"Yes, he is the best. He is very helpful."

When the fire was up and they had settled, the children asked for a story. "I don't know if that's a good idea, children. It is now late and we must continue our journey early in the morning."

The children looked to the matriarch, as they did when denied by their father. "Please mother, just one," they pled united.

She looked at Gamu and gave him a nod. "Okay, just one, but a short one." The group fell silent as the flames flickered in the pitch darkness.

"Very well, children. Should I tell the tale of the arrogant tree?"

"Oh, not that one again," Chiiko voiced.

"Or should I tell the tale of the dead cannibals that roamed the savannah looking for human flesh?" Both Gamu and Chiiko growled savagely sending Kayalethu and Kushinga into a wild shriek.

Tanaka squinted her eyes. Loudness could arouse the suspicion of jackals and night spirits. "Enough of that, boys. Tell them that tale about the nyaminyami. That is more appropriate, don't you think?"

"Yes, of course . . . sorry." He scratched his neck and cleared his throat, then began. "With scales as dark and shiny as obsidian rocks and a tongue larger than a python curled around a thick tree branch, the nyaminyami commanded all life in the aquatic world. Before the Akuwa had made what is now the Stone Houses their seat, they settled by the banks of the River Khumalo, but fell under the rule of the usurper, Gorekai'Yi of the O'Ziumbe, after he slayed Farakaii the Full Moon. Gorekai'Yi decided to construct a dam despite the Oracle of the High Bushveld, Mezahkulu's warning.

"Do you know why they called him Farakaii the Full Moon?" Kayalethu cut in. Gamu shook his head.

"Because he only ruled for one."

"Quiet, Kayalethu. Don't interrupt your father," Tanaka reprimanded. "Or anyone for that matter, in the middle of a tale."

Gamu continued. "The oracle warned the usurper that the nyaminyami would not allow it, for it would disturb the balance of nature, but nonetheless, construction continued. Halfway through the building, the sky suddenly darkened, the air dampened and the waters that were once calm became fervent. The chief and his men had to hold onto their headdresses as the wind howled, harkening a frighteningly loud screech that killed every bird in flight. From the feathery canvas emerged the nyaminyami as its tongue lashed like a whip. There stood Gorekai'Yi next to his three sons . . ."

"Apologies father, but can I interrupt just one more time?" It was hard being mad at Kayalethu, not when she smiled like that. Tanaka had the same smile, but Gamu hadn't seen it for a while. He nodded solemnly. "Seven sons. Gorekai'Yi had seven sons." Kayalethu was smarter than her age would suggest.

Tanaka normally would have reprimanded the girl's petulance, but her husband's storytelling had seduced her into a trance – by the crinkling at the side of his eyes, and the animated fashion his jaw would stiffen and relax as the tale wove along. These moments reminded her that despite his shortcomings, she truly did love him. When she finally came to from her spell, the story was well on its way again.

"In front of the leviathan atop his half complete dam, Gorekai'Yi took out his bow and sent several arrows toward the creature. It roared and lashed its tail sending a small boat into splinters, then flung its jaw toward a fisherman's boat. The village folk screamed in horror, as did the men from the pain of decapitation. Next the nyaminyami turned its attention to the half built dam. It whipped its tail back then lashed hard, over and over until the construction disappeared to the bed of the Khumalo. The creature returned to its grave, but not before it unleashed a flood of epic proportions, drowning hundreds. For days, Chief Gorekai'Yi waited by the riverbanks hoping his sons would return to him. On the third day, Mezahkulu approached the chief as he sat by the riverbanks, peering into the dark waters, searching, waiting. What was he waiting for? He did not know. His sons were dead because of his foolishness, because of his arrogance. He thought he was greater than nature. The oracle instructed the chief to make a sacrifice. One hundred of his finest calves were slaughtered by the riverbanks and their blood released into the waters. The next day inflated corpses decorated the riverside when the first fishermen arrived. It took all morning, but finally the chief had recovered his sons. Gorekai'Yi died thereafter from grief and the seat returned to the Akuwa."

"Why was the nyaminyami so mean, father?" Kushinga began to yawn.

Gamu scratched his head. He thought he had already explained this. This happened every time he told a tale. He just wanted to finish the story and be done with it so the children could go to sleep. He knew he did not have the means to support another child, but Tanaka was already pregnant. Before he had a chance to answer the boy, he and Kayalethu were well asleep.

Of the children, now only Chiiko was awake. "What happened next, father?"

"I'll finish it another time. It's time to go to bed. We must continue our travels before dawn. I need you to be strong for all of us. I am counting on you son." The boy nodded and laid his head on the mound of grass and twigs he had fashioned into a pillow and slept.

Kayalethu usually had trouble sleeping, however, the last day's travels had taken a toll on her. Other nights when her siblings' heartrates matched the song of the black, she would stare at the stars and overhear her parent's private conversations. It happened more than she would have liked. The night was their solace, a time when the children should not witness it, but Kayalethu did. Gamu and Tanaka tried to keep a brave and united face in front of the children, but a quick glance behind the drapes exposed the truth.

Once they were happy, but bad luck had put a heavy dent on their marriage. Tanaka was upset Gamu had turned down work as a laborer, carrying heavy bags of manure. He had assured her they had to stay strong and wait for something more suitable, but Tanaka had grown impatient. He could build weapons and construct furniture. He could even do pottery. His dream was always to own his own shop where he could work creatively all day with his son as apprentice . . . *or my daughter.*

Sometimes when the family was settled, he would spontaneously decide they had to leave. He would convince Tanaka they would be all right for the next few months. By then he definitely would have found decent work using his wood talents.

"That's what you said several moons ago, and here we are. This is not the first or second time you have done something like this. You are so reckless and irresponsible. Remember that time you lost work as a carpenter when you broke your thumb fighting with that man?"

"He insulted you," Gamu protested. "I was defending your honor." She shook her head in disappointment. She had a good argument. They were cold and hungry. He knew she was just as scared as he was, but he had to take a chance. He was getting older, if he didn't do it now, he never would.

Tanaka had suggested they return home to her parents, but that was out of the question. He wasn't willing to swallow his pride and return to his wife's village with his palms open begging for some grain. He had a better plan.

"Not again with this Yago and his stories. I don't like him. Whenever you two are together you return home smelling of beer."

Gamu didn't want to get into that now. *It's not even the point.*

"I don't trust him. I don't like the way he looks at me when you are not around. While you were at work he came by the hut and asked if there was anything he could do to help us. I told him we were okay."

"Listen Tanaka, there's a man in Hippo Valley who runs a utility store, Mzilikele. He is a relative to Yago and Yago told him about me when he visited. He is a master woodsman, and he's looking for a man with my skills. He means to expand his business. It's perfect for us."

"You mean perfect for you."

Where does she get this? All I do is for my family. How dare she, I'm raising a child that isn't mine! He wasn't going to bring that up, not ever again. Last time he did, she slapped him hard. When the neighbor ran in to see what the commotion was about he stooped towards Gamu in respect, revering his right to discipline his disobedient wife. Gamu spent the next few days trying to avoid his neighbors. "Please don't turn this into another argument. Yes, it is what I have always wanted to do, but it is stable. It is what is best for the family. Accommodation shouldn't be hard to find once we have settled in, and we can build a little hut and have a decent plot of land to plant our crops. Trust me, it's going to be great. Wait until you see the Stone Houses, the homestead of the Akuwa royals. They say it is impregnable, only succumbing to Changamire and his mighty elephant, Bazeka." He thought some general knowledge would melt the frost in her gaze. He looked up to meet her eyes but they were still suspicious and full of malice. "We must have faith. The ancestors do not reward those without."

Tanaka wanted to trust her husband, but her hungry children made it hard. It seemed sometimes, she had no choice but to trust him and have their fate in his hands. "Do you still love me, Gamu?"

"Of course!"

"Even now, after I have mothered six offspring? Sometimes I just feel like you see me only as the mother of your children, not your wife."

"*Mudiwa*, don't ever say that again. I love you more and more as the years go by." Gamu used his rugged finger to dry her tears from her wet cheek. He found his hand cupping her breast, continuing down her body until one of the children had a bout of coughs.

Tanaka pulled his arm away, smiled at him and gave him a kiss. "Time to sleep, the baby needs rest as well."

"Good night wife." The couple lay side by side, with Tanaka held tight in Gamu's embrace. As he slept he felt a slight shove on his back.

"Gamu," Tanaka whispered. "Are you awake?"

"Yes *mudiwa*. What is it?"

"Let's go to Hippo Valley."

"Are you sure? Is this what you want?"

She hesitated and then nodded. "Yes, I want you to be happy. You are my husband, and I am your wife. I will follow you wherever you go."

"I am so lucky to have you. I am truly blessed." He kissed her lightly on her forehead. Albeit for just a moment, Gamu smiled as he looked around at his little brood, sleeping peacefully. He wanted to give them the world, title, respect. He wanted to give them something they could hold long after he was dead and one with his ancestors. *Now let's hope I can find Mzilikele before it is too late.* They were a couple of days away from Hippo Valley. *If I do not get this work, we are all doomed. Ancestors if you are listening, help me.* Finding some sleep now would prove more difficult.

CHAPTER 6

Prince Themba woke up in a panic, late again as his head throbbed mercilessly from the last night's gallivanting. He needed something to help him overcome the attempt on his father's life, so sought some comfort from *umqombothi*. In his dreams, the mighty hippo fought valiantly, holding the attackers back, but as he stomped and trampled on his foes, others formed, until the king was surrounded by a ring of violet tinged flames, that crept closer, and closer, until he and Comrade Chengetaii swooped in, and extinguished the flames with a hail of cylindrical and half-moon strokes.

He looked to his left to discover a woman lying cozily under the layer of animal hides. He rubbed his head. He had hoped she would be gone when he awoke, but that was not to be. He wiped the drool from the side of his mouth, yawned and gave the young girl a shove. It took another one before her eyes finally opened. Themba welcomed her to the living as he tossed her earrings onto her lap. "Why are your earrings wooden? My mother's and sister's are made of pure gold and silver," he asked in apparent solicitude.

The girl shrugged. "Not all of our parents are kings and queens."

Themba was perplexed. "As you say Tsitsi, that's your name isn't it, Tsitsi?" Themba grabbed his spear, inspected it, making sure no one had molested it whilst he slept. "My mother has plenty lying around. I'm sure she wouldn't miss them if I gave you a pair. You are too beautiful to be wearing such shoddy ones."

The girl's breasts rose as she lifted her arms to yawn. It was a warm morning. Her body glistened with sweat like she was a mirage imagined by weary desert travellers. Themba had to be on his way, but the temptation to stay was too much. He put down his spear and crept back under the hides.

"But Themba, didn't you have princely business to take care of? Who is to govern?" She had to forcibly palm his hands away from her lap. "Your father . . ."

He interrupted her protests with a soft finger and brushed it slowly up and down her lips. "Hush now. My father can wait. He won't notice anyway." Themba was startled by his openness. It was unlike him to discuss his feelings, especially ones concerning his father with a wench with wooden earrings. He slipped his fingers under the hides and moved his way toward her nether regions. There was a sudden knock on the door. Themba tried to ignore it as he moved his other hand on to her stomach and proceeded until he had her breast firmly clasped in his hand.

"Themba, someone is knocking."

"Forget it. They'll go away, just ignore it." Now he was nibbling softly on her neck as he caressed her thighs. The salty taste of her skin felt good to him.

There was another bang on the door. "Themba, wake up."

"Quiet, it's my brother." He jumped to his feet and frantically searched for his garb. "Just a moment Simba, I'll be right out." *By heavens, where did I put my spear?* It was hiding under a hide he had thrown onto the floor carelessly during his passions. He picked it up and turned to the girl. "I hope to find you gone when I return. We do not need a scandal." She nodded quietly, as she coiled about on Themba's soft mat. He reached into his pouch and tossed her a copper piece.

"I don't want your copper." She threw it back at him.

His eyes widened as he frantically placed his finger on his lips. If they were discovered, his mother would punish him for sure. His father would do worse. There was another knock.

"Stop being such a baby," she teased as her hand disappeared. "That is no way for a fearsome prince to act, scared like a little rabbit." Her eyes rolled backward. "It will heal."

Themba partially forgot his brother was waiting for him outside, banging on the hard wood like a spurned lover at a rival's door. Blood trickled down the bridge under his nostrils and settled at the top of his plump lips. He licked it off and took to the door. "I have reconsidered. Upon my return you'd better be laying there waiting for your prince, just as you are."

She smiled the most mischievous of smiles. "Yes little hippo, and perhaps next time bring your brother. I hear you two are inseparable and in the cover of the night, I won't be able to tell who is who. Two hippos are better than one," she giggled.

Themba tried to smile, but it came out awkward. "Sure," he replied, and exited.

Simba greeted him outside with disappointment in his eye. "Rough night little brother?" Simba handed Themba a horn of water.

"Don't you have something stronger?"

"Haven't you had enough?"

Themba ignored his brother's condescending tone and continued sucking. It felt good on his tongue. It wasn't beer, but it would do.

"What were you doing in there? You have been acting suspicious lately." When they entered the shade of the large jacaranda tree, with its plum and orchid leaves spread out across its balky veins, Simba grabbed his twin, applying a tight head lock, rubbing the back of his head with his bare knuckles. "Come on brother, I want to hear all about it." Simba pondered for a moment. "You have a girl in there don't you?"

"Let go of me," Themba irked in pain. "It hurts, you piece of hyena dung!" He wriggled free, but it took great effort.

"Calm yourself brother, it is merely jest. What's with you today? You're usually more of a laugh."

"Just let me be, I'm not in the mood. I was doing nothing, overslept that's all."

"Are you sure?" Simba revealed a chipped tooth grin. "There's nothing you want to tell your brother?"

"How many times do I have to say it? I have a headache. I'll tell you all about it later. We need to make haste. Father is likely to kill us."

"Correction, Themba, kill you – he sent me to come and get you. This is one killing you will endure alone."

"Why didn't you wake me up on your way?" His eyes began to swell.

"Brother, you have to learn to do things by yourself. When I am king, when I am away, you will rule in my stead. What if something were to happen to me? Look what they tried to do to father."

"Enough with that nonsense. Nothing will ever happen to you . . . or father." Themba had taken the attempt on the king personally. He wanted to have been there to protect him. "Not as long as my spear hand is able."

"And I the same." Simba put his hand on Themba's shoulder and looked at him, a mirror image. "It will be tough at first. I cannot recall any moment where you weren't by my side, but we are not children anymore. Soon the desert locusts will descend upon us ushering in the draught and with that, invaders. We will need to be strong. That is the only way the tribe can survive."

Themba nodded meekly. *You're always right aren't you Simba?*

"Did you say something, brother?"

"No, nothing. Nothing at all."

Two Amakazi greeted Simba and Themba at the entrance to the king's audience chamber, bowing as the young princes appeared. King Farakaii's body glistened as a servant tended to his wounds from the botched assassination and rubbed red oil up and down his legs. Adjacent to Themba sat the feared General Shato and next to him his son Taonga, Princess Nonkuleko's newly betrothed. Next to them sat General Moyo, various high-ranking members, and Sekuru Rwizi. Though the ancient spoke in a ponderous whisper, as the most senior griot in Hippo Valley, his word was revered so highly people would silence themselves, and strain their necks like giraffes reaching for the highest figs, to hear what the ancient had to say. Chief-Treasurer Mutasa sat next to him in his fine garb, as ever quick to offer his hand to the ailing ancient when required.

Ganizani, the young Amakazi crept into the hut, crawled to the king and whispered in his ear. The way his father received the information, Themba knew life was just about to become more interesting. Jorro Moyo, the son of General Moyo appeared at the entrance. The young man crouched until his cowhides caressed the floor and hopped closer to where the king was receiving his daily grooming. "Our father," the young man began as he fell on his face.

"Have you apprehended him?"

Jorro nodded.

"Well what are you waiting for then? Bring him in for all of us to see, so we can question him." A man with a ragged sack covering his head was ushered in and pushed onto the hard stone floor as he kicked and struggled.

"Here is the treacherous cretin my lord. We found him northeast, by the Python's Creek. When one of my informants sent word of a stranger spending frivolously at a local tavern not far from the Lion's Den, I knew we had found our man. However, when we arrived, he somehow got wind of us and escaped from our clutches. Nonetheless we caught up with him in the end. We believe he was headed toward the Eagles Nest."

Farakaii pulled off the sack covering the suspect's head. "Who are your other conspirators? We know your spear is clean. We know that all you did was house these men and their property." The king's eyes widened when the prisoner tried to speak. "You took out his tongue?"

"Yes *mambo,* he tried to escape and accused you of many abominations, too heinous to say here." Jorro walked toward the mighty hippo and whispered in his ear. The king listened attentively, nodding his head. "I beseeched he hold his tongue and wait for your justice, but he couldn't. I had no choice. If I had let him continue, he would have cursed us all."

"Do you think I perform these vile acts my brother has relayed to me?"

"Of course not. Never!"

"Then why remove his tongue, young Moyo? Is his tongue more valuable attached than not?" Jorro stuttered, lost for words. Farakaii was a formidable man and was now visibly peckish. His nostrils flared wildly as he glared at the young Jorro.

"Seems someone was desperate the man remain silent," suggested Mutasa.

"I resent such claims you make against my son," General Moyo rebuffed. "Let us settle this outside. I will not suffer weasels like you accusing my kin of conspiracy. I'll eat your heart, you hear that, boy?"

Mutasa, ever so calm replied, "No one is accusing anyone. Though your response suggests someone guilt ridden."

What was there to be done? The man's tongue had been cut off and thrown into a bush for the ants and lizards. He wasn't going to grow one back. Farakaii had given them instruction to apprehend the suspects alive, but two had turned up dead and now the third, with no tongue to confess. The king had always been suspicious of the Moyos and their motives and had encouraged his sons to be leery of them. They were an old family whom had emigrated from the south many generations prior. They came with their own regiment of well-trained warriors and had initially been a thorn to Akuwa chiefs, until Kubulani the Consolidator unified the region. Sure Farakaii was supreme ruler of the Akuwa Kingdom, but he still depended on the strength of other clans.

General Moyo raised his voice first. "Let us be done with it and hang him. Hang him from a jacaranda tree by the gates so that every passer-by sees it. So they know that this is what happens when you go against your king."

"But your excellence, if I may," Mutasa politely interrupted. "Should we not keep him alive? We could learn more about his co-conspirators. Somehow, there must be a way. Let us not be bloodthirsty and too quick to draw blood."

"That's because you have never wielded a spear. You lack bravery. You and all your ilk," General Moyo spat back.

"Enough," the king shouted, bringing both men to their knees. He hovered above them with his spear in hand, seemingly in deep contemplation. Mutasa could not help but notice its sharp serrations glisten threateningly. He was in a nice elegant cup, neatly bowed, but you could tell by the bead of sweat on the aging general's forehead, he was finding the crouching painful. When the king was satisfied by their submission, he waved them up. "Then what do you suggest, chief treasurer?"

"Give him to me. My men will have him talking in no time, no time at all."

"Are you blind, treasurer?" inquired General Moyo.

"Not at all," the treasurer replied, somewhat taken aback by the general's insinuation.

"The man is without a tongue. How does one confess?"

"Dead men do not talk and neither do those without tongues . . . but they can illustrate."

"Preposterous!"

"We cannot prove he is guilty either," Prince Simba silent until now voiced, as Themba watched casually. "All we have is the ivory and the rhino horns we found on his person. The ancestors teach us to be certain when dealing with the judgment of death."

"What do you know of the ancestors, young prince?" General Moyo looked similarly bemused by Simba's words. "There are still many things in life you must learn, like this man," he said and pointed his finger at Muchita, "is guilty. Look at him. It is as clear as day. Even if he isn't, what difference does it make? Like you said, the ivory. The thoroughfare yearns for blood. They are asking themselves, what is Farakaii going to do? Our neighbors are already beginning to think we are becoming weak. They smell blood. Heed my words. A clear message must be made."

General Shato had been silent until now, like a python basking on a rock, taking in an afternoon sunbath. "The elephant and the rhino remain sacred animals," he whispered. "Cursed is he who taints their spear with the blood of these creatures. I propose we send him to the Forest of Abominations. There he can be the spirits' problem."

Muchita's eyes widened, and his face turned white with fright – like a cadaver. The stench of feces and urine now engulfed the king's audience chambers despite the sweet licorice smell of silver-bush that sailed from smokers' pipes as it wreathed around the room. The prisoner twisted his fingers. It was all rather perplexing to the chiefs and elders in the room, but after a while, Simba understood. He rummaged in his satchel and produced a rock with sharp edges and handed it to the defendant who knelt and began scribbling on the floor.

In obvious discomfort, Rwizi had already started making his slow shuffle to where Muchita knelt and inspected the scratches. "I think it says" He paused to cough. "It says he wants a trial by combat."

It was before noon, but they had been served enough surprises to keep them satisfied for the next two moons. Farakaii raised an eyebrow. "You do realize when you die, and you will surely die, your body will be quartered and thrown into the four edges of the Forest of Abominations and your parts will be ravaged by scavengers, your eyes will be plucked out by vultures and your skull will be the home of snakes and insects. Your soul will roam in eternal terror, constantly chased by dead cannibals and a tribe of tokoloshe." A fearful murmur sounded in the room upon hearing the frightful name of the creature. "Furthermore, your wife and children will never find solace, only the shame you shall leave. All your property, though it is not much, will become the property of the Akuwa peoples and your children will inherit nothing."

Muchita nodded.

"So be it." The king raised his spear, a blade so sharp he used it to trim his beard in the mornings. "So, who is eager to avenge his king? Who will carry out this justice on my behalf?"

Just when it looked like Ganizani the Amakazi was about to make his declaration, a voice rang out: "Use me as your instrument of justice. I will not fail you." The whole room turned. Themba stood up, cleared his throat and with a cracking baritone proclaimed his spear against Muchita. "I will see to it his blood stains the earth." The crowd raved in shock . . . *skepticism.* Themba, though physically strong for his age, was at the end of the day but a boy. No one saw this coming, not even Themba himself.

"Sit down, son," the king commanded. "We all admire your courage and devotion to carrying out the people's justice, but I cannot allow it."

Themba cleared his throat again and pleaded for the room to fall silent. He was going to have his moment. "I am now a man, father. I proved myself at the rites of passage, returning home with a dozen lion pelts, one which I wear this very day. Not many can claim such a feat." Numerous nodded their heads, acknowledging the prince's exploits. "I have also taken a girl. Several even." The crowd laughed, even harder when Themba reached into his loincloth, pulled out his private parts and gave them a good boisterous tug. "You can ask all the young girls, some mothers too, how man I am."

"Put that away," the king commanded. "Spare us of your perversions. There are men of title in this room. You will act with dignity, not like a clown. We already have that position filled so there is no need for this, if it is meant as an audition. Besides, Adele the Craven was known for leaving his spear in battle and also having a member as great as a donkey."

"Forgive me, father, it was merely jest, but the truth remains, it is my right. Any man able can be the spear of justice, and as I exhibited, I am a male. Besides, Goromonzi the Nyaminyami slayer was only two fists young when he defeated half a dozen bandits with a herding staff."

Rwizi, undetected, had shuffled himself to the center. He caressed his beard, an entanglement of course white hair and raised his staff. "I am afraid the boy tells it true, mighty hippo." The room fell silent. Listeners mystically moved forward despite themselves. "It is the law, since the old days." Rwizi paused and exhaled the most horrible of coughs. ". . . Given to us by our ancestors and the basis to which this civilization has thrived since we emerged from the Khumalo. Themba has made the challenge, and it is only up to him to release himself from his oath."

Farakaii frowned. For the first time in a while, he felt powerless. Although he was the mighty hippo, he too like all men answered to the ancestors. "Have you come to your senses, son?"

"The ancestors say a man who walks up to a lion and challenges it must stand and fight because he is lost when he turns his back and runs. You taught me that father. I am your son and will die before I besmirch your name with idle threats. I mean to make this man pay."

Muchita must have been shocked by the turn of events. He had been expecting to face one of the king's fierce warriors like Chengetaii or Tulu the Water Dancer, however, the ancestors had chosen a fresh-faced boy who had barely sprouted pubic hairs. If he killed the prince, he would be deemed innocent in the eyes of the ancestors and would thus be able to keep the ivory. Who needed a tongue then? He could spend the rest of his days wealthy, with many wives.

"Very well, Themba, if this is your wish." The king turned to the congregation. "With a heavy heart I have been left no choice but to sanction the trial."

Mutasa rose and bowed his head. "My lord, I propose we postpone it to the Festival of Tusks."

"I concur," General Shato lisped, bowing graciously. "Such an event would bring thousands more to the festival. It would be great for our markets and generate some much needed gold."

"But this is my son we are talking about. I will not allow it to be a spectacle."

"But my lord," General Moyo interrupted. "Not only is this man a mutinous conspirator, illegal poaching is not just an offence to the ancestors, but an offence to the community as well." The congregation nodded in unison. "The people have to witness the justice. They demand it, so they too can quench theirs."

The king took a deep breath. "Do as you will. If the boy weren't mine, the decision would have been an easy one. My late father, resting with the ancestors, taught me to rule by example, as did his. Justice and fairness must be uniform, no matter the number of titles." The drum beat, ending the meeting. "You are all dismissed."

General Moyo stood up. "Your excellency, I want you to know that my best men will look under every rock until we find more co-conspirators. Also, the issue of the diamond mines, and hunting permits. I have many petitions I need to discuss with you."

"You are all dismissed," the king reiterated, this time louder, barely looking up. General Moyo understood fast, bowed and slid away.

Themba's heart sunk when the mighty hippo finally looked at him. "What are you waiting for? Be gone from my sight and sharpen your spear."

When Simba finally emerged from the king's audience chamber a few minutes later, Themba asked curiously what their father had said to him.

"Nothing you need to worry about. The words between father and son are sacred."

"But I am his son too."

"You are, Themba, but right now he is disappointed in you. It's up to you to earn his trust again."

When the twins were alone, Simba unleashed a quick jab, connecting hard with Themba's lip. Soon thereafter, the wind was knocked out of his stomach. He knelt down, desperate for air, but before he knew it, a foot flew his way. Themba landed on his back, spread out like a star. Simba hovered over him covering the sunlight that had been blinding his vision. "Why are you doing this brother? I fear for your life. I will never forgive myself if something happens to you. You are my little brother. I don't want any harm to come your way." He stretched his arm out. Themba rubbed his bruised lip as he sat on the earth, his eyes as sorrowful as they had ever been. "Father and I worry for you. I know you'll win, I have practiced spear with you every day since we were strong enough to hold a stick. I just know it . . . but, as your brother, I can't help but worry. Have you thought how mother will take this? Sekuru Rwizi has been sent to her hut, just in case she falls ill with grief when she hears."

Themba hadn't thought about that, but in time she would understand when he stood before the tribe with Muchita's head aloft the adoring crowd.

"Come, embrace me broth . . ."

As quick as a flash, Themba unleashed a fast right, knocking Simba off balance, sending him hard into a large clay pot behind him. Simba groaned: "Good one, little brother, produce the same punch against Muchita and it's as good as won."

"That's the thing Simba. I will always just be your little brother."

"But Themba we are equal. We came into this world together, hand in hand. You and I are the same. Sure I will rule, but only in name."

"You will never understand." Themba shook his head and walked away leaving Simba rubbing his jaw.

CHAPTER 7

They were close. Gamu could feel it. He was after all returning to the land of his fathers. He could see the large waterfall that lurked behind the Hippo Valley plains, and if weather permitted, one could faintly make out the giant walls that protected Akuwa royalty in the Stone Houses. "Careful now children," Gamu warned as they cooled their bodies by the riverside. Carelessness was a crocodile's best friend, the wise men taught. It wasn't uncommon to hear tales of children, even some grown men larger than Gamu, dragged into the current never to be seen again.

As he contemplated their next meal, the earth began to shake and a herd of cattle thundered past in great haste. *That's odd*, Gamu thought. The commotion had rattled everybody's nerves. "Stay calm. It's probably nothing, just some renegade cows. The owners are sure to catch up with them later and return them to their cage."

Tanaka looked at him and beckoned him to the side for a small chat. "What if they do not have an owner?"

"What do you mean?" Gamu replied as he casually scratched the rash on his neck to his wife's irritation. She had been worried when it showed up, but alas what could they do? The little he had could barely pay for food, clothing or shelter. Where was he going to find the copper pieces to buy some herbs from a witchdoctor to relieve him of this ailment?

"I mean," she continued, looking around making sure the children were far enough to not overhear them. "If we were to take one, the owners would be too grateful to have their cattle back to care that one was missing."

The look on Gamu's face turned from uninterested to appall. "Have you gone mad? Do you know what they do to cattle robbers around here?"

"Yes, I know what they do," she replied as she rubbed her husband on the chest.

"I don't think you do. If you did then how can you ask this of me? Is this what you want, for me to get killed? Not to mention what they would do to you and the children after." Tanaka began to cry. He looked down at her dark brown eyes, almost black when she was upset. He did not like being harsh with her, as delicate a flower as she was, so lithe and petite. Despite that, he offered her no respite. "A man's relationship with his cow in these areas is sacred. These people, Tanaka, they are different from you and I. A man's life is worth very little to them." Her cries turned into sniffs as she gradually calmed herself. Gamu pulled her close and embraced her. His long limbs made it look like he was a daddy long-legged spider with its tentacles around its prey.

"I am so sorry, Gamu. I don't know what I was thinking, for even suggesting that. It's just . . ."

"Hush now. It is okay. Everything will turn out well, I promise." Gamu wasn't sure he believed that himself.

A while later a heavily panting man, hairier than any man he had seen before, appeared round the bend. Gamu immediately grabbed his pickaxe and commanded Chiiko to do the same. When the man was close he fell to his knees and crawled toward them like a hound. Tanaka quickly grabbed a skin of water and watched as he drank thirstily. "Do you have any food? Perhaps some fruit," the stranger asked. The Savannah was often an unforgiving terrain, especially at that time of the year. The majority of the trees Gamu and his brood had passed had been picked dry and every plant, desiccate. Tanaka reached into her sack and took out a half-rotten guava. As soon as she had given it to him, it was gone.

As the strange man sucked frantically on the skin of water to the children's amusement, Gamu pulled Tanaka to the side. "He's a criminal," he whispered.

"What? How do you know? He seems like a decent man in need of help, like us."

Gamu put a finger over her lips. "Lower your voice." He looked to make sure the children were okay. "Look at his sack." Just peering over the edge of its mouth was the tip of a creamy white object.

Tanaka's eyes grew wide. "Ivory," she blurted out, shocked.

Gamu quickly covered her mouth, lest they alerted the weary traveler. "Just trust me for once."

She looked at him like he was asking for much. "Okay then, what should we do?"

He used his eyes to direct her toward the children and turned to the traveler. "What was your name, stranger?"

The man hesitated and coughed as he beat on his hairy chest, no less impressive than the densest parts of the Domboshawa woodlands. "Erm, Dingani, my name is Dingani."

Gamu took some time to study his face. It was a mundane one, like any you would find around village thoroughfares, with thick hair flowing from the sides of his jowl. "You mean like Dingani the Bobcat?"

"Yes, just like the Bobcat, Dingani."

"Oh okay. Well, nice to meet you. We've been travelling in the wilderness for a few of days now."

"I'm so lucky I ran into you. I have been running for days without food and little water. Which way are you and your party going? I have nothing to give."

Perhaps some of that ivory in your bag, Gamu thought.

"But perhaps I can help you with directions. I know the region well. I could even knock a day off your journey with some short cuts."

"We are going to the Lion's Den," replied Gamu.

Tanaka's eyes grew wide. What was her husband up to? She thought they were going to Hippo Valley. Had he been lying to her again?

Dingani began to laugh. "Are you suicidal? I wouldn't recommend taking that route. The only thing you will find there is bloodshed. I was at a village just off the Lion's Way, where the Akuwa Kingdom meets the Shumba. Beasts run amuck, and not your typical large cats. I am talking the supernatural. I've seen it myself. It was dark and the beasts moved so fast but I saw them all right. I hid behind a large rock and watched as they devoured everything in sight, women, children and even men great in stature. I watched as a child got torn apart in front of me, limb by limb, and soon thereafter, the mother. One of them leapt up onto the thatched roof and from there it saw me."

"So what are you doing alive?"

"I've asked myself that everyday since, but what I can tell you is, I remember hearing a drum, however faint it was. My sister always said I had good hearing. When we were children she used to call me Dog Ears. Such was my talent. Sometimes I would hear things no one could, but it was more painful than anything. It made my stomach hurt. Anyway, why am I telling you this?"

Gamu thought the same.

"There I was, curled behind that stone, as this night creature growled. I could barely see them, but I could hear them. Even their heartbeats. Solid thuds, like the morning drummer. However, as dark as it was, when it roared, the red of its tongue illuminated the night sky. The roar shook the earth as its blood soaked companions followed suit, each as grisly as the other. I soiled my loincloth, this one that I wear today, as you would, if you were there! Fortunately for me the ancestors answered my prayers. The beasts suddenly turned and followed the faint drum deep into the night. If I were you I would stay away from that area at all costs."

Gamu found the story improbable, but there was something in the man's eyes that made him wonder. "Sure. We will stay away from there."

"Good. So, tell me about yourself." Dingani poured some water over his head, and shivered as cold beads trickled down his sun-beaten back.

"I am Gamu, and over there is my family. The little man on the left is Kushinga. He is my youngest. The tall one next to him is my eldest, Chiiko and the little lady is Kayalethu. I'm a woodman. Give me a tree, a saw, a few nails and hammer, and I'll make whatever you want . . . I mean not right now, considering the situation, but keep in mind, if you need a new kitchen table for your hut or a door fixed, I'm your man." Dingani nodded dismissively. Gamu continued nonetheless. "I was born in a small village in Hippo Valley, but I haven't been here for many years. That there," he gestured toward his family, "is the only tribe I need. Everyone greet Dingani." They waved reluctantly. "So friend, how about some *umqombothi?*"

"Yes please, I was wondering when you would ask, but make it quick. I need to be on my way."

"Yes of course." Gamu went to fetch it. It wasn't the best beer to begin with and the sun beating on it did not make it any better, but it had to do. "What business are you on, to make you in such haste?" Gamu took a sip himself before he passed it on to the strange man." When Dingani had two hands around the leather skin, and mouth planted over the mouthpiece all the way down to its neck, he was too preoccupied to see the large bony fist heading his way. Gamu couldn't have hoped for a better strike. He hadn't had to use his fist in a long time. It seemed like time had slowed as the man who called himself Dingani, flew back, landing a few meters away out cold pasted on the dusty pathway, spread out like a new born child.

When Dingani came to, Gamu stood above him with his sandals, an entanglement of brittle wires and cheap hide, pressed hard on his chest. He grated and tried to force his way up, but Gamu's foot stood heavy. Beside Gamu, a younger face appeared, mid or early twenties with long frog-like lips and a deep cleft on his chin that resembled a zebra's bottom.

"Get him up," a voice commanded. The young man made to grab this Dingani, but Gamu stood in the way.

"Who are you and what do you want with this man?"

The frog-like man screwed his face, appalled by Gamu's assertiveness. "I do not answer to peasants like you, boy."

"I am no boy."

In truth, Gamu was dressed not too different from the herd boys that tended their father's cattle. The man tried to shove Gamu out of the way with the back of his palm, but he had underestimated the wiry travellers strength. He did not try again. It was not worth the humiliation as his others looked on. "I am Jorro Moyo, son of Jocko Moyo, chief of the clan Moyo and General of King Farakaii's third regiment. This man," Jorro pointed down at Dingani, "is a fugitive and now my prisoner."

"I see. Who is he?"

"He goes by the name of Muchita . . . a peasant farmer from what we hear, and a traitor."

"He told me his name was Dingani. I knew he was false."

Jorro burst into laughter. "Dingani, you mean like the cat?"

"Yes, I know."

"You have good instincts, traveler. They're all the same, his kind. A truth from their mouths is as rare as the ghost lion with its red fiery eyes." He studied Gamu then looked at his family who up until now had only been spectators. Jorro smiled as to dilute the sting on his insult.

Two men jumped off their zebra's as Gamu finally moved out of the way and set Muchita on his knees, tied his wrists behind his back and began striking him with the blunt ends of their spears. Jorro meanwhile took off the rug that hang over his round shoulders and slipped off the bracelets about his wrists, so he could join the brutality.

"Please stop, I had nothing to do with it. I am innocent," Muchita pleaded.

"Then what are you doing with this?" Jorro lifted the sack worth at least fifty cows.

"I thought, I thought . . . It's not mine. I was only holding it for someone else. Some men . . ." he fretted. "They came to me, they gave me a few gold pieces and said they just needed me to keep it for them for a few days." He looked at Jorro. "I didn't know who they were, I didn't know they would . . . you know . . ."

"Enough peasant, keep your mouth shut and come with us."

"I'm not going back. You're going to kill me, most likely torture me first. Do not think I am stupid. My fate is sealed. Curse your father's house." Amongst the Akuwa, this was the worst thing one could say to another.

"Take it back," Jorro threatened. "Take it back or I'll take your tongue." Muchita did not. Jorro's eyes widened into perfectly shaped spheres, little beads in a sea of white. Gamu looked back at his family to make sure they were okay. When he turned back,

Muchita's tongue was flying in the air. Gamu had never seen anything like it. He was saddened his children had to see that as well. They were too young to witness such viciousness. The youngest started crying, but Chiiko didn't seem too fazed but rather enthralled.

Blood was soon plastered over the soil. Muchita clucked like a chicken, unable to scream as blood oozed out from his mouth and over his chest. To Gamu's surprise, Jorro's men found great humor in it. "This is disgusting. I want no part of it. Shouldn't he get a fair trial? This is just barbaric."

Jorro shoved him to the side. "This does not concern you, peasant, be on your way." He pointed toward the pathway as blood dripped from his spear.

"If what I have heard about King Farakaii is true, he would never stand for this. The village folk profess how noble and wise he is."

"You know nothing, peasant. This man is a fugitive of the law."

"Says who?"

"Says I. Your better," Jorro poked, flabbergasted by Gamu's gall. They had been hot on the illusive Muchita's trail, but had been sidestepped at every turn, until now. They were all tired. He could not suffer being questioned by a beggar. He meant to take the suspect away swiftly, with little fuss. "Take your wretched brood and be gone from my sight," Jorro sneered, trying his best to darken his voice.

"You're right . . . it was none of my business until I caught him for you. My family and I are not leaving until we get compensation."

Gamu put a sturdy hand on the young man's shoulder. He had never seen such ugliness as Jorro's cleft deepened and his eyes squinted into smaller, darker beads. It was uncustomary for a peasant to touch noblemen unless permitted, but something kept him defiant. He was prepared to go to fists if need be but it would never be a fair fight.

"Sheath your weapons brothers." Jorro smiled and quickly reached for his side. Gamu's heart froze, but instead of a dagger, Jorro unveiled a bag of copper pieces.

Gamu felt its weight, tucked it into his loincloth then said: "It's not enough. I want more."

Jorro chuckled until he saw the peasant meant what he said.

Gamu could see the confusion on the faces of his children and the fury on his wife's. She came running and fell on her knees and pled. "He means no trouble . . . It is the sun. It has beaten hard on us. He does not mean anything. Please, Gamu let us go."

"Stay out of this, Tanaka." He turned to Jorro. "Your reward is generous, but it is not enough. This Muchita I captured is worth more than a petty thief."

Jorro studied Gamu up and down. "Far less greedy men have been stabbed and thrown into the Forest of Abominations." He paused. "But humor me. What more do you want?"

"I want you to help my family and I through the capital gates."

Jorro laughed hard. "Is that all? I thought you were going to ask for a hundred cows or something and then I would have had to kill you, and then enslave that lovely family of yours." He smiled at Tanaka and then his brood. "Yes, you do look like a group of vagabonds. Hippo Valley is the greatest city known to mankind. We are selective about the type of people we allow into our human and genteel protection."

"Sure. There is a man there I seek. His name is Mzilikele. Perhaps you might have heard of him? He is a great woodsman."

"Does this man know you are coming?"

"Oh yes. A good friend of mine, a former neighbor, Yago, notified him of my impending arrival."

Jorro found the story hard to believe but there was something about the peasant. He liked his courage. "It is going to be tough." He thought for a moment, fingering his cleft. "Very well peasant, grab your measly possessions. Men, help these people, we are taking them back with us."

Gamu could not believe it. He wanted to cry tears of joy, but he had to control himself.

They arrived the next morning, entering the gates as the suspicious guards manning the barricades saluted as they rode by. "You're on your own from here, woodman. My journey continues. I am going up there."

There it was, up on a hill high above the Hippo Valley thoroughfare. *The Stone Houses*, Gamu muttered, mouth agape. It was the home of the Akuwa royals. Gamu had never been there, but he remembered his mother describing it to him when he was a child. He remembered her vivid description of the narrow alleys and the ancient architecture made when man used stones as tools. "Thank you for the help, Jorro. My family and I greatly appreciate it. You will get no trouble from us. Isn't that right Chiiko?" The boy nodded shyly.

Jorro gave his rein a strong tug and kicked lightly with the back of his bare heals. "I would say goodbye, but something tells me destiny has other plans. Stay safe Gamu and out of trouble."

CHAPTER 8

Queen Zandile did her best to maintain a motherly air, the personification of decorum as she held court. "I want to thank you for the sack of pumpkins you sent us, mother," thanked a woman, ashen of hair and several years older.

"You are welcome priestess, but it is my husband you should thank. He worries so much for the orphans. Their wellbeing is very dear to him."

"May the ancestors continue to bless our beloved king's reign."

The queen gave the priestess a brusque dismissal before Sekai, her oldest friend and trusted aide, announced the next visitors. A man and woman carrying a child were ushered toward her and fell on their knees. The man presented himself and began: "Most beautiful and righteous queen, this is our first born, it is a girl. We have travelled the whole day so that you may bless it."

Sekai collected the child and placed it in the queen's arms as she sat. Zandile smiled as she held the baby, peering down at it as they locked fingers. It sent memories flooding back, back when Nia was just a baby. Of all her children, giving birth to her was the most laborious. Whilst the others had come out willingly, Nia had taken days and a handful of the land's best midwifes. She had screamed so loud, perhaps hoping her husband heard her cries wherever he was, be it ruminating on the slopes of Mount Pyyros, reaving by nearby villages, or hunting game. Of all her children, he had only been present for the first and even then all he did was lift the baby's miniature loincloth and confirm he had begot an heir. Instead, Zandile took comfort in Sekai, who had always been there as long as she could remember. Zandile had wanted many daughters, but the ancestors thought it wise she only have one. She too was the only daughter amongst the Moto chief's brood. "She is very beautiful, my sons will fight over her in the future, just you wait and see." Zandile paused, allowing the congregation to laugh heartily. "What is her name?"

"Yeni, after her grandmother," replied the father.

"That is a beautiful name. What do you desire for Yeni?"

"We pray she finds an upright husband and produces many sons, as numerous as the stars."

"Is that all? *Do they not want more for their child than to be a breeding creature?* Nothing else comes to mind?"

The father scratched his head, as though summoning all his brainpower. "Oh yes. May she fetch a good dowry? Many, many cows," he chuckled, using his hands for emphasis.

The queen shook her head in disbelief, but the proud new father still had that stupid grin on his face. "Very well then, let us close our eyes." Zandile rose. "Bless this child, may she grow healthy and strong, and become a good, moral and righteous child, one that abides to the will of the ancestors and the spirits of yesteryear. May no evil come near this child and may it find a husband with a good dowry." *May what happened to me, never happen to this sweet child,* she muttered under her breath. "Go and be blessed." The young family thanked the queen, bowed and slid off.

Zandile was now spent, although it was just past midday. She would have to rest later, for it was time to prepare supper. "Where is that child?" Nia was supposed to have been with her, observing and learning what it meant to be a queen. "When you see her, send her to my compound." Sekai nodded and continued her duties. *I hope that child is not making a nuisance of herself, with that boy.* Zandile shook her head and made way to the queen's compound.

She arrived just as Atakachi, her eldest, and Mukina, her second-born arrived from their hunt. She smiled as Atakachi approached her with an antelope perched on his shoulders. He smiled back and threw the animal in front of her. Its blood from the open wound smeared the copper earth into a rusty brown. "I see it has been a successful hunt," she exclaimed, examining the animal. It was a fine acquisition with large spirally twisted horns, and its belly, which was once white, was now a mixture of red and misty rose smudges.

"It has," Atakachi could not deny, and his teeth glistening in the sun said it all. In Mukina's hands were some rabbits he held by the ears. "It is not much, but he is still young and eager to learn from his brother. He almost got a boar, but it escaped in the last moment. I am sure he will get one next time. Won't you Mukina?" The second in line to the Piripiri throne nodded shyly. He wasn't blessed with the sureness Atakachi was born with, or the natural charm that made everyone who came across Alinafe enthralled.

Zandile accepted the gifts and began skinning the rabbit, discarding the hair, guts and head as her sons sat under the jacaranda tree next to the kitchen hut. The antelope, she would save for later. Its preparation was more arduous, and she wasn't in the right mood. The horns she would use to make medicine for fever, the meat, she would use to feed visitors she was expecting. When the boys were settled, she brought forth *umqombothi*, which they accepted graciously. As they drank, Alinafe, but a fist of age came skipping along. He had smelled the aroma of the rabbit cooking, and knew supper wasn't far. He was the greediest of the bunch. *It is good*, Zandile thought. The boy did need some more meat on his bones. "Where is your sister?" Alinafe shrugged his shoulders, seemingly not caring. He was now wide eyed in fascination of his brothers' spears, long, with razor sharp black stones gleaming in the late Pyyros sun.

When she was done cooking, a bowl of warm water went around the boys to wash their hands. She prayed for the food, and then began to eat.

"What's for dinner?" Nia appeared at the door. Her plate was already prepared for her. "Ooh, nice, rabbit and pumpkin." Before she sunk her fingers into the bowl, Zandile gave her a stern look. "Oh. I forget."

"You always seem to," Zandile replied.

All Nia could do was smile and do as tasked. After washing her hands, she sunk them in and began to eat.

"You've been making a nuisance of yourself, haven't you?"

"No, I haven't," the princess replied with a mouthful.

"You missed the morning meetings."

"Oh, that was today? I forgot. Sorry, mother."

Zandile was not sure about that. "You must promise not to miss the next one, or you will be sorry. How are you supposed to know how to run a household and govern your people if you are always getting your knees dirty and idling away?" Nia promised she would not miss the next one, but Zandile was not convinced. "A good visit to a witchdoctor is what you need. Perhaps they can find what's wrong with you."

Nia's nose wrinkled. She turned around to find Uncle Machupa staggering in with red eyes, and a haggard physique, like he hadn't slept in weeks. Zandile shook her head. "Hello brother, I trust you have had a productive day."

"Yes, very productive," he stammered, taking a swipe of his skin. Zandile went into her hut and came back with a plate for her brother-in-law. Machupa's was a sad story. Unlike Maghedzi, he was gifted with a naturally homely face, but he drank so thirstily, his looks had evaporated despite his moderate age, not much older than Zandile. Whilst the king was short and squat, Machupa was naturally slim with long legs, but his nonstop drinking had given him a round stomach and spindly arms and legs. His face hallow, and hair, patchy and uneven. Despite that, the children, especially Alinafe was fond of him. "Where is my brother?" Machupa inquired.

"Only the ancestors know." Zandile replied. "He is either in the Fire Shrine praying, or looking into those damn fires up on the slopes of that hideous mountain." Zandile was not from Pyyros. The mountains quiet rumbling and the smoke it exuded was something she could never get used to.

"My brother needs to learn to enjoy himself sometimes," Machupa slurred. "There is much to be enjoyed in life. The stars, the moon, *umqombothi*, and the beating of a good drum." He hollered for more beer. " . . . Love." He gesticulated toward Zandile, who moved away before his hand could reach her thigh.

"I think it is time for you to go brother," Zandile said. Machupa rose from his stool, wobbled like he had rickets and took down some beer. Before he could say his goodbyes to the children, he fell backward and before long he was snoring. There was laughter, and even a smile from Zandile. "Children, help your uncle to his tree. Let him wake up there for Maghedzi to find when he decides to come home."

Prior to their marriage, Zandile had been warned Maghedzi was rigid and cruel. At first, he was anything but. Outside he was a warlord, however, inside Zandile's warm hut, the same one in which the king was raised, he was a baby again. They became confidants in family and state matters. She had his ear as she did his heart. She remembered fondly the stories he told her, cusped in his arms. Stories like the 'Curse of the Chameleon', the 'Rabbit and the Baboon' and legends of the fire gods from Pyre Mountain, Gyiku'o and the first men.

Legends had it only one mortal man had ever reached the top of the lava spitting Pyre Mountain and gazed upon the face of the Ifirit. At the beginning of time, in the age of immortals, in exchange for eternal life the gods warned against interfering with the savage tribes that lived outside the shadow cast by Pyre Mountain. The immortals enjoyed fruitful lives, living off the rich lands they had been blessed, made tools with the shiny black stones laden on the mountain slopes and bred many offspring. They had no want or need. Game was bountiful, the water was crystal clear and there was no such thing as drought or the tsetse fly. Like all things, that all ended the day their leader, Gyiku'o, ventured from the sacred shadow and took a savage into this hut, shedding his seed in her womb. This infuriated the gods. That was the end of immortality and the paradise that they had resided in.

Such stories, Maghedzi would relay to Zandile as a large fire raged in his thatched chambers. That was until the feast announcing the birth of her youngest, Prince Alinafe. He was sour throughout, hurt the Akuwa, Shumba, as well as other notable patriarchs from the Snake Pit and Eagle's Nest had failed to attend. He became sloshed and stumbled into what he said he supposed was Zandile's hut. *What was I expecting?* Zandile thought. It was customary for men to take as many wives as they could – especially a king. Maghedzi shrugged his shoulders as though absolving himself as he pleaded his case. She could take sharing him with the other wives for it was their custom. She was always going to be number one, the soil where the future Piripiri seeds were planted, however, she could not suffer being made a fool. "How could you do this to me, you dog?" she had screamed. "Have I not given you all the sons you wanted? And in return, you shame me in front of the tribe. Even my servants are laughing at me. Wait until you sleep. I will cut it off. I wish father had sold me to Farakaii!" Zandile regretted what she said immediately, but she was too proud to take those words back – that name, *Farakaii*.

Maghedzi's eyes darkened, making her feel like her feet were stuck in a thick, unforgiving pit of sand. He stammered then raised his hand, but rather than cowering, Zandile stood defiant, even offering her cheek. She could hear his teeth, like two jagged bricks rubbing together. He did the unexpected. He turned and walked away.

It was never the same again between Zandile and Maghedzi. For years they were estranged, with the king picking up wife after wife and frequenting their palaces, rather than hers. Despite that, in the eyes of their subjects, the couple perpetuated a united front. Tonight, as it seemed, she was back in the king's good graces. He was tender, even sweet, holding her just like before. When he was done, he wiped the effort from his forehead, sat up and poked his finger through the flame. He let it stay there extraordinarily long before he turned and looked at her, setting an intense unease in her spirit. She had tried to keep Nia's womanhood a secret to preserve her youth and innocence just a little longer. She had even cast the girl's cloths into the flames for she could not even trust her own servants. Blood or not, Nia was still a child.

"The ancestors have been good to us," Maghedzi confessed.

Zandile didn't particularly agree, but she acceded nonetheless. She didn't want to make a debate over it. "They have, husband."

"Our waters are flowing, our reserves are filled with grain and game is plentiful. No tribe in the region resists us and I have begot many sons."

Zandile could not disagree with that.

"And now, our only daughter together, has become a woman."

Zandile could now see she was foolish, thinking she could keep such an important detail from the king.

"Now that she is a woman, I do not see why we should stall on finding her a suitable betrothal."

The world was asleep when Zandile woke. She looked to her side. Maghedzi was well asleep, snoring frog-like croaks. She rose from the mat and crept to the wall. She felt for a gap, and pulled out a brick. She reached in, rummaged, and then came out with an object wrapped around a soiled cloth. She turned around to make sure he was still asleep. She unveiled a sharp black blade made of obsidian rock and crept toward the sleeping king. When she was close enough to hear his now light breaths, she brought the knife down and cut off a small piece of the king's greying hair. The king awoke in a panic, wide-eyed, looked around, and just as suddenly as he rose, he instantaneously fell back to sleep and the loud snores he had been performing.

She put on a dark cloth over her head and shoulders and crept out of the hut. There was no one there, but she knew there were watch guards patrolled around. What she needed to do relied on total secrecy so she proceeded with caution toward the Fire Shrine. There was no one there when she arrived. She entered the chamber, knelt in front of the statue of Gyiku'o and began to pray. "Please forgive me for this ancestors, but I have been left with no choice. Nia, my only daughter, she is still too young." She was crying when she pulled out her blade and cut a line down her palm. She winced in pain and unveiled a straw doll from the cloth, let her blood drip over it and fastened the chunk of kingly hair onto the doll. She grabbed one of the torches that kept the shrine bright and set the doll on fire.

CHAPTER 9

It was at the dead of night when the Sangoma and Reza finally arrived a short distance away from the Pyre Fortress gates. It had been an arduous journey from the Forest of Abominations. He had to make his way through rotten carcasses and skeletons that decorated the forest threshold. When he had finally exited, he gasped and sucked in the air. It was fresh, devoid of the smell of decomposing flesh and mold. He had forgotten the beauty of the wild, the sprawling umbrella trees and lilac jacaranda trees that decorated the savannah. "You, stay here," he commanded Reza. "Do something useful for a change. Go hunt, go find yourself a hare, or if you are as good as you think you are, try catching some boar."

All the memories came flooding back. Back to a different time when Reza was just a pup, and he was just a priest. Reza was there at his first purification. They had fled together when a group of farmers ambushed him, weapons in hand, after the rains he had promised had not come forth. He remembered fondly the day he found Reza, hidden in a bush after its family had been killed by a ferocious lion. Now they went separate ways. Sneaking into the palace was hard enough alone. He did not need a lazy hyena slowing him down. "Master has serious business. Wish me well. I will return when I return."

The dirty animal giggled squeakily, turned and trotted merrily into the darkness. When she was far enough, the Sangoma turned and giggled loudly, mimicking his companion.

"Did you hear that Masuku? Why, that sounded like a hyena," said one guard to another, manning the gates.

"That's strange, a hyena roaming this close to the walls? Impossible."

The Sangoma giggled again, just in case the men thought their *umqombothi* was getting the better of them.

"Perhaps one managed to evade the rangers. Come on, put your beer down. We better scare it away before it steals into the walls and drags our royal family out, by their throats."

"That wouldn't be too bad would it?" one snorted.

"No, it wouldn't. I would fancy spending one night in that luxurious hut. Or one night with the queen." Masuku added. They both chuckled. "Come on, let's go."

When the guards left their post, the Sangoma slipped through and hid behind a clay hut. A watchman passed by, waved his torch around, turned and walked back. The witchdoctor darted toward a large tree with thick leaves that protected him from the moonlight. He heard a pig-like snore. He turned and looked down, frantic, fearing discovery. However, he calmed himself and chuckled lightly when he realized what was making the groans.

Now, it was about patience. There was only one guard left between him and destiny. His opportunity came when the guard manning the entrance followed the sound of a feminine voice into the night. His long, black nails dug into the earth, giving him a burst of pace. He hopped over a water fountain like a springbok then jumped into the air and seized a branch. His body, starved of nutrition, swayed slowly from side to side like a monkey amongst the vines. He looked down upon the window of death, however there was no noose around his neck. He kicked hard into the tree, sinking his toenails deep into the thick balk, climbed then hoisted up. He sped down the thin tree branch and jumped into the dark purple sky and over the wall, rolling twice as he landed. He produced a miniature bow and arrow, armed it with a sharp twig and shot. He pumped his fist and almost hollered in reverence of his perfect strike, but he controlled himself at the last second. It had pierced the watchman's neck, which he swatted away, as one does a mosquito. All the Sangoma had to do now was wait. When the watchman finally succumbed, he repositioned his mask, making sure it was in place, and patted down his hides. The large door creaked as it opened.

"Who goes there?" a grizzly voice commanded. In a matter of moments, the Sangoma had a sharp blade pressed against his neck. "You're that priest I exiled, the one that called himself the Sangoma. Yes, I remember you. How can I forget such a grotesque?"

"Excuse me, King Maghedzi, but the ancestors never sleep and they are very talkative."

"And they talk to you?"

"Yes, your eminence. I have been blessed with such abilities . . . as well as others." He looked around. It was a dark and humble room with the air of gloom.

"What abilities are these? The only powers I remember you having were the ones of deception and blasphemy." There was a grunt, like someone had started to laugh but stopped a tenth of the way. "I have it in my right to have the Desert-Snake open your skinny neck and let your vile blood decorate my beautiful animal hides. His shotel has not tasted human skin for a while, and I fear he is growing anxious. Why have you returned, to curse my house and bring my tribesmen to ruin? Or have you come for my life?"

"No," the Sangoma refuted indignantly. "I am not an enemy." His armpits moistened as he looked around and noticed the two mounds of skulls, just as tall as he was and as wide as a full-grown bull. The hollow eye sockets seemed to look at him. *Help us*, they screamed, *help us*. Some were layered in grime and mold, no older than a few months with strands of hair stuck on them. One was so crushed a shiver went through his spine when he noticed the large club hanging on the wall. Unfortunately, his business here was for the living, not the dead. *I cannot help you now*, he assured, *but I will in time.*

"You are my enemy, Sangoma, yes you are. Were you not banished? Sent away, never to return?"

"I was, I had nowhere to go, so I went to the dark forest hoping to die and suffer for my sins, but I am alive as you can see."

"That is a lie. No man has gone into the dark forest for countless generations and lived to tell about it."

"I am living proof," the Sangoma confessed.

"How do I know you are not a spirit, a ghoul, come back to prey on my people?"

"The blood on your guard's blade is evidence I am no ghoul. That I am not spirit, but man."

"You might be many things, Sangoma, but you are no man." The king, but a shadow, rose, walked toward the flame that burnt and became flesh. He was a short package, but strong, with legs thick like they had walked the entire northern desert. "Raise your mask." The Sangoma hesitated momentarily, but the king's eyebrow was raised, and his nose was screwed up into a tight wrinkled knot. His freakishly wide jaw rippled like a calm wave caressing the shore. "You haven't aged at all, black mage. You look just as ugly as the last time I saw you, a small, decrepit little creature. You entered my chambers unscathed. You are resourceful indeed, however, it also says much about my security. That I will deal with after I have dealt with you. You see, Sangoma, I cannot suffer insolence and carelessness." Maghedzi paused and thought for a few moments. "I ought to execute you and add your head to this impressive collection I am developing, but our harvest has been healthy enough, so you may find me a little forgiving. State at once what you came for and it better be good, or you die."

The Sangoma took a quick look at the mound conveniently in his view and cracked a bead of sweat before he cleared his throat to begin. "I have had a revelation. The ancestors came to me as I lay deep in the Forest of Abominations . . ." The witchdoctor could see the discomfort the name created in the young protégé who loosened the pressure against his neck. From a young age, children were taught to fear the dark forest. "The ancestors came to me with a stern message, and with it, a revelation of future events and what must transpire."

The king seemed slightly amused as he listened carefully and compelled the Desert-Snake to set him free. "And what are these things that must transpire? What happens to me? Are my enemies destroyed? Do I succeed over the Akuwa?"

The mage could sense the incredulous nature of the king's tone, but continued nonetheless. He had come a long way and survived insurmountable obstacles in the Forest of Abominations: "Your destiny is greater than even you can fathom. You are the architect of peace." The Sangoma did not see the slap coming that sent him flying into the furniture. When he opened his eyes he was face to face with a skull. "I do not seek peace. I seek what belongs to my people, what belongs to me."

Leave Sangoma, the skull lisped, *or you will surely die . . . like me.* The skull began to chuckle, and then laughed louder and louder until the witchdoctor began to scream in fright.

Maghedzi slid off the leather belt that held his dagger and set it about the cowering Sangoma. It went on for half a minute until there was silence. The king was not young anymore. "Take him to the dark huts and seal him," he huffed, out of breath. "Make sure a priest performs a protective spell around his prison. I will execute him on the morrow."

The Desert-Snake grabbed the priest and carried him off like a little baby. The Sangoma suffered further agony as the clip that fastened his mask snapped, sending it, and his headdress flaying to the floor and landing with a crack.

CHAPTER 10

It was an arduous walk from the king's chambers to his little hut. Sekuru Rwizi had been taking this route for countless years, up and down the spiraling staircase to give council to the various kings over the ages. For many he had served as wise man, griot, tasked with giving sound council and aid to the king with his vast knowledge of the natural world and keeping the history of Hippo Valley alive. *King Netsai*, he remembered fondly. He had been the first Akuwa king he had counseled. *A good king he was*, he reflected, but his reign came to an end by a sudden chill.

Netsai had left no heirs so his younger brother Gotsi became king. He was an ambitious ruler, who had grand plans to make Hippo Valley great again. He had attempted many reforms, but that caused a division between him and the nobility who liked things as they were. He was assassinated, and his son, Gondo, was proclaimed king though he was only three years old. Tsorai Shato served as interim king until Gondo came of age and used his time in power to the betterment of his clansmen.

The Akuwa took back power when bastard-born Bolasi in exile, with the aid of the Shumba, took back Hippo Valley after a prolonged siege of the Stone Houses. It had taken ten years. No force was strong enough to break the stone walls, so they used cunning instead. Bolasi with the aid of Hoza, smuggling themselves in through a secret passage. There they hid in Ife, Tsorai's twentieth wife's hut and under the cover of the night, opened the main gate from inside, allowing the rebels in. Rwizi had been standing next to Tsorai when Bolasi speared Tsorai through the heart.

Bolasi took the throne for himself. That presented a problem in the future when the calf, Gondo, became a bull. This sent the realm back into civil war, which ended when both men were killed in battle by the River Khumalo. The realm needed a king swiftly, before anarchy ensued. So Sekuru Rwizi with the aid of the fierce warrior, Gyid'o and the three dwarrows, Jag'd, Mud'k and Mamdab'o made the journey to the top of the Sacred Hills to seek the council of the Sisters. They faced many perils along the way, encountering mythical creatures and the fury of nature, but finally they arrived at a great cost with only one dwarf surviving. The Sisters declared that the Akuwa throne must go to one that is courageous and pure of heart, and it was Rwizi's destiny to determine who that was. The wrong choice would mean the end of Hippo Valley, and their people, reduced to wonderers of the known world.

Rwizi went to Bolasi's son, Bageti, at his homestead and spent several nights there, questioning him on life and what it meant to be a king. He then went to Gondo's son, Kudakwashe, and did the same. After seven moons had come and gone praying with only water for nourishment, he finally got up and proceeded toward the new king. On his way he happened upon a boy, perhaps three fists of age, herding cows. He met eyes with the boy and immediately fell on his face, took out the Akuwa staff and hailed, "Long live the mighty hippo." That boy was Anesu, who went on to rule for many drought-less and prosperous years.

That was many years ago now. Rwizi could not remember the vast number of his years, but however old he was, what was certain was climbing the stairs up and down the Akuwa hill grew more difficult as the years passed.

"Sekuru Rwizi," a voice hollered, several times before the ancient turned his head. His sight was almost gone, and so was his hearing.

"Oh, it's you," he said, as the blur became Xolani.

"Here, let me help you down the stairs." Xolani grabbed the ancient's satchel, took one of his hands and helped him to his hut. It was a small and dark place, and it smelled just as old as the ancient was rumored to be.

The old man coughed hard. "Sorry young man. Where is my pipe?"

Rwizi looked around despite it being right in front of him. "Oh there it is," he chuckled, lighting up the camphor leaves, inhaling deep before he let out a mushroom-shaped cloud toward the thatched roof.

"Where is Tjingii?"

"I sent him on an errand. He should be back soon." Prince Tjingii, third in line to the Akuwa throne, had been spending considerable time at the ancient's hut, rather than the training grounds with the rest of his peers. "So, young Xolani, why do you visit this old man? Don't you have other things to do?"

"I just thought to pay you a visit, that's all."

Rwizi chuckled, and coughed at the same time. "What do people call me young man?"

Is this one of the ancient's trick questions? Xolani deliberated. "The wisest man in all the land?"

"Then you should know you couldn't fool me. Sit down, young Xolani, tell me what troubles you."

The boy took his time before asking: "Sekuru, what do you know of the nyaminyami?"

Rwizi stroked his long white beard before he answered, his lengthy nails cutting into his coarse shrub of hair. "They are mythical creatures, cryptids. Xolani, why do you ask?"

"Just curious that's all."

"Well, they are water serpents capable of growing the size of several huts, with command over water and rain, lakes and rivers. Generations ago, villagers said they brought ultimate abundance, prosperity and good fortune. At first they were considered beautiful, friendly, and wise. They provided divine protection and vigilance. Temples and statues were erected in their image. The nyaminyami is said to have even fed the villagers from its own meat during times of famine. In exchange the people would perform ritual dances. However, that all ended when fishermen started disappearing without a trace." Rwizi looked at Xolani. "Between you and me, these are just stories young man. Maybe the nyaminyami lived amongst us, but as a man of knowledge, I have not seen one myself."

You old fool, Xolani thought to himself. "How did the nyaminyami communicate with the ancient people?"

The old man laughed. "I suspect as a snake, or any reptilian creature would."

"Is there anything more you can tell me about them? What they like to eat? What kind of powers they have?"

Rwizi scratched his head and began. It was a good while when the old man stopped mumbling. Xolani's neck was sore from having to lean toward the ancient, and his head ached from trying to decipher what he was saying. After a while, there was silence. He looked up to find the ancient snoring. *Might as well,* he sighed. He had promised to meet his half-sister, Princess Nonkuleko. He picked up an animal rug and placed it over the snoring wise man.

***

Xolani giggled as he finally let his half-sister go and helped her to her feet. "I'm so sorry Nonkuleko. I couldn't resist."

"That's the last time I let you teach me anything."

"Don't be like that. It was just jokes. Swimming is really easy. You did well. You'll get it soon." He got out of the pond and like a monkey, climbed the mango tree all the way to the top. There was a rumble as birds flew out, chirping, upset at their peace being broken. When he finally slid down with small bird feathers stuck in his hair, he had not only one, but three mangos in his hand. Nonkuleko's large eyes widened and the frown she bore evaporated and turned into a line of perfect little white teeth. She waded through the water and made her way to the bank where Xolani waited, proud. She looked down at her bare chest. "Curses, I lost my necklace in the water. Taonga gave it to me. I really liked it."

"Oh that's a shame. I'm sure he can get you a new one. You and he are to be married soon. You must be excited."

Nonkuleko looked down. "Yes, very much so. Taonga is gentle of heart and an excellent archer."

"They say it is the most important day in a woman's life."

"Yes, that's what they say, but . . ." The girl sighed. "I don't love him Xolani." Her eyes swelled to the precipice of tears. "I don't know why I feel so much despair. Father loves him, like a son. He comes from an old family and has good manners. Every day he has sent me a jacaranda leaf, but still . . . I can't find myself to . . ."

"Have you told your mother how you feel?"

"Yes. She didn't care. She said it was my duty. She said my comforts in life say I can't decide whom I marry." Sibongile had summoned a few Amakazi and taken Nonkuleko on a tour around the back ends of Hippo Valley. She was shown the small water well peasants used to retrieve water, a far cry from the bountiful wells to which she was accustomed, with carvings of hippos and nyaminyamis. She was taken to the market square where beggars roamed, looking for what they could to eat. Sibongile had pointed at a small hut and explained that a large family lived in it. When one of the girls from the household appeared, Sibongile held Nonkuleko by the shoulder and pointed. "Look, you see that girl." She had no beads, nor jewelry. Not even wooden bangles to decorate her wrist and ankles - just a dilapidated leather skirt to cover her private parts. "That girl can marry who she wants."

Nonkuleko finally raised her head. "I never asked for any of this . . ."

Xolani felt awkward. He didn't know how to comfort her. He was saved when familiar laughter appeared behind them. "Sorry to interrupt your play time, sister, half-brother." Xolani turned to find Themba sitting on his great zebra. He bore the look of a prince elders told stories of, who performed heroic and valiant deeds.

"Oh, hello, Themba. You're not interrupting. It's such a hot day, so I thought I would teach Nonkuleko how to swim. Join us if you like."

Themba hurled himself from his zebra, landing with the deftness of the spotted cat he wore around his waist. He pulled Xolani's spear from the earth and launched it high into the afternoon sky until it cut through the water, only after momentarily seemingly disappearing into the clouds. His chaperones, Takunda and Sipho cackled like hyenas. "Nonkuleko will be in the pot carrying competition at the coming festival. She should be practicing, and bringing water to my chambers, not frolicking in water with the bastard brother."

The princess was not impressed by Themba's tone. "You should learn how you address me, little brother. The only reason you can speak to me that way is because you have wood under your loincloth and I have not. Remember that."

"That matters naught to me. Get your things. Mother has sent for you." He turned to Xolani. "What do you say you and I bond a little before my big fight?"

"I have plans." He had fresh meat for Aku the nyaminyami, but he couldn't tell Themba that. He struggled for something . . . *anything.* Improvising he said, "my mother sent me to get some things."

"And here you are, taking a dip with my sister, in the middle of a chore? Do you presume I am foolish?"

Xolani thought nothing at all.

"Get your things, we are going for a hunt and then later, there is a banquet at the Moyo farm."

Xolani could see he had no choice in the matter.

"Takunda, see to it my dear sister returns home where she belongs."

Reluctantly, Nonkuleko collected her things and prepared to go. Xolani whistled, made a sudden dash toward the pond and dove in, in an elegant, erect swoosh. It was a while before he remerged with his spear and also Nonkuleko's necklace. She smiled widely, thanked him and off she went with a bag of juicy mangos.

It was a grueling ride for Xolani, as Themba had been going on for ages about what he called the art of hunting, likening his technique to that of the jaguar. Xolani had grown up arms-length from his half-brothers, but he knew the prince well enough to know silence and patience were not his strong suits. "I've killed many kinds of animals," the prince boasted. "Boar is pretty good, but if you can catch an antelope, then you are hunting at a high level." He halted his zebra, and unveiled his hunting bow. Shiri hooted violently when Themba's beast came closer.

"Shiri," Xolani commanded sternly, "Quiet!" The zebra yipped a couple of times more before it calmed itself.

"Here, feel the bow strings." They were thick and strong, little threads of hide bound into a strong, elastic string. "Feel how smooth the wood is."

Xolani caressed it and found himself in the pond where he played with Nonkuleko, but this time it was just he, waist deep in a dark red liquid. He tried to move, but thick metal chains pinioned around his wrists and ankles held him down. He quickly took his hand away to watch Themba's mouth move. He hadn't heard what the prince had said, but he nodded politely. "Darkwood?"

"Yes. This will go through a wildebeest from a hundred meters. However, there is nothing more glorious than bringing home a marshbuck."

"Have you ever got one?"

"No," Themba sighed. "Maybe one day. Only the true masters can catch one. It takes true experience and talent. Father has got one. If you've been in his chambers, you'll see its head plastered on the wall. Sometimes it takes days before spotting one and even then actually catching one is something else entirely. Such evasive creatures they are, like girls, if you know what I mean?" the prince winked.

They entered a cave and emerged in the Monomotapa hunting grounds. An offshoot from the River Khumalo ran through, providing water for the vibrant wildlife that lived within the forest. In a matter of moments, the boys were slick with sweat. It was a humidity Xolani had never experienced. He reached for his skin of water, but Themba was quicker, offering his. "Go ahead," he encouraged. The humidity and the beer coupled with the identical numerous tree trunks and twisted branches made Xolani drowsy in no time. Little light shone and could only be seen from the sporadic cracks in the thick canopy. Although it was a beautiful place, one could not be deceived. It was a treacherous domain, with creatures of vicious varieties. "Do you know the tokoloshe live here?" Themba revealed.

Xolani's eyes widened as he made to run back but instead he fell flat on his face as he tripped over a stone.

Themba held his stomach in laughter. "Just joking, skinny one. I have been in these forests many a time, and I have not encountered any tokoloshe." He reached out his hand to help Xolani up.

"But that doesn't mean they are not here," Xolani said, dusting himself off and rubbing his bruised knees. This was after all, a boy that had encountered a water dragon, not long ago.

Themba pulled Xolani close and covered his mouth. "You know what, I doubt there ever was a nyaminyami, but that's just between you and me." Themba climbed over a large chest high root and reached out his hand to hoist Xolani over. "Watch this. You will love it." He walked into a small opening in the large tree, seemingly disappearing.

"Themba, where are you?" There was no response. He peered into the dark hovel. It smelled of mold and age, like old Rwizi's hut. "Themba?" *Where could he be?* Suddenly Xolani could feel a presence behind him. He slowly turned his head and found himself face to face with a gremlin with large pointed ears, a porcine round nose and a row of sharp teeth protruding from it.

"I have been looking for you Xolani. It is time you meet death." Xolani took two steps backward before he opened his mouth and began to scream.

"Xolani," the goblin fretted. "You're scaring away our game." The creature took off its mask to reveal Themba laughing hysterically.

"That's not funny." Xolani threw his tiny fist into Themba's shoulder.

"You should have seen your face. You were about to cry."

"No I wasn't," Xolani denied, though his eyes were still glistening. "How did you do that?"

"There's another exit at the other side of the tree."

"Okay Themba, you are great. You had me."

"I did, but that is in the past now. We have some killing to do."

"You will have to teach me how to move as quietly as you did."

Themba politely nodded.

They had been circling around the dense forestation when Xolani felt something under his foot. He fell to the ground gnashing his teeth and lifted his leg revealing a bee with its wings still flickering with the minuscule life it had left. Themba ended its misery with the other end of his spear. "Lift your leg." Xolani was reluctant, but soon submitted. "The stinger is still in. I have to take it out. Are you ready?" Xolani nodded as sweat dripped down his forehead. Themba held the leg up with his left hand, then pulled the sting out with the other. "The bee is dead. They do not survive a sting. At least you have now killed." Xolani did not find that funny, the pain he was feeling was anything but. Themba let go of the leg and lifted up his skins.

"What are you doing? Are you crazy?" Xolani turned his head in disgust and shut his eyes.

"We will need urine to heal that, otherwise it might fester and your dreams of becoming Amakazi and donning that pretty blue cape will sink to the bottom of the Khumalo."

"What about water? We have plenty." Xolani looked around for his skin.

"That won't work, I'm afraid. Trust me. I've been stung many times before." Themba moved uncomfortably closer and let out a golden stream, pouring onto Xolani's foot as the boy squirmed. Somehow Themba's healing brought great satisfaction to him as he bore a grin as his magic liquid flowed. When he was done, Themba let his loincloth fall and ripped off a leaf from a nearby tree. "We could have eaten it if it were not a female. Wasps are really tasty. Almost like locusts. Here, clean yourself up." As Xolani opened his mouth, Themba placed a finger over his lips and slowly reached inside his quiver and pulled out an arrow. Xolani looked but he couldn't see anything. "Right there, near that mahogany tree over there. The large thick one, about seven or eight feet in diameter."

The trees were indigenous to the northern tribes. Long ago, when Kubulani the Consolidator returned from his travels north, he was so enthralled by the majesty of the hundred and fifty foot trees, he came home with a bag of its hairy seeds. Sadly, only here in this green sanctuary is where they had survived.

"Yes, I see it now, there behind that bush."

"Here, I want you to have the pleasure. It's not much, but it is a good start." Xolani grew sweaty around the neck.

"Urm, you should do it. I insist."

Themba pulled back his string, aimed momentarily and let go. The prince smiled as they walked to the kill. He picked it up by the ears and inspected the wound it had left through its stomach. He pulled out the arrow and handed it to his brethren. "This is better than a woman." Themba paused and looked up to Xolani. "You haven't had a woman have you? What are you, a couple of years younger than me?" He shook his head. "You are no fun. I'm tired of hunting rabbits. I can do it with my eyes closed."

"I have a cloth in my bag if you want. We can blind fold you."

"Very funny brother, but I suggest you stand very still." Xolani protested, but Themba quietly insisted.

"Why are you looking at me like that?" In a flash Themba flung his fist toward Xolani's face and past, grabbing a snake mid strike. He quickly gripped it with his other hand as it twirled and tried to open its mouth.

"Do you know what this is? This is an eastern green . . . boomslang snake. This is one of uncle Munyaradzi's favorites. What a wonderful creature it is." Xolani wasn't sure how Themba could find beauty in such a perfidious animal, the symbol of all treachery and the source of betrayal. "The ancestors are watching over you, Xolani. If it weren't for my keen eyesight and excellent reflexes, there's a good chance you would be dead by tomorrow." That sent a shiver down the boy's spine. "Its venom is deceptively effective. Most times it takes about a day before the poison begins to work its mischief. Remember Haraki? After he got bit he went to sleep thinking he was okay, but awoke bleeding from his nose, ears and even his buttocks." The prince giggled. "Grab me my knife . . . There." Blood squirted from the decapitated head as all five feet of the snake coiled around frantically on the fallen leaves. He threw the head into the bush, picked up the rest of the snake and handed it to Xolani. "Here, put this in your bag." Xolani, reached out, still shivering from his near dance with death. "Give it to your mother, and she will know what to do. It's getting late. We should be on our way to the Moyo's." They exited the hunting grounds and returned to their zebras and made their way to the Moyo farm.

They were greeted well by Jorro and as they were ushered into the gates. The sun was dying, but the torches lit and the fires burning helped guide their way. After they had sat down and passed the bowl of fermented milk around several times, Jorro was recounting when he took off Muchita's tongue when loud screams rang out and then all hell broke loose. The air quickly became thick with the sound of men wailing, praying for their ancestor's mercy whilst women and children cried as they sprang for shelter. Xolani hadn't the faintest what they were running from, but the trepidation in one woman's eyes painted an uninviting picture. He got up to run, but he was so drunk he could barely keep his legs straight. He turned his head to see a woman desperately trying to open the hut door, but as quick as a flash, a shadow blew past like a gale and there the woman remained, at the foot of the door, with an open back. Another girl lay on the ground with her wooden doll clutched firm in her hand. She was still alive. Xolani knew it by her lungs that stood out, inflating and shrinking slowly. Everything was moving so fast, but when he turned his head, bright eyes shone in the darkness. The shadow growled in the midst before it turned its attention into the night and sprang away only for Xolani to hear the sound of bone crushing and flesh cutting. "Themba, where are you?" Suddenly he was trapped. He rubbed his eyes hoping to sober up, but that did not work. He could smell them, encircling him and sizing him up. He wasn't much, what were they waiting for? He commanded them to depart with the most authoritative voice he could summon. "Away with you, dark spirit. I am not afraid of you." He clutched his spear tighter, but what hope did he have of protecting himself with such a blunt instrument? Furthermore, the beasts could not understand Akuwa. He held firm, with his feet tucked steady in the soil. Suddenly, blood fell on his face. He didn't have time to wipe it off before more sprinkled his loincloth. Observing their fallen brethren, the other beasts fled. First a luminous object appeared, and then following it emerged Themba who casually walked to the dying beast that lay on the dark Moyo soil. He did not say a word. He just raised his spear over his head with both hands, and then let it crash down into the center of the beast's crane. "Here, take this," Themba said, offering his spear and pulled out his club before he turned in a sudden movement and back-handed a beast headed his way.

"Thank you," is all Xolani could muster before a light growl sang, and so did the prince's club, crashing the side of the beast's head.

Jorro followed shortly, emerging from the dimly lit Moyo thoroughfare. "Did you see that? What was it? They were moving so fast I could barely see what they were." He looked down where Themba's spear and club had worked. "Ahh, I see, mountain cats. What are they doing so close to the capital? You should have seen the look on Jabo's face. His face bloated like a fish fleeing a crocodile." His jest was interrupted when he turned to find his wife. He looked at what she was carrying. His better eye widened and there in her arms was his son Korokoro.

CHAPTER 11

The Sangoma had now lost count the number of days he had been confined to his dark cell. Throughout all his years dabbling in wizardry he thought it sad he couldn't find a single trick to escape his abyss. A guard came in every once in a while to change his chamber pot and deliver his meals. "Why am I alive?" he would ask to no response. "What is Maghedzi doing? Tell him his subject loves him. Tell him, he is the one the ancestors have chosen. Tell him he is our salvation . . . When will you let me go?"

"We'll let you go all right, soon enough." The guard had replied chuckling before shutting the door.

After supper, he knelt and raised his spindly arms to begin his prayer. As he commenced, so did a commotion outside. He cursed with a tight fist. He liked to pray in silence. That way he could hear the spirits clearer. He wanted to pray for Reza's safety. The watchman Wasike had warned him: "Just you wait, when I find that bitch of yours, I am going to kill it and make a nice loincloth with it." He remembered the guard well. He had greyed in some places, but his roughcast features remained the same, and his fervent application of his duties. Those words had haunted the witchdoctor in his dark abyss, so he gnashed his teeth until they bled and begged the ancestors to watch over her.

Many days later, Wasike appeared at the door wearing a frown, holding a bucket and a piece of cloth. "Clean yourself up and don't waste time, you have been summoned by the king." The Sangoma loathed bathing, having not taken one for ages. However, bathing was the least he could do if it meant leaving that dark, damp and smelly cell.

He was greeted at the entrance to the king's grounds by the Desert-Snake. His large hands gripped around his arm like it was a child's wrist. They entered the room where his new adventure had begun and there was Maghedzi grim as ever, as two flames flickered leaving a trail that sailed into the thatched roof. The Sangoma fell on his face and waited for the king to speak.

"I trust you are pleased with your accommodation?" he began as he caressed the skull that was resting on his thighs. It had a large gap in the middle of its teeth, and its eye sockets were wide and hollow. It seemed to be grinning about something. "Do you know who this is Sangoma?"

"I'm afraid not, my lord."

"This is Akinyemba the Sparrow. They said he was a great warrior, so I made it a point to collect his head. If only I could kill him but another time." The king frowned. "Alas, a man only lives once."

"I am sorry for that, pre-eminence."

"It's not your fault." Maghedzi looked at the Sangoma suspiciously. "Or is it?"

"Never, I swear."

"Then why do you apologize?"

"I-I-I-" the wizard stammered.

"I-I-I-" the king mocked, before he grew silent again and turned his attention to that flame he seemed to be entranced by. "That night half a moon ago when you foolishly snuck into my hut, after I sent you to your cell, I received word that my son Alinafe was horribly ill. We thought it was just a chill and would go away after a few cups of herbal tea, but the fever persisted and his condition worsened. I sent out my fastest zebras far and wide in search of the best healers and even offered vast sums of gold to save the boy's life."

The Sangoma didn't know what to say. How could he affect the events of the living, when he was trapped in an abyss?

Maghedzi offered a boiled egg. "Go on, it is not poisoned if that's what you think. That is the work of women and cravens, which I am neither." When the witchdoctor was done and had egg yolk crumbs mixed with spittle and paste around his mouth, the king continued. "I want you to perform your magic. You are my last hope. If it is true you have been in the dark forest and returned unscathed, you must possess some real power. Heal my child and I will give you a king's reward."

The Sangoma liked the sound of that. *A king's reward*, he repeated to himself.

"Alinafe is a good child, an obedient one. He has done nothing wrong." The king looked down and shook his head. His beady eyes were red and raw from the lack of sleep, and his cheeks had turned almost pink. "I have been thinking." He paused and looked up straight into the wizard's eyes. "The same day you came with all this talk and me giving you the beating of the season, is the same day my little boy fell ill. Is it a coincidence?"

"It was no coincidence at all," replied the Sangoma.

In a flash, the Desert-Snake rose to his feet and had his shotel licking the back of the mage's neck. "You see, like I said. He brought this illness into your household, father. He admits his witchcraft. Please, let me take his head before he works more of his mischief."

"I have brought no curse to your son, my lord," the wizard protested. "However, the ancestors see everything. Our ancestors frown harshly on those who strike a messenger of the spirits, king or not."

"So only you can lift this curse?"

"Yes, I will prove it and you will see that I have been chosen to guide you."

Maghedzi studied the frail-looking midget for a minute in total silence. "Very well, sorcerer. Desert-Snake, take this creature to the boy's hut. See to it he gets everything he needs. I do not want any excuses. If he fails, bring me his head. See to it."

It was the third night and the boy's fever had not receded. The boy's muscles were still sore, and his mat was drenched in sweat. Sporadically, the boy would scream in horror as pain engulfed his little head. With Queen Zandile's help, the Sangoma tried to make the boy eat, but he had lost his appetite. Zandile cooked the boy's favorite dish but shortly after, a mixture of kidney beans and carrot soup came spewing out of the boy's belly. The boy muttered nonsensically, and his lips were lined with cracks. The witchdoctor had chanted all night and sprayed the room with incense and herbs, warding away avenging spirits, however, Alinafe remained in critical condition.

When everyone had gone, he thought to close his eyes – just for a moment. A few moments later, he awoke to murmurings. *Is it the spirits talking to me?* "Talk to me, tell me what I must do to save the boy," he pleaded. The sound came again, however it was no spirit . . . it was Alinafe. He quickly felt the boy's forehead. It was still warm, but drastically cooled. He called out to the servant to get some fresh water. Zandile and Nia walked in. They too hadn't slept. He could have sworn she had aged at least ten years in the last few days. He placed a long bony finger on his lip and beckoned them over to the bed. "Listen carefully."

"Mother," the boy stammered. "Father, where am I? Where's Nia?"

Zandile and Nia's eyes widened with joy. "He's awake, he's awake," They screamed, jubilant. The rest rushed in, brothers, cousins, aunts and well-wishers.

The Sangoma had done it. He had broken Alinafe's fever, but he was not surprised. Now, he was even more resolved to his destiny, carrying out the will of the ancestors, and receiving a king's reward.

"The king summons you," bellowed the guard, Wasike.

The wizard winced in pain. His body was skin and bone and the guard's grasp was as hard as tongs. "Mind how you handle me from now on. You forget I just healed the prince."

"All those people might think you saved that boy, but I know better, I do not believe in none of your craft."

"Then you are lost my child." Wasike gave him another shove and off they went.

The Sangoma entered the king's chambers with a huge grin his mask did well to conceal. Maghedzi sat on his throne whilst the Desert Snake sat by the window seat plucking on his *mbira*, somber and melancholy chords. When the Desert Snake was done and replaced the *mbira* for his curved blade, the king whistled and in came two men carrying a chest. One of them was Wasike, who as always, performed his duty steadfastly and with glee. They opened it, revealing a chest full of gold and silver pieces.

The Sangoma rubbed his hands together and licked his lips. It was enough for him to retire from wizardry and buy himself a farm. *Who knows? Maybe now I can find myself a wife, and have children, like normal people do.*

"You have done well, Sangoma. My family and I would like to thank you for what you did for us, saving our son. It is very admirable, however . . ." the king said plainly. "This good does not wash away your past. You broke into my palace and entered my chambers uninvited. My wife, the queen needs an invitation. What gives you such privileges? Where you not stripped of your priesthood and banished from my kingdom?"

"Yes . . . yes, I was, but . . ."

"Forget it Sangoma, there are no laws that can save you. You should know. You are well versed in our customs. Wasike, take this creature away and hang him from a tree with his reward."

"But," his voice broke. "I saved the boy."

"And there is your compensation for your fine work." The king pointed at the chest. "A king's reward. Make sure no one takes down his body until the crows and ravens have had their fill. When there is no more flesh for the vultures to pluck, take his remains back whence he came from and cast them there, where his bones will lie for eternity. I assure you he will not return a second time."

There was a small crowd outside by the village square. The Sangoma was miniature in stature, so they didn't need to search long for a tree that could support his little frame. By the time they sat him on a donkey and tied the noose around his neck, he had run out of ancestors to pray to. The hooded hangman performed a solemn prayer, loud so the crowd could hear. "Be happy his grace didn't give you to the flames." Those were some fine words of solace. When the hangman kicked the donkey, off it went and so did the Sangoma as the rope tightened around his neck.

CHAPTER 12

Gamu had now been circling around the Hippo Valley market for hours trying to find this illusive Mzilikele his friend Yago had told him about. He prayed he wasn't too late. It was the busiest time of the day as merchants buzzed around bartering their goods and the blue sky had been replaced with a thick cloud of dark smoke. Street boys loitered in their threadbare loin skins doing what they could to earn a few copper pieces, carrying wealthy men's sacks and bartering what they could. It smelled like any other busy market center with meat roasting on skewers and people making merry drinking their *doro*. Carpenters and stone carvers worked quietly under their little thatched roofs as their products decorated the pathways. *It is decent work,* Gamu acknowledged, *but it lacks heart.* On the other side of the wide pathway, chickens rattled in their cages, perhaps aware of their impending fate whilst oxen, goats and sheep paved the thoroughfare with shit. High up, looming over them on the Akuwa hill was the large towers and stonewalls that housed the king and his court.

It was a task asking directions, as everyone was too busy and preoccupied in their daily duties to stop and assist enervated wanderers. There was the ever-familiar heehaw of donkeys and the wild grunt of oxen as they carried baskets up and down the thoroughfare. Transportation of goods was a thriving business, now that they were enjoying their most favorable weather in a while. Markets were busy struggling to keep up with the ever-increasing population that had settled around the thriving region as the drought slowly descended upon them. Tanaka had suggested Gamu start his own transportation business, however, he wasn't so keen. Back in Pyyros, she had met a neighbor who boasted her husband had just entered the carriage business and said they were doing fairly well. For proof, the woman showed Tanaka the copper bracelet her husband had bought her. Gamu didn't like these stories. It made him feel worthless as a provider, and the longer he kept this up the sooner Tanaka would get fed up with him.

What he wanted was to erect state of the art huts and make row crop cultivators superior to the counterfeit products that dominated the markets. He wanted to fix ploughs that everyone thought unsalvageable in the cool shade of his shed, away from the treacherous sun and watch his children grow until someday they ventured off into their marriages. By then he hoped he would have a healthy ranch with at least fifty cows.

Gamu found himself outside a large shed, lined with bamboo gates. He could smell the *umqombothi* cooking as he walked through the entrance. It was almost empty with a man passed out on a table with flies hovering around him. Another couple talked quietly in a dark corner with their long spears placed on the table. He tightened his fist. *I have to be careful. I have an ever-growing family that depends on me.* "Excuse me sir, are you the owner?" A man nodded, wider than Gamu and his family combined. "I am looking for a man."

"You are not from around here are you?"

"Well, technically I am, but I moved away when I was younger."

"Is that so? The runaway has returned to his ancestors. Isn't that nice. About time don't you think? I say to my son who wants to go away, where are you going? There is nothing for you there. All they do there is drink and waste their copper on women. They take these foreign women into their huts and adopt their religion, forsaking their ancestors. They create nothing for themselves and do not send gold, silver, or even copper to their families back home. You have done good young man, returning to us."

"Sure."

"Do I sense sarcasm, young man?"

"No, not at all. I am just looking for a man named Mzilikele. He owns a store somewhere around here. I mean to work there."

"Praise the ancestors. Work these days, so hard to come by. It's all these Gudo's and Rwaivi's rushing into our great city, taking our pastures and labor. Even if you find work, it's not enough. Back in the good old days a man only worked half the year. He would plant his crops and watch them grow, and you fed your family. Nowadays it is hard for most of us." He gave him a toothy smile. Gamu noticed the gold bracelet he wore around his plump wrist and a black and white beaded headdress with black shiny feathers. Despite him being a lot shorter, he still made Gamu feel small. "What's your name?"

"I am Gamu, Gamu, the woodman."

"A woodman you say?" The middle-aged man pulled down his loincloth exposing his private parts. "Look at that."

Gamu was horrified by what he saw, and the man's piggish chuckle. He turned away as fast as he could, but he had already got a glimpse of it.

"My woodpecker was working just fine, but now," the man frowned. "Can you fix it?" The otherwise quiet room now had laughter, with everyone looking his way.

I really don't have time for this. He was tired and hungry.

The man put his faulty equipment away realizing the jest had worn off. "Just jokes traveler, Akuwa humor."

"It's okay. No need to apologize." *You should probably have a witchdoctor look at that.*

"Let me introduce myself. I am Gwadza, and I am the owner of this fine establishment." The man used his hands to illustrate the entirety of his ownership. Raising his arms seemed quite an effort. Gamu thought he saw a bead of sweat crack at his temples. The fine establishment was dark with rotting wooden stools and bamboo walls layered with grime. That was without mentioning the man's rotten teeth.

"Nice to meet you. Do you think you can help me?"

"Hmm let me see." Gwadza scratched his head in thought. "Mzilikele you say? I know one, but he's a butcher and there is nothing great about him."

"Surely there is more than one Mzilikele in this village?"

"True stranger, but I've grown up here all my life. I inherited this beer hall from my father, and he his father's father, you see. If there were an Mzilikele who owned a utility store, I would know about it. It is my business to know these things, you see."

"Are you sure about this?"

"Yes, you can ask around, sure the market is big, but if you find the Mzilikele you are looking for, come back to me and I will give you a whole night of drinks for free."

Gamu's world seemed to be crashing like two rhinos charging head to head. His thoughts went immediately to his wife. What would she make of this? Next, his children . . . . They were still young, but when they were older and looked back, they would see that their father was a failure.

"Whoever gave you that information probably tricked you. I say he made a proper fool of you. He took you like a man takes a wench over one of my old dirty tables. Too bad, it looks like you did not enjoy it. Don't feel too bad stranger. It happens to everyone at one point or another." Gwadza's face turned to one of solicitude. "Because I like you, come back later tonight, and I will give you the first round of *umqombothi*, free, and perhaps her." He used his brow to point toward a young girl lurking in a corner, who smiled back at them. "To show our hospitality and sincere empathy for your troubles."

Is this man serious? I'm married, plus what good will beer do right now? I have travelled half way across the land for work that doesn't exist, in search of a phantom. A lie. A con. He wanted to grab hold of something and break it, but he couldn't do it here, they would surely make him pay for it. "Thank you, but no thanks." Gamu walked off as the innkeeper continued rearranging the tables and the stools and doing his best to remove the filth on his benches.

He had been duped and played the fool that he was. How could he go back to his family? He thought of something, something to make it right, but nothing came to mind. At least he had the bag of copper, his reward. He felt for it. It was still there. *Wait till I get my hands on Yago's skinny neck.* He had been so blind. He had let his superciliousness cloud his judgment and allowed Yago the opportunity to outmaneuver him. Their supervisor had suddenly fallen ill and died. When such things happen, people got promoted. Yago would earn a few more measly copper pieces every moon. Gamu could not believe it was enough for the ultimate betrayal.

As Gamu reached the large jacaranda tree just outside Gwadza's entrance, something compelled him to turn around. He was shaking as he approached the beer monger, who stopped what he was doing and stood waiting with his fat fists planted on each of his rotund hips. It took a while to say the words, but they came nonetheless: "About that beer you promised?"

***

Tanaka and the children were still waiting by the time the sun began to descend. With some of the money they had received from Jorro Moyo, Tanaka bought herself and the children some food. Chiiko was first to finish, discarding his chicken bone before he latched at Kushinga's bowl. The boy began to cry, alerting Tanaka. She bridged her eyebrows and grabbed Chiiko's ear. "What did I tell you about stealing your siblings' food?"

The boy squelched in pain. "Mother stop, I'm sorry."

"Sorry for what?"

"Sorry for stealing Kushinga's food." Tanaka tugged harder. "I'll never do it again. I promise."

"Good boy." Tanaka finally let go. She hated punishing her children, but someone had to do it as she considered Gamu too soft. "Your father should have been back by now. It is getting late, you should go out and find him before the black descends upon us. You are old enough to go alone, aren't you?" The boy nodded. "I will wait here with your siblings. Off you go."

Chiiko had been circling around the Hippo Valley market for a while now, but couldn't find his father. The black was approaching. The sunset looked beautiful, in its full glory, but he did not have time to admire it. He had asked everyone he could, and all of them told him the same thing. He followed the scent of goat stew to an inn.

"Sorry, little man," the innkeeper said. Chiiko couldn't help but notice her large breasts and even larger stomach. "He passed by here, but that was ages ago. Seemed like an upright man. He was looking for some master craftsman, Mzilikele. Have you tried Gwadza's? He's probably there, that's where people go to drink."

"What would he be doing there?" Chiiko was incensed by the notion.

"Just saying, child, your father looked like he needed a drink . . . or two." She chuckled again.

He ignored that. "Can you give me directions to this place? I am not too familiar with these areas."

"Young and fresh I see. The young girls and even some mothers will love you."

Chiiko found himself feeling rather uncomfortable. "Look lady, I'm just trying to find my father, that's all."

"You truly are his child, no time for small jest. Sure young man, I'll show you out and point out the direction." She walked Chiiko out, onto the pathway and pointed toward Gwadza's *Umqombothi*. "Be careful, young man, I'm sure you can take care of yourself, but there are many bad men about and they come out in the dark. Best be on your way before then."

The boy thanked her and ran off.

As he approached Gwadza's, he could hear loud cheering. He added an extra spring to his step. His sandal's leather sole was weathering away. He could feel pebbles and the stones as he ran. It hurt, but he continued nonetheless. The entrance was blocked by a large mass of people, shouting and screaming. He used his elbows to sneak through the crowd. Though taller and thicker boned than most his age, he was still a child, so it wasn't long before he had burrowed to the end of the tunnel of drunks.

Father! There he was, lying on the hard floor. Gamu wiped blood from his chin, sprang up and leapt forward toward a large man, perhaps two meters in length. The giant skipped out of the way and with the heel of his feet sent Gamu back to where Chiiko found him. The giant sprang forth, but Chiiko leapt forward to protect his father from a further beating.

"Out of my way, junior, this is none of your business."

"Please, leave my father alone."

"Your father stole my *umqombothi*," the beast of a man roared. "No one takes my beer without paying the price. Get out of my way."

The boy refused to heed the burly man, putting up his fists and steadying his legs the way his father had taught him. The giant rubbed the bruise Gamu had left. "The little boy has heart I'll tell you . . . like his father. Not very clever though." The crowd of drunkards laughed, bashing their metal cups onto the tables. The giant made to continue his attack, but Chiiko stood strong and determined.

A man with a lithe frame and genial smile whistled and everyone fell silent. His garb was expensive, an assortment of gold and silver jewelry all over his neck, arms and ankles. "That's enough, Tulu. I think the traveler has learned his lesson. Besides, would you beat an already defeated man in front of his son?"

Finally, Tulu was compelled to stand down. "Okay child, take your father home before I change my mind. I hope you have more sense than him. Thank Chief-Treasurer Mutasa."

Chiiko picked up his father by the armpits and helped him out of the beer hall. He was panting by the time they reached the exit, fighting hard to hold his tears back.

"Please don't tell your mother," Gamu slurred as a mixture of saliva and blood dripped from his open lips. He opened his mouth to continue, but before long, he was snoring on his son's shoulder.

When he came to, it was pitch black. "Where am I, how . . ." The words stuck in his throat when he caught Tanaka's gaze.

"We need to talk."

"Do we have to do that now? My head is throbbing." He felt like someone had sunk a splinter through the back of his head and out through his forehead.

"Yes, we have to do it now."

"But there are people around - can't we take this up in a more private setting?" Tanaka had found a camp where travellers could stay for a small fee.

"No Gamu, now."

He sat up and groaned from the pain. He felt like his ribs were aching to rip through his insides and escape his cavity.

"What happened? What have you done?"

"It's nothing. Just got into a scuffle that's all. I'll be okay. I just need to rest."

"You're a warrior now?" Gamu had never seen her so upset . . . for a while. "Chiiko is going on about you fighting Tulu the Water Dancer. Are you crazy? You will get yourself killed and then what are we going to do?"

Gamu was too tired to respond. All he wished for was to be left alone.

"Did you find this man you were looking for?" Gamu shook his head, unable to meet her eyes. "Okay, but you know where he is and we will find him tomorrow?" Gamu shook his head again. Tanaka paused and thought briefly. "What's that smell?" She wrinkled her nose, grabbed him by the cheeks and forced his mouth open. Her eyes widened. "Is that what you have been doing all this time when we thought you were looking for this Mzilikele? Drinking?"

Gamu wanted to beg her to quieten down, at least for the sake of the other travellers, and he didn't want his failings being broadcast for all to hear, especially his children. Alas, he was too weak and too sloshed to do anything. Tanaka inhaled in an effort to calm her escalating nerves. This was not good for the child brewing in her belly. Her mother warned her against stress during pregnancy, but it was hard living by those words in the current situation. "Does this Mzilikele even exist?" Gamu did not move, didn't talk, he didn't even breath it seemed, perhaps too ashamed of his ghastly breath, the foul sour smell of a cocktail of sorghum malt and yeast. "Okay, we still have the copper . . . right?"

Gamu reached for his loincloth and felt around it. He began to tremble, and then a tear began flowing down his cheek.

"You bastard," she screamed, "What were you thinking going to that place? Are you thick in the head?" Her voice broke: "You have children, Gamu."

"You don't understand, Tanaka, I'm so sorry, the beer peddler, Gwadza, he tricked me."

"Sorry?" Tanaka slapped him hard. "How dare you," she reproached. "I followed you everywhere and put my trust in you, and this is how you repay me? You are a failure Gamu, an utter disgrace. Thank the ancestors your father is not here to witness this." She shook the children awake.

Gamu tried to rise but a bolt of pain zapped through his body, crippling him. "Tanaka, where are you going?"

"Anywhere. Faraway. Home." She rounded the children and grabbed their belongings. It didn't take long. Kushinga and Kayalethu were now walking zombies.

"We can't just leave dad here, mother, he's hurt," Chiiko pleaded.

She gesticulated toward his ear, cowering the boy. "Do as I say, now." She ripped off the hematite stone necklace Gamu had given her on their wedding night, the only thing his mother had left him when she joined her ancestors. "I'm going to sell it. Gamu, enjoy your life."

CHAPTER 13

As the Sangoma wrestled for his last thread of life the rope around his neck was wrenching, he could hear the wails of women. He opened his eyes just one last time to find an arrow headed his way, zipping past and cutting through the rope that was draining his life force. He coughed and groaned as he struggled for dear air. He looked up into the distance to discover the Desert Snake thundering toward him with bow in hand atop his great zebra. The sound of drums followed, growing louder and louder. He knew what that meant. It wasn't the drum heralding the birth of a prince, or the period of mercy. It was the drum announcing the death of a prince.

When the Desert Snake arrived, the Sangoma was still trying to catch his breath. "Get up," he snarled between gritted teeth, grabbing him by the arm and pulling him up onto the zebra.

"Where are you taking me?" The witchdoctor had now finally regained his speech. He turned his head and met eyes with a limp corpse impaled on a tall wooden stake. Its skin was pale, and bloated, but the eyes were alive. *The boy*, the voice whispered. *The boy*. "The boy," the Sangoma cried vociferously. "The boy, we must save him. We must change direction."

"Not a chance, Sangoma. The king has other plans for you."

Another voice spoke to him, compelling the little priest to give the Snake a shove, sending him to the dust. The Sangoma took over the reins and powered toward little Alinafe's quarters, following the somber melody of grief for navigation. People wept outside the hut as they looked on. He shoved his way through the herd until he got to the entrance.

"A spirit!" the guard Wasike wailed, white with fright. "Look what you have done evil spirit, the prince is dead."

The Sangoma managed to peer through quickly before the guard's large hands were upon him. He could just make out Queen Zandile as she wept by her dead boy's side, however, though Alinafe was a lifeless pale, he noticed the faintest of twitches only a falcon could espy. At first he thought his eyes were playing tricks on him, for the Sangoma was no bird of prey, but it happened again, this one fainter than the last. "I can resurrect him," he declared as priests prayed for the boy's safe passage.

"How can the dead save the dead? Look at him," Wasike pointed at the boy. "You did this. I always knew you were up to no good in life, now you return to terrorize us in death. Be gone evil spirit."

"I am not a spirit, look." He exposed his neck, revealing the rope marks from the hangman's noose. "Please Wasike, you do not understand, I am here to help."

"I think you have helped enough, lizard." Just as the guard raised his club for a thunderous strike, Queen Zandile walked out.

"I can help. I can resurrect the child," the Sangoma pleaded.

Even though the queen's eyes were raw with grief, they could not match the red that radiated through the cracks of the Sangoma's harrowing mask. What could she do? Her son was dead and there was a mystic who claimed he could save him. In her heart, she felt it was her fault. Had someone seen her that night she stole into the Fire Shrine and performed the dark magic? She had been trying to save one child, but in turn, had cursed another.

She had been warned as a child when she and Sekai stole into the woods to seek the aid of a mystic. Sekai had fallen in love with Zandile's brother, Neo, but sadly he had not reciprocated her affections. Zandile had dreams that he and Sekai would marry. Life would be blissful, for she and Sekai would not only be friends, but true sisters by marriage. She had praised Sekai's virtues in her brother's presence, and even lent Sekai advice on a woman's wiles, but no matter what they tried, Neo barely noticed Sekai for he was in love with another. When Zandile overheard her father, brother and their counselors devising a marriage proposal, she decided they had to act. "This way," Zandile said, leading Sekai into the forest just outside the village.

"It is too late, Zandile, Neo is to marry Chief Mukonikoni's daughter."

"Not if we can do anything about it. Go back if you want regret to follow you for the rest of your life."

Though it was still afternoon, it was dark in the forest, for the thick leaves had created a canopy light could not penetrate. They tip-toed through, evading the numerous whistling thorn trees and their sharp leaves until they reached a short flight of stairs leading to the mystic's hut. They collected themselves and then knocked on the wooden door.

"Who goes there," asked a voice from inside.

"Zandile and Sekai. You are Azai the Prophetess of the Thorne Forest, are you not?"

An old lady with large dry breasts sitting around her navel opened the door. "I have counseled chiefs, warriors, desperate farmers and impoverished peasants, but never a chief's daughter."

"We are not here for me, it is for my friend."

The old woman looked around at nothing. Her tongue stuck out, like she tasted the air. "What do you have there?" the mystic pointed.

"A chicken, for payment."

The prophetess turned and walked into the dark hut. "Then enter and tell me what troubles you, young girls."

Sekai was apprehensive. "Are you sure this is a good idea? She smells. She might butcher us in that hut . . . and eat us," she fretted.

"Nonsense. Stop being so craven, Sekai. She knows my father is the chief. She wouldn't dare." Zandile grabbed her by the wrist and they entered. "Prophetess, we come seeking . . ."

Before Zandile could finish, the sorceress cut in. "Your friend is love struck. But her object of desire loves someone else. You seek a remedy to that."

The girls looked at each other in astonishment. "You see, Sekai, I told you she was good." Zandile turned back to the witchdoctor. "How did you know?"

"The spirits," she replied. "They send messages across the plains, over mountains and over the rivers, across the savannah and even the deepest and darkest of woodlands."

Zandile was clearly impressed. "Very well then, can you help Sekai?"

"Do you not need the same help young princess?"

Zandile pursed her lips, dumbfounded at the mystic's insinuation. "I do not need such. Some call me the most beautiful woman in the entire kingdom. Besides, I am the daughter of a powerful chief. I am likely to be a queen one day."

"So be it." The old woman shuffled slowly to her shelf and brought down a vile with a liquid. "Put this into the desired target's drink. If you time it right, when he is most vulnerable, he will be yours."

Sekai and Zandile smiled at each other. "Then we will be sisters," they screamed in unison. Whilst both were tall for their ages, Sekai was more slender at the hips. Whilst both girls sported finely made bead belts and bracelets that covered most of their torsos and arms, Zandile's were more numerous, with the odd gold and silver laced tapestry that marked her as the daughter of a high ranking chief. Whilst Sekai's head was elongated with soft plain features, Nia's head was heart shaped with a face as though it was carved out of obsidian rock with long thick eyelashes and perky duck-shaped lips.

Azai the Prophetess handed over the vile. Sekai grabbed it with glee and pulled, however, the witchdoctor's eyes lightened into a luminous green, and her voice changed into a deeper, darker croak. "Be careful what you ask for, child."

Sekai nodded wearily, and off the girls went.

A chance to slip the potion into Neo's drink had not been forthcoming, and Sekai was running out of time. Now she had just one day left. She looked at the vile in the darkness of her hut, rubbing her thumb up and down its texture. She had no choice. It was now or never. She found the prince preparing for a hunt. "Sekai," he bellowed. "Fetch me some beer for the hunt."

The gods are indeed good, she thought. "Yes, delighted to." She inserted the *umqombothi* into a leather skin and so no one could see, slipped the potion in. "Here you go," she said bowing elegantly.

Neo ripped off the top and took a sip. He looked up and smiled. He looked just like his sister, Sekai thought, but with a rounder nose, wider lips and cheeks filled with sparse hair. "Thank you, Sekai." He looked at her in a way he never had before. "I shall return soon, my sweet lady." She found it rather pleasing.

It's working, she said to herself. "Yes, Neo, I will be eagerly awaiting your return with a big dangerous leopard resting on your strong shoulders."

He smiled, whistled and off he and his entourage went. That was the last time she saw him. That was the last time Zandile saw him too. Neo never returned and after weeks and weeks of searches, all that had been found of him was the skin of beer Sekai had prepared for him.

Now grown up, Queen Zandile nodded and ushered the Sangoma into Alinafe's hut, despite Wasike's reluctance. The witchdoctor danced in to the hut and set about his work. He erected twelve lamps around the room and wreathed the space with incense as he chanted and danced around the boy's limp body. He muddled some herbs in a large wooden calabash and then commanded Wasike to bring him the blood of an innocent. Soon thereafter, he was stroking the cheek of a lamb. "Yes, this one will do." He turned to the queen. "Leave," he hissed, "Leave at once. The magic I am about to perform is very dangerous." He hummed and shuffled his feet as his shoulders began to rotate.

Zandile had no choice but to yield. She crept out of the hut, with tears flowing down her cheeks. She sat outside all night as mosquitos made a feast of her, but she did not care. Purple and black smoke raged from the chimney as the Sangoma wailed until the wee hours of the morning and continued through the day and into the next.

After nodding off behind his mask, he awoke to soft coughs. He assumed it was Zandile. She had caught a chill over the night from sitting outside in the cold. He crept up to her as she slept and let the warmth of her breath blow on his mask. There was another light cough, and then another, but it was not from the queen. He looked down at the boy and then set his lips by Zandile's ears. "Ssshhhhh," he whispered, barely keeping his saliva in his mouth. "The boy lives, the boy is alive!"

Later that evening, the Desert-Snake approached the Sangoma as he ate gleefully outside the lodgings he had been given, now reunited with Reza the hyena. The sandman's curved blade danced around his hips as his thick dark hair blew behind him and over his shoulders, evaporating the smirk of triumph lodged across the mage's fat lips. Most people were cautious approaching the Sangoma with Reza nearby, but this one was unperturbed. "I ought to put my spear through that mask of yours, sorcerer," the foreign man snarled as he unsheathed his sword and pressed it on the mask's temple. Reza began to giggle angrily. "Send that creature away before I cut it up." The wizard whistled and waved Reza away. "You would be dead if the king had not summoned you."

"Summoned me? I wonder what for?"

"Get up. Father waits for no man." The Desert Snake sent the bowl and its contents tumbling to the floor for the ants and pulled the Sangoma by the arm.

Maghedzi's back was turned when they finally arrived on the mountain slopes of Mount Pyre. Sweat began to form under the Sangoma's armpits as the mountain huffed and puffed and exhumed a terrible ashen cloud and the frightfully foul odor of sulfur. There were a lot of things the spirit-medium had missed from his days at Pyyros all those years ago, however, the persistent smell of rotten eggs that lingered around the volcano was not one of them. When the king finally noticed them, he immediately fell to his knees. "Sangoma, forgive me, forgive us all. I doubted your powers and it almost drowned my seed." Tears ran down Maghedzi's eyes. "But you resurrected him."

"Our ancestors teach us to forgive, even our enemies. What matters is what you do to make amends. Only then can the spirits be appeased."

"And how can we appease these spirits you speak of?"

"I will show you the way, the road to your destiny as supreme ruler."

"But I am already supreme. My subjects obey me without question." The large pile of skulls he kept in his hut was testament to that.

"In this realm, my lord. However, the world is large, larger than you can imagine." The Sangoma felt like a giant of a man, looking down upon Maghedzi's raw face as the king knelt. "When the fire gods gave your ancestors dominion over the realm atop Pyre Mountain, what did they say?"

"The land promised to you is as far and wide as the eyes can see."

"Then you must gain the eyes of a hawk. I can show you how." He offered his hand and helped the king up. "Look into the flames." At first Maghedzi had the look of irritation as he searched, only seeing the dull flow of the lava streams, but then his eyes widened.

CHAPTER 14

Xolani squinted his eyes, shying them away from the unrelenting sun that cut through the jacaranda's shade as he bathed Shiri. He had just returned from the Moyo homestead, still grief stricken by the sad affair that was Korokoro Moyo's funeral. He had begun to cry, but wiped away the tears before anyone saw. He had been there the night the beasts attacked, sloshed and cross-eyed scared. He too might have been mourned on this very day with the rest, had it not been for Themba's timely intervention.

His mother had promised to punish him for his misadventure, but the passing of little Korokoro and the others had united the king's court in a cloud of sorrow. The Moyo, whose totem was the heart, strongly believed in its power. Xolani had to shy his eyes away when a priest with a large bone pierced through his nose, slashed across the boy's cavity, stuck his hand in and removed his heart. The priest paraded it around for all to see before dicing it into small cubes and setting it on the blazing brazier. When it was well cooked and the fat fizzed, one by one he went to each of the boys' immediate family and helped a portion of the boy's heart into their mouths until all that remained in the brazier was the fat residue. Xolani had wanted to vomit, observing the Moyo's strange and rather gruesome ritual, but managed to hold it in and hurl in his mouth. The Moyo believed by eating the dead's hearts, they lived within them forever. To Xolani, it sounded oddly poetic, but still, he doubted he could bring himself to eat his brothers' hearts if tasked to.

"There you go," he said, casting the brush back into the wooden bucket of water. "What do you think, Aku?"

"Shiri has never been cleaner," the creature confessed. The zebra stomped its hooves into the red earth creating a small cloud of dust and flared its nostrils wildly as it yipped noisily.

"What's she saying?"

"She says I am one to talk, the way I smell."

When the laughter died down, Xolani asked the dragon how he ended up in the Khumalo. The dragon hissed before it looked down, coiling itself into a neat cup. "I don't remember. I don't remember anything from my former life, just the images of my parents . . . and eyes, a deep purple easily mistaken for black."

Xolani became distracted by an approaching image prompting him to grab his spear. "Someone is coming, Aku, you should be on your way." The water dragon dove back into the river creating a red stain. Xolani tried his best to look threatening, forwarding his chest and gnashing his teeth. "No further, stranger."

"Calm down, young man." The man's triceps flexed as he stroked his agitated donkey's spikey hair. "We mean you no harm." He looked down and studied the prints the water dragon's talons had left, and the snake-like tracks of its tail. "Sure it's safe here, boy? Those are some large tracks there."

"It's nothing, just a crocodile," Xolani lied.

The man looked suspicious, but left it at that. He looked closer at Xolani. He recognized those eyes, a dark brown one could mistake for black. He even recognized the ears, slender and pointed at the ends. "Wait, you are Xolani, Chipo's little boy . . ." The man instantly jumped off his donkey in one fluid motion, his necklace, an entanglement of bark and reeds swung from side to side as he moved closer. "Do you not recognize me? I am your uncle . . . uncle . . ."

"Batusai?" the boy inquired, unsure. It had been many years, and Xolani was very young, but Batusai's face was a handsome one, and not easy to forget. "Uncle, you've come back!"

"Good ancestors, you have grown. You are now a man," Uncle Batusai laughed.

"Mom will be so excited. Here, let me take your things. You must be tired and hungry."

"That won't be necessary boy, I do not have much, but some boiled pumpkin and greens would be nice."

Xolani had not seen his mother happier when he and Batusai appeared at the entrance to her compound. "Mother, look what I found." She dropped the threads and equipment she used in her weaving and ran to welcome them.

Chipo smiled. "It is good to see you have not been completely idle. Go and catch some chickens, we are having a feast." She stood back so she could get a better view. "Look at you." Rather than the loincloth, cow tails and magnificent cape that once donned his shoulders, Batusai now wore an archaic green-dyed cloth wraparound, and a similar band wound around his head, darkened by the dampness of his sweat. His wrists bore an assortment of red, yellow and green beaded bracelets, across his back was a straw quiver and a bow, and in his first hand, a long savage spear. "The ancestors are good. They have kept you well, though your stomach is too flat. We need to get some food into you."

The whole afternoon they laughed and reminisced. There was much to catch up on. They carried it on into the dimly lit supper. "The ancestors have truly blessed us," said Chipo, as she dipped the serving spoon into the cauldron and fished out a drumstick. It was customary for the most senior male to eat the best piece.

"No thank you, Chipo. I will just be having some pumpkin and greens."

That took Chipo by surprise. Boiled chicken and pumpkin had always been Batusai's favorite dish as they were growing up.

"My tongue has not touched flesh for years. I have made an oath to never eat meat."

The thought was rather perplexing to Xolani. There was nothing he loved more than chucking down red meat, chunk after chunk, until it was finished. Xolani discerned awkwardness, so quickly intervened. "Uncle, have you captured any poachers?"

"Some, but not enough I'm afraid."

"There was an assassination attempt on father, you might have heard?"

Batusai hadn't, he had been out of touch for many years now. Once upon a time, it was his duty to protect the king's person.

"They found one of the bad men with elephant tusks and rhino horns." Xolani could see the utter disgust in his uncle's eyes as he relayed the story. "Themba is supposed to fight him in a trial by combat at the Festival of Tusks."

"I pray that he makes things right." They all nodded their heads. "All this is great, but I have other reasons for my return." Xolani and Chipo waited in anticipation. "I have come to see the king . . . your husband. I come representing the Green Rangers." They were warriors tasked to protect the Akuwa sacred animals, the ones kings and chiefs expected to inhabit in the afterlife. "We were attacked in the bush by a pack of wild dogs. I was injured gravely, but managed to fight them off before a Tsavo herdsman saved me.

It happened after me and my fellow rangers had been on the trail of poachers. When it became dark, we built a fire, but in the middle of the night we were ambushed by a pack of wild dogs. They first tore out Geko's throat, and began eating Pumile alive. His screams, I can still remember until this day."

That sent a cold chill down Xolani's spine as the events at the Moyo farm vividly resurfaced. He waited with bated breath for the rest of the tale. "I stabbed one, and sliced an ear of another, but they kept coming. I looked to run, but there was no tree to climb. I performed a silent prayer and prepared myself for my ancestors. One attacked, sending me back, slipping over a stone. Now I was on my back with only my spear to protect myself. I tried to scream, to scare them off, but that didn't work. One jumped on me and attacked, but its teeth caught the shaft of my spear instead. I wriggled my spear free and it flung its teeth again. I was sure I was dead. I had no energy left to fight. One had bitten me on the side, and another had taken a large chunk of my thigh. However, as its teeth came my way, I heard a drum in the distance. The dogs stopped in their tracks, turned and began to bark. Not long thereafter, they disappeared into the night. When I got up, there in front of me, he stood."

"The Tsavo herdsman?"

Batusai nodded. "As he nursed me in my anguish, he revealed to me some things. He told me that man was not superior, or equal to animals, but lowly, an unholy specimen. I laughed and showed him the wounds he had just stitched." The green ranger reached into his bag and produced a smooth hide with a drawing on it. He placed it on the table and turned the light upon it. "You see that there? That is a *quagga*. It looks like a zebra, however instead of black and white, its colors are a mixture of tan, majestic whites and gold. Like the king of the Savannah." One could see the passion he bore, the way he described the creature. "Though our primary objective is ensuring the king's rhinos, elephants and most importantly, the hippo, remain safe, there are plenty more animals which need his help."

"I'd love to see one, uncle."

"I wish you could, Xolani, but these creatures are almost extinct. Finding one in the bush is rarer than an unmolested cactus in the drought." His eyes darkened and the thick veins on his hand stretched as he tightened his fist. "Earth, our mother, is very upset, Xolani. She talks . . . she lives!"

Chipo's arms were now crossed and tightly kept to her body.

"We are in the bush so much, we have seen some things you would never believe." Batusai opened his mouth, then hesitated, stopping his course of speech. "We need help, Chipo. There is an ever-growing threat our dwindling numbers cannot help prevent." The Savannah is sprawling, reaching far and wide, further than any eagle could see. There were numerous caves, mountains and rivers where poachers could find refuge and avoid the law. "Look at my spear, Xolani." The boy received the instrument, brushing his fingers over its edge. It was razor sharp and made a small crack on his tips. A lot of spears were decorated with animal hides but his was bare. "That spear has not touched an animal's flesh. It was sworn to be its protector." Xolani's eyes widened as he indulged himself in his uncle's spear.

"Your uncle needs a refill." Xolani could have sworn his uncle's calabash had been refilled recently, but Chipo's stern look had him up on his feet and on his way.

When the door was shut and Xolani was gone, she turned to Batusai. "What are you doing?"

"What do you mean?" he replied, appearing unaware of his alleged crimes.

"Do not think you can come here and take my child away from me."

"Take your son? I have no intention of that."

"Could have fooled me, the way you're selling this cow dung you are spewing. Xolani is going to his rites of passage, and then after that, he will become Amakazi."

"Calm down, Chipo, I have nothing but good intentions for the boy. I love him like a father."

"Only you are not." Chipo spat, with words meant to sting.

"I am not, but nonetheless, we are like family, you and I."

"Then why did you desert me?"

Batusai did not answer, but Chipo only needed his eyes for the truth. In fact, she had seen that look before. It had been in front of her for most of her life, as they grew up side-by-side.

"He made me join the Green Rangers to keep me away from you. He told me if he ever saw me again, he would kill me, but my cause is greater than my life. That is why I am here, and also I . . ." He started moving closer toward Chipo until the door opened and in came Xolani with a wide smile and a fresh new calabash filled to the brim, unaware of the apparent discomfiture.

"Here you go, uncle. It's nice and cool."

"Thank you, Xolani," said Chipo, curtly, but sternly. "Now say good night to your uncle. He is tired and will retire to the guest hut." The boy wanted to protest. Such was his irritation at being sent to a pointless errand, and it wasn't even that late. Batusai grabbed his spear and drawings and moved to the door. "I will pray on what you have said. Good night." She curtsied and clapped her hands.

The next morning, Batusai awoke to banging on the door. Two large men appeared at the foot of his guest lodgings. It had been a while since he set his eyes on the blue capes the men donned, and the gold chain that kept the ensemble together. "Grab your things and follow us," the taller said, with respect for the position Batusai had once occupied when he was Amakazi.

It was a meandering path through the Stone Houses, a myriad of thatched huts and stone pavements protected by towering granite walls, some twenty, other parts thirty meters in length. It was no wonder they said the Akuwa lair was impenetrable, Batusai thought, but no walls, meek or great could hinder nature once it had endured enough – the green ranger was sure of that. It was what his teacher had promised him amongst their conversations, some which extended well beyond the break of dawn. Batusai wondered how many wildebeest were denied their grazing lands to establish this grand civilization of which the Akuwa were so proud.

When they arrived, the guards took his spear and threw him in front of the waiting monarch sitting upon his throne. "Batusai. It has been a long time indeed. I thought I would never see you again. Raise your head." The green ranger did as commanded, but kept his palms unified. "Chipo informed me that you had come, but I thought it false. Not after our last encounter. I initially refused to grant your audience, but a man cannot deny his wife, late in the hour."

"My king," Batusai began, "First I thank you for seeing me, considering our past. Kill me if you may. It is your right. As the mighty hippo, my life belongs to you. However, I wouldn't have come here if it were not for a righteous cause. When you stripped me of my blue cape and exchanged it for the green, I was admittedly bitter, for my ambitions were far greater, but now I see you were acting through the ancestors."

The king looked taken aback by Batusai's frank speech.

"I have come here to seek men and resources to help in our fight against poachers of your sacred creatures. I'm afraid they face extinction."

It was no surprise to the king. He had seen the contents of Muchita's satchel and duly set them into the fire. It was not a gamble inferring there were many more such bags around the kingdom, not when one could be rich.

"I have sworn to protect your creatures, but unfortunately, we are losing the war. We are underfunded and facing a race against time. Right now we stand at a meager thirty-two. Even if we do find poachers, we cannot hope to catch them on the donkeys we ride. If we carry this on, our children will not feel the joy of seeing a western-back-rhino, a mountain gorilla or a clouded-leopard."

"The world will be better for it," joked Chief-Treasurer Mutasa, ever present amongst the king's flock, patting down the fine animal skins that decorated his shoulders.

Batusai was not swayed by the laughter. "Mighty Hippo, your love for the natural world is spoken of across vast lakes and rivers, and shouted from mountaintops. We ask that you provide us with more men, food and weapons."

"Our ancestors teach us that nature is sacred. They teach us to be upright in life, for the wicked return as dung beetles, spinning feces in the searing heat, and the righteous, a leopard, an eagle, or better yet the hippo, so as you see, I am sympathetic to your cause." Farakaii stroked his beard as advisor after advisor whispered in his ear. Batusai remained where he was, on his knees and palms touching. "You have shown great courage and obvious belief in your cause by coming here today. Regrettably, I do not have any warriors to give you at the present moment. My first duty is to my people, and then the animal kingdom."

"Besides," Treasurer Mutasa cut in. "These animals that you say are on the brink are all as good as dead come the draught. It is a waste of time. Perhaps it is the will of the ancestors." Many about nodded their heads in agreement.

Batusai's mouth remained ajar as the king continued, but his mind had already shut off. He had failed. He had travelled halfway across the land and would now return empty handed. "I wish I could grant you what you seek," continued the king. "But all I can offer now is some food and some old spears, clubs and bows. I wish you and the rangers luck in your righteous endeavors and the ancestor's mercies."

Batusai stood up and prepared to leave when the heir to the Akuwa throne, Prince Simba, suggested, "What about the prisoners? There are many able men there. Some women condemned of witchcraft." Everyone seemed perplexed. "I was talking to the honorable Mutasa the other moon. He said the prisons were full. Instead of hard labor, they can help protect your precious creatures and stop being a burden on our dwindling resources."

This did not go well with some. "But these are criminals – murderers and thieves. Men who lack honor, mere beasts in man's loincloths. What use could one have with such filth? What's to say they would stay? What would stop them from running away and murdering honest village folk in their sleep?"

Batusai's eyes narrowed and became steelier. "Death," he answered plainly. That word sent a breeze through the room. A chill one could cut like the frozen glaziers atop the southern mountain slopes.

After much deliberating, the king admitted proudly, "I think it is a good idea. Simba, I will trust you and the treasurer to handle this. See to it that Batusai has a good meal, and then take him to the prisons. He can take whoever is willing to join him."

"Thank you, thank you," Batusai exclaimed, falling to his knees.

"Do not thank me, thank Prince Simba." With that he was led away as the king continued his day of judgment.

The next morning Xolani sprang as fast as he could to see off his dear uncle. "There you are, I thought I wouldn't see you before I left," admitted Batusai.

"I ran as fast as I could. Did you find what you were looking for? Did father help? I'm sure he did!"

"I don't know, Xolani. All I have are the dredges of society. The chief-treasurer picked all the healthy and strong prisoners for his own purpose and left me with this lot." It was a sorry crew Xolani had to admit. "It's better than nothing I guess. Perhaps it is the will of the ancestors. We need all the hands we can, if we are to win this war." He fastened a large basket on the back of his donkey and turned to Xolani. "I have something for you." Batusai pulled out a red, gold and green bracelet made of tightly combined beads. "These are the colors of our order. There is much honor to be found as a Green Ranger. I see that now. I know your dream is to be Amakazi, but if you change your mind, we need boys such as yourself." Chipo whistled in the distance, alerting Xolani. "Man is no different from a zebra, or a monkey, or even an ant. You hear me? Only we are worse. We are the worst creation of them all. Take care, Xolani. Your mother is a good woman. Take good care of her."

Batusai turned to the chained prisoners and wondered how he was going to get this lot up to the task of saving the animal kingdom from man's greed. "From now on, I am your commander. You can call me the Hangman if you like. Some people call me that. I have always been good with ropes. Could tie all kinds of knots when I was younger, but nowadays, I'm just good at tying a noose. All of you have chosen freely to join the Green Rangers. I never had that say, the ancestors made that choice for me. Some of your brethren opted to stay in their cages, but although you are now likely to die sooner, a day breathing free air and enjoying nature and its wonders is more worthwhile than a lifetime trapped."

"Could you spare us the speech and get us moving, pretty boy?" said a corpulent man, oval like a pumpkin, and similar in girth.

"Who said that?" The portly man stood forward, defiant with a large satisfied grin on his face. Batusai did nothing but whistle. A few moments later a black cat emerged from the bush, sprang onto the fat man and buried its head into his tires of fat, unleashing an avalanche of blood down the man's body. The rest looked on half surprised, half soiling their cloths as the cat dragged the man toward Batusai as blood pumped from his neck. Batusai took out a noose from his bag and threw it over *King Farakaii's* head and fastened it around a tree branch. When he came to, the sound of farts and excrement erupted as the fat man swayed slowly from the jacaranda tree. He chuckled. "They do this all the time."

CHAPTER 15

It was a joyous occasion for all as drums beat and the mellifluous sounds of *marimba* pleasured the senses, as did the sweet aroma of meat burning on skewers as the Festival of Tusks finally began. Despite that, Comrade Chengetaii stood stone faced, gently caressing the groves on his dagger like a musician fingering the metal strings on his *mbira* as the various clans paid their respects to the mighty hippo who sat atop his kingly seat. Despite his rank and the titles he had collected in a spectacular military career, Chengetaii simply wore a leather loincloth, but was loath to wear the Amakazi cape around his shoulders. He found it cumbersome and impractical, but Farakaii had insisted he wear it as the Captain of the Amakazi – at least during the festival.

The heir to the Chitemo chieftain stepped up first, keeping himself ten paces away from the king. Despite Farakaii's protests, Chengetaii had insisted on this. "A king who is afraid of his people is no king at all," Farakaii argued.

"Better a false king than a dead one," Chengetaii had replied. The assassins weren't likely to leave it as it was. They would strike again soon and what better occasion than a festival with all the commotion and strange faces descended upon the capital.

The Chitemo prince wore a beautiful brown dashiki with little red pickaxes sewn all over in fine detail. They were a proud and ancient clan who were renowned for their agriculture. The red symbolized the blood their forefathers spilled on the brown soil, tilling away in the heat. "Mighty Hippo," he began, genuflect.

"Stand up, young man." Farakaii waved him up. He found the face familiar, but a younger one. Now he had long dreads sat over his shoulders.

"I am Sifa, son of Sifa Chitemo, Chief of the Chitemo Clan of Mazowe. My lord father regrets he could not come in person. Gout has restricted him to his hut. He sent me with gifts." Sifa unveiled a tuft of silver-bush. "This is a symbol of the friendship between the Akuwa and the Chitemo which has existed for thousands of generations and long may it be preserved. My lord father asks you accept two tons of silver-bush. Our donkeys almost died bearing the weight."

The king chuckled. "It is sad to hear my old friend Sifa is not feeling well. His courage and uprightness is a shining example to all of us. Your father and I served side by side on many campaigns."

Sifa nodded. "He has recounted to me on many occasions, the day you slew Shapiro the Giant."

"Yes, he was gravely injured during that battle. Everyone thought he was done for, but we thank our ancestors a healer was nearby to clean and patch him up before the wounds festered. Everyone talks about my battle with Shapiro, but they forget the others. Your father was something. We would have never defeated the rebels if it weren't for his brave efforts. We will never forget that, young Chitemo."

Sifa bowed and slid away as he came, with his hands clapping.

After all the clans had received the mighty hippo's blessing, Prince Simba led out the hosts clad in his traditional ceremonial garb, with cow tails wrapped around his limbs, which gave the young prince the gravitas of kings and heroes long past. The crowd danced around as he took his giant barefooted steps. A leopard skin apron covered the prince's thighs. The rest of Farakaii's brood and an assortment of competitors from prominent families had to be content with cheetah skins. Despite that, Simba did not need kenspeckle garments to stand out from his peers. His calves threatened to tear apart the garters that held his cow tails in place. He wore no headband as he was not married, but his brick jaw and confident stride told everyone who he was. King Farakaii had once had that youthful look. Now he was regal with greying hair and a shortly cropped beard.

Young girls blushed as the prince passed, full of poise and purpose. Mothers and their mothers' whispered in each other's ears. "I hear he has been betrothed to the Salt-Fish Merchant's daughter. There is no male heir, so Simba will inherit his vast fortune," one woman whispered to another.

"Where did you hear that from? My second cousin is friends with a servant at General Moyo's homestead and she overheard them saying he was to wed the general's daughter."

"Let's pray the child takes after the father then, lest we have a frog for a queen."

The pot carrying competition opened the rivalries for the day. Princess Nonkuleko steadied herself at the starting line and placed the large pot on her head, using a soft cloth to cushion the weight. Though she opted out of the traditional ceremonial outfit, she still dazzled in her simple blue and white beaded skirt, exposing the bottom of her buttocks, ample and orbicular. The drum rang and off they went. It would be a while before they came back. The rest would eat and drink, sing and dance. Comrade Chengetaii would do neither. He hated these occasions. One could not walk in peace as touts harassed and begged whoever passed to buy their products. "Captain," one shouted. "Fine work, no?" He lifted a rosewood hand-carved mother nursing a child. "Touch it, feel how smooth the wood is. This one your grandchildren can inherit."

There was a familiarity about the face on the statue that turned Chengetaii melancholy, rehashing images he had tried to bury a long time ago. He reached out to it and clumsily rubbed his fingers over its rosewood cheeks, then lips, and closed his eyes.

"For a warrior of your repute, only five silver pieces."

The commander contemplated for a moment, then snatched his fingers back and shook his head. "Sorry."

"Come on. Four silver pieces . . . three," he exclaimed. My family is hungry. I have not sold anything today."

"No," Chengetaii spat. When the tout was about to throw out another number, the captain grabbed the statue with both hands, raised it above his head and cast it to the ground sending splinters flaying over the red thoroughfare. "Here are your five silver pieces and then some." He flung the pouch to the floor contemptuously and hobbled off, leaving the tout open-mouthed in gleeful amazement as he counted his newfound riches.

Prince Tjingii's drum rang into the afternoon sky, signaling the pot carriers' return. Chengetaii immediately lifted his head and made way toward the finishing line. When he arrived, Sanaa from the Crescent crossed first, closely followed by Nonkuleko and the rest, a Tsavo girl with stretched ear lobes, a Chitemo, a Timba from Domboshawa, A Tsuro, Nyati, Tsavo, and other representatives from the great houses that comprised the Akuwa's vast kingdom. Everyone fell silent with anticipation, even the adolescent boys who thrived on mischief.

The master of the ceremony peered into the girls' pots and lifted his staff as he announced the winner. "The women's pot race goes to Princess Nonkuleko of the Akuwa." The crowd roared and Xolani was the loudest, jumping and whistling enthusiastically. Though fastest to complete the route, Sanaa had spilled too much water, unlike Nonkuleko who had the grace of a swan, not spilling a single drop. Though Sanaa took the loss hard, she collected herself enough to congratulate the Akuwa princess as the entire clan sung her name. "Non-ku-le-ku, Non-ku-le-ku, Non-ku-le-ku."

In the evening, when stomachs were full, and people's heads were light with *umqombothi*, the revels began. King Farakaii was in pleasant spirits that night, even taking from his stool to lead the dancing, forming a line of synchronized dancers. Left, the king went, kicking into the air, and then did the same to the right. He thrust his spear into the sky as he stomped into the earth, bellowing over the frantic drum. The king had lost some of his natural physique, but he had not lost his voice.

Soon enough the whole banquet was in song and dance, giving Xolani a chance to venture off into the wild and see how Aku, the water dragon was faring. He cut junks of meat from the lamb on the skewer, wrapped it with leaves, and threw it into his bag. He looked around for his mother. She sat with Aunt Rabia, his stepmother, Sibongile and other notable women of court. Chipo looked at him and smiled. He waved, and slipped away into the bush, taking the longer route, as it was safer during the night. He hopped over crop fields, and waded through thick and long vegetation until he heard a faint sound ahead. When he got closer, the sound became that of a woman wailing. He clutched his spear tighter and dashed to the scene. When he finally emerged from the bush, rather than a damsel in distress, he found a man knelt by a large jacaranda tree and under him, lithe and petite hands grasped the heaving masculine back. Xolani froze and parted his lips, but before he could turn back undiscovered, the man turned his head and met his eyes. They were similar eyes, but whilst his bore surprise, the ones he met bore carnal excitement. Before he ran back into the bush the man raised one of the hands he used for balance and waved him toward them. Xolani's eyes burgeoned in disbelief and embarrassment, and he disappeared into the bush. *Why did I take this route?* he asked himself. He wished he could forget everything he saw, but he could not take it back. He had heard the wails of a woman, and had prepared himself to fight off bandits, or wild dogs, but the look she bore was not unease, or grief, but rather the antithesis. He would have to visit Aku another day. He returned to the banquet, but rather than join the rest in the festivities, he went straight to his hut, shut the door and went to sleep.

The next day's games began with the marathon. There was an anxious mood around camp as three clans were still vying for the overall honor as victors of the year's competitions. Chengetaii expected a home victory. He had made his warriors run for hours on end, barefooted, sometimes for whole days, along the sacred hills, the Great Waterfall, up the Khumalo and the banks of Lake Nhahara until one with superior eyesight could just make out the Frosted Hills. It was the training they needed to become strong. If one couldn't complete the rigorous training methods, they did not deserve to wield a spear, an axe pick or a rod to pound sorghum was more suitable.

After a few hours, when the mood was beginning to wane, enthusiasm erupted anew when Simba appeared around the bend, a clear distance ahead of the trailing Sifa Chitemo. As Simba powered toward the finish line, at the last straight, Sifa slipped, landing in a thud. The sound of bone cracking horrified those that were close enough to hear the wreckage, stopping the galloping prince in his tracks. When he saw what had happened, he ran back to Sifa, clutching at his broken ankle. After a few exchanged words, Simba extended his hand, helping his rival up and wrapped his hand over his shoulder, and the two crossed the line in unison. Hippo Valley united in celebration of Simba's great gesture of sportsmanship as young maidens rushed to the finishing line to aid the participants with cold water.

Meanwhile, Prince Tjingii was excelling in the *mankala* competition, making quick work of his opponents in route to the final where Zaza the Tsuro defeated him at the last hurdle. Chengetaii was amazed by the mechanic way Tjingii surveyed the playing board and moved his pieces around, until he had devoured all of his opponents. Tjingii, unlike his brothers, preferred to play these games of strategy rather than practice spear, and had mastered several instruments, the *marimba*, the *mbira*, *ngoma* drums, the horn, and *shekere* to name a few. Tjingii had even taken a liking to alchemy, and herbalism. Farakaii had begged Chengetaii to be patient with the boy, insisting Tjingii would one day take to spear . . . eventually. Eventually never came, nor would it. If greatness was achieved through the spear, Tjingii had to find a different avenue. It was unsurprising to Chengetaii when Tjingii could not help himself but cry. Though Chengetaii's cheek had remained dry for eons, he vaguely remembered the feeling of disappointment. When he had lost a duel in his youth, he had wept bitterly, but he learned to harden his heart. Simba ushered his inconsolable brother away, however, Themba was not impressed. "Look at him, he shames us all," he spat churlishly.

"Shut up. You are drunk. He is just a boy," Nonkuleko retorted. "You were a cry baby too. Ask mother."

Themba wiped Gwadza's fine brew from his little moustache. "It's different. Not in front of our enemies. I know these Timba, Chitemo, and Tsuro types. They will think we are all soft."

"You should go and comfort your brother," Sibongile compelled. "Tell him he did well and will win it next time for us."

Themba shrugged his shoulders and with a cool insolence, slipped into the crowd.

"That boy is too stubborn for his own good," Chengetaii ceded.

"He will come around. He is a good boy. He will apologize to Tjingii," the queen assured the commander.

"Be sure that he does, or I will use my own disciplinary methods. Tjingii is not like his brothers, but a true warrior protects the weak."

"How will Tjingii learn to be a man if we keep protecting him?"

"He is your son, do as you like. It is not my place, but as long as I am commander, I will teach my boys how to be warriors in body and spirit." With that, Chengetaii took his leave as he felt faint raindrops on the top of his shiny bald head.

"Look what you have done Themba." Nonkuleko's eyebrows bridged. "Now the ancestors punish us." Rain began to trickle, thunder erupted, then a few moments later, they were all drenched.

CHAPTER 16

Now that the Sangoma had won King Maghedzi's trust, and been installed as chief-witchdoctor of the Piripiri Kingdom, life was not too shabby. He had even been bestowed a nice little hut not far from the Fire Shrine, so he could be closer to the Piripiri spirits. He had found it hard settling into his new environment, but the smooth clay walls and clean water brought in by servants every morning was something he could get used to. He had even received a surprise visit from Princess Nia, who had given him a flower – a token of gratefulness for saving her brother. The Sangoma discerned fierceness in the girl's essence – a tremendous presence for one so young. She had even come alone, undeterred by his appearance and reputation.

"Everyone around the village says you are a bad man. They say you have put a horrible spell on my father. Is that true?" the girl had inquired.

"See for yourself." He ripped off his mask and twisted his face, making himself even more grotesque.

"You don't scare me," said she. Most girls her age would have fainted at his sight or turned and run away in tears, but not she. Embarrassed, the Sangoma quickly refastened the mask. "I was overhearing people talk. They said that you were banished from Pyyros. Is that true?" Nia did not need a reply. "Why?"

"You are too inquisitive for your own good, young girl." The princess reminded him of himself when he was smaller. "Your young mind will never understand."

"Try me. My friends . . ." the girl hated lying, the only true friend she ever had was Wafula, and the last time she saw him was when she left him alone deep in the Fire Caves, the night she bled. "My friends say I am pretty wise . . . even my father once said so."

His eyes flared, like two torches in the black. "I was banished because I wanted to heal."

Nia took a moment to reply. "But that's not a bad thing?"

"Like I said, princess. It is complicated."

She moved closer and slowly reached for his mask. The wizard hissed like a viper's warning. "It's okay, I don't mind looking upon your face. It is the face our creator has given you. Besides, you must get hot and sweaty under there."

Nia stayed all afternoon. He showed her some of the new concoctions he had made and jars with different animal parts. "This is the heart of a silver back gorilla. Do you know what that is?" The girl shook her head. "It is just like a chimpanzee, but bigger, and stronger, with hair as black and shiny as your father's spear head. They dwell deep in the jungles and are a constant menace to the Uche."

"Have you seen one?"

"Yes, but different ones." The Sangoma's tone changed. "Ones you will never want to see, in the Forest of Abominations."

In the dark forest, he had encountered an inkanyamba as he foraged in shallow waters, an elongated fish, eight or perhaps ten meters in length. It had attacked him, but the Sangoma was nimble, dashing out of the creature's reach. Legends said inkanyambas controlled the weather, so the Sangoma sought after one to study its powers so he could wield it. It was easier said than done, for they were dangerous creatures, with razor sharp teeth and an unquenchable thirst for human flesh. He had encountered a school of kongamato and ran for dear life as they flapped their featherless wings high above him. One had even dropped a large smelly stool his way, staining his beloved mask. He had rolled his fist into a tight knot and vowed revenge, an idea that had the Sangoma licking his lips by the prospect. He thanked the gods he had not encountered the impudululu, adze, and the worst, tokoloshe. His voice calmed. "Anyway, this gives one strength and agility."

Nia reached out to it. "Can I have it?"

"Get away," the Sangoma spat. "This is not made for children, besides you cannot afford it."

"Sure I can." The girl calculated everything she had and came to nothing. "What about this one, what's this?" She pointed at an old wooden container engraved with strange patterns and symbols and motioned to open the lid.

"Do not dare, child." The Sangoma's eyes flared luminously, like she had performed the gravest of violations. "That is my greatest possession." He smiled proudly like a parent, holding aloft a new born baby.

"Are you going to say what it is, or?"

He initially hesitated: "Fine, as long as it is our secret." He looked around the hut, but the only others present were Reza and the python he had never come around to naming. "It is an elixir I concocted. It induces prophecy."

Why did the Sangoma have the best toys, the girl thought, whilst she had a sewing kit? "Can I have some? I want to do prophet things too."

"Absolutely not. There isn't much left, it has to be used sparingly."

"But you made it right?"

"Yes."

"Then you can make more."

The truth was he couldn't. It was all the work of the lazy hyena, Reza. The hyena's antics had created a concoction so great it made him the greatest prophet, in any generation. No mystic could hope to match him, not even the legends like the Oracle's of the Sacred Hills, nor the Green Leafed Nganga. "Of course I can." He snapped. "Enough, it's time for you to go. Some of us have to work."

"I will, but only if you do a spell for me."

The Sangoma hesitated. His power was not something to be used frivolously, but he could see that the girl was truly troubled. "Fine, what is it?"

"Can you make Wafula forgive me?"

"Who is Wafula?"

"A boy."

"Ah, I see, young love."

Nia curled her little paw and struck the Sangoma on his shoulder. "That's disgusting, never. We are not in love. He is my friend, but I was mean to him."

"Very well, as you say. Close your eyes, child." He raised his arms and shrieked, deafeningly. He clucked his tongue and began chanting as he slammed his feet into the ground. "It is done!" The Sangoma readjusted his mask and headdress. "Now go, but remember your father has already tried to kill me twice. If he were to hear of this little meeting, I shan't be so lucky the third." The girl nodded and skipped down the pathway.

When the princess was gone, the Sangoma turned to Reza. "Do you remember the Desert Snake? Oh, how could you? You were just a little troublemaker then. Now you are the cause of my misery." The witchdoctor walked to the hyena as it wagged its short tail, patted it on its spikey back and from nothingness produced a large bone. "Even then, though my powers were still in development, my body shook when I felt the little boy's spirit. I need to find out more about this mysterious foreigner." When he noticed Reza wasn't paying him any mind, he kicked the bone away from its range. The hyena giggled and looked up, baring its teeth.

It had been a busy period for him. He had officiated four marriages in the last moon and also attended dozens of baby ceremonies. He had slaughtered so many lambs his right shoulder was now swollen and sprained. He even noticed signs of bulk growing. *Maybe it's not too late for me. Maybe I too can have a beautifully sculpted figure like the Desert Snake.* It was long and tiresome work, but in the end, it would be worth it the day he performed his favorite ceremony. He missed it dearly, the singing, the dancing and the campy atmosphere, but now sadly, few practiced it. It was what made being a witchdoctor worthwhile. He would have to be in his best shape. He had performed the miracle on the daughters of chiefs and men of great title, but he had never performed one on a princess. He pulled out the withering jacaranda leaf Nia had given him and caressed it as he hissed. He was resolved to do right by her, but only if he could make Maghedzi see.

"So, the ancestors have chosen me to save mankind from annihilation?"

"Yes, father," replied the Sangoma in the darkness of the sparsely lit room. "Through blood and fire you shall unite the tribes under the fire gods and save us from the real threat."

"Then their temples will fall? And their knees will descend in praise of our gods? That I shall become a judge of man wielding power over life and death? You place too much faith in me, Sangoma. Has it ever crossed your mind that I might not be this savior you speak of?"

"Never!"

"How do I do that then, have they told you that Sangoma? The Stone Houses is impregnable, as is the Lion's Den, and only the

Uche know their jungles. Furthermore, who knows the allegiance of the rulers at the Snake Pit."

The Sangoma grabbed a chicken, cut its neck, and let the blood fall into the flames. The fire roared and then began strange voices. "I understand," the spirit-medium replied.

"Are you talking to the ancestors?"

The priest nodded. "They say we do not need to invade the Stone Houses. That we can savor for later. We will see how long they can hide behind their stone walls as your warriors scorch their fields, take their cows and women."

The king licked his lips, and for the first time, cracked a smile, as wry as it was. "For that I would have to take Domboshawa."

"Domboshawa? Why?"

"My new warrior units need spears, bows, arrows, clubs, but I lack the wood to sustain a war of the magnitude you speak of, one that will crown me emperor of all the kingdoms. By the banks of Lake Dombo there is plenty. The finest wood you can find in all the land."

"Ahh, I see now. This is what I saw in my visions. A woman, walking with a group of men, but rather than at the back she walks in front down a pathway decorated by the heads of great men."

"What does that mean? Is the general dead? Ask them."

The Sangoma reached into his bag and this time pulled out a snake. It lashed its tail and threw its head toward the Sangoma's hand, and sunk its fangs. The mage hissed as though merely irritated by a mosquito bite, grabbed it by the neck and duly slashed, letting its blood pour into his calabash. He set it on the flames and let it warm until it bubbled. He waited for it to cool and then drank. He twitched a little, babbled and then said in a dark voice, "No, he is alive - if that's what you can call it. I see a living corpse, walking through a desert of skulls, all crying for his justice."

"Very well then. The people of Domboshawa will rejoice in their liberation, but first, I need the blessing of the ancestors. Will you speak to them on my behalf?"

"That all depends."

The king chuckled: "You do have man parts after all. Very well, bless my campaign and after I have taken Domboshawa, I shall add Chief-Witchdoctor of Domboshawa to the titles I have already bestowed upon you."

"But there is already a chief-witchdoctor installed there, your grace. A powerful one reports say."

"That can easily be fixed," replied the king.

"You are as generous as you are wise, my lord, but what of that matter we have been speaking about?"

"You mean *you* have been speaking about." The Sangoma had come to the king on a weekly basis since his return, preaching the virtues of purification, and how the Piripiri gods yearned for it. How the future could only come to fruition with a great sacrifice. It was the only way, however each time, the king had grunted an incessant no, before shooing him away as one did a wasp. "You are persistent, I'll give you that."

"I am tireless in applying the will of the ancestors, my lord."

"Will this ensure that I prevail over my enemies?"

The Sangoma hissed.

Maghedzi placed a finger into the candle burning on a cabinet, thought for some moments then finally replied: "So be it."

CHAPTER 17

The canoe race was now Xolani's last chance to convince the elders he was worth a place at the rite of passage, after his poor performance at the archery competition. When the sun finally returned after a wearisome day and a half, Xolani was first out of his hut, sprinting toward the start of the Khumalo's banks. Due to their uncle Munyaradzi's delay, the strapping Taonga Shato stood in as the fourth man. Simba climbed into the canoe last, praying before he entered. He knelt in the front, whilst Themba knelt in the back, Xolani behind Simba, and behind him, Taonga.

"Don't ruin this, like you did the archery competition, Xolani," Themba warned.

"Get off my back. It is Taonga you should be worried about. Our canoe is likely to sink, as big as he is." They all laughed, though Taonga found nothing amusing. The Shato's were notorious for their lack of humor.

"Enough!" Simba shouted. "Taonga, you have grown up with us and soon we shall be brothers by law. Let us remind our neighbors who reigns in the aquatic." The boys cackled like hyenas as Tjingii's drum sounded.

Sibongile and Chipo were amongst the crowd that had gathered to cheer on the competitors. Although the two mothers did not always see eye to eye, for the sake of appearances they showed solidarity, smiling as they shared a chat. "I'm so happy that our boys are getting on so well," Chipo revealed to the queen.

"I can imagine you are. Xolani is a good boy, obedient. That is a strong virtue. He will serve my boys well."

Chipo smiled and nodded. "Have you seen our husband recently? How does he fare?"

"This morning actually. He is in good spirits," replied the queen.

"Oh, that's wonderful. I was in his chambers just last night."

"Farakaii is very keen to add more sons. I have been truly blessed. A fourth son would make him very proud, but how tiring it is. So much effort involved. How's it going for you sister? Any plans on extending your household? Xolani must be lonely."

"Soon enough, sister. I am still young. There is plenty of time for that." Both women grinned and waved as people passed.

Meanwhile, the boys were in total focus, rowing hard, but for every blade that cut the frenetic water, the Timba and the Rwaivi's efforts matched it. The Chitemo were not far behind either, but the Tsuro were now out of the race. As they made their way down the final stretch, it was now only the Rwaivi that rivaled them. Xolani found himself in a strange state, like he was asleep, but somehow still paddling. All the fatigue was now drained clean from his lithe arms. He didn't even see the harsh currents or the sharp rocks that sprung out wherever they would. He rowed faster and faster until he heard the crowd roar. When he opened his eyes, the first thing he saw was Nonkuleko's beautiful smile as she helped him climb out of the large canoe. They had won the day. They were heroes. Comrade Chengetaii appeared before him, closing out the sun. His face bore curiosity. "The water, around the canoe. It turned red, like blood. Did you see that?"

The boy shrugged his shoulders. "I think your eyes are getting old, commander," Xolani teased.

Chengetaii had only seen that a long time ago, in another lifetime. He looked at Xolani for a moment with suspicion. "Forget it. You implemented my teachings thoroughly. Here, this is for you." The commander handed him a pendant of the head of a hippopotamus.

Xolani's eyes widened. He wanted to scream and shout, perhaps dance, but the Commander of the Amakazi stood before him, and his giant cape cast a shadow over him. He instantaneously erected himself and tightened his jaw. "It will be my honor to represent the mighty hippo at the rites of passage."

"Your father will be glad to hear it. Now go. Show the bloody thing to your mother. I am sure she will be overjoyed." With that the commander was off, his cape flapping behind him, returning the sunlight onto Xolani's face.

When Chengetaii arrived at Farakaii's hut, he found his brother stretching and performing exercises. "There you are."

"What in the ancestors name are you doing?"

"What does it look like? I intend to take part in the wrestling competitions."

Chengetaii looked his brother up and down and smirked. "No offence, but when was the last time you came down to the armory and performed some drills?"

Admittedly, it had been a while. "That's true, but I still feel fresh. You saw me against the assassins."

"Those were amateurs. If they were true assassins, you'd be dead. You are in no shape to wrestle. Don't think your wild coughs have passed my notice. You need some time off, in the country, tending the cows. What do you say? Just you and I, like when we were boys."

"And then who would rule? Moyo? Shato? Mutasa?" The king laughed. "There is too much to be done. The boys are not ready. Simba will be a great ruler, but he is still too young. He has not been tested by life. Themba . . ." the king paused. "Themba is

Themba. I have decided he is to seek a betrothal with the Piripiri girl."

"What about Xolani?"

"Maghedzi would never agree to that. Xolani is not in the succession line. Themba shall travel to Pyyros and with the ancestors' grace secure an alliance between our clans. Munyaradzi shall accompany him. If there is anything he is good at apart from drinking, it is woo. He is suited to aid Themba in this endeavor. Mutasa shall join them as well, as my ambassador."

Chengetaii thought it a bad idea, but the king seemed resolved. "As you say. You are the king after all."

The king did not disagree. "How is my boy? Have you been keeping a stern eye on him as I tasked?"

Chengetaii nodded. "Of all your sons, he resembles you the most, in body and spirit."

"I hope Sibongile never hears you say that," the king chuckled. "You know how she is about that."

Chengetaii nodded. He knew all too well.

"They all did well at the canoe race. It is no easy task defeating the Uche. You have instructed the boys well. I hope you are not breaking their backs on the training fields."

"Nothing they can't handle."

Farakaii was not so sure.

"Xolani has been growing stronger every day and appears to be a serious child. Do you know that he tamed Shiri?"

"The zebra that kicked Tulu and bit Goden so hard they had to amputate his hand?"

Chengetaii nodded. "And he has also been admitted into the rites of passage." Pride shone through the king's eyes. "Are you ready, brother? We are running late."

The king extended his arm, signal enough for Ganizani to place his spear in his hand. A servant crept up and placed the king's feathery crown atop his head. After the servant had fastened the cow tails around the king's arms and legs, off they went, continuing their conversation through the winding pathways and corridors as Amakazi guards led the way. "I really do miss the matches, the intensity – studying an opponent and unveiling their weaknesses." Guards saluted and villagers fell on their faces as the king and the commander passed the Stone Houses gate and made their way down the winding staircase surveying the waiting crowd.

"Let them stay memories. Let the people remember the warrior you were, the one who felled Dingani the Bobcat, Misisipo the Mute and the Red Grasshopper at the Pyyros tourney. That afternoon you were peerless," Chengetaii testified proudly. "I was just fortunate enough to have been there to witness it." They passed by the chief-treasurer, Mutasa, who bowed as did Moyo, Shato and other notable men of title from clans that belonged to the Akuwa Kingdom: The head of the Tsuro, Nyati, Timba and other opulently dressed potentates from the luscious graze-lands of the Tsavo herdsmen, to the rocky isle of the Rwaivi.

"You over exaggerate, brother."

"I remember it vividly. You went through the contest with relative ease, slamming your inferiors into the red dust with such graceful brutality. I fondly remember Maghedzi's face when he had to crown you champion."

"Oh yes," Farakaii chuckled. "It was grudgingly to say the least. That's how he's always been. Even when we were boys, he was always peculiar."

"And now he is old and peculiar with an ever growing army."

"I was watching Tulu training the other day. I would put good salt on him, though he has to get through a tough group of warriors like Nanduri from the Chitemo clan. Twenty heads in battle he has collected, some say."

Chengetaii was not impressed.

"En-Kai the fearless cattle herder from the Tsavo is also one to watch for."

Chengetaii had to agree. "I had the chance to see Amare, the young prince from the Rwaivi tribe. Do not let his delicate looks and carefree attitude fool you, he is a contender."

"Aye brother, I have seen his father Kilele in battle, as a friend and foe. We never went head to head, but I saw what he did to three of my best warriors. He shot three arrows in one go, as his boat sailed to shore. He would have planted one in me if it weren't for General Moyo knocking me out of the way at the last second. Though we defeated his forces, there was no questioning what warrior class Kilele Rwaivi was."

Finally they arrived at the thoroughfare. They had built a platform in the center with four large pillars decorated around it with giant elephant skulls to show the might of the hippo. The throne was cut from rich darkwood with a seat layered with soft leopard skins. The front and hind legs had small hippopotamuses carved skillfully in to it. It was topped off with large eagle feathers atop the chair rail, shaped in a half moon, matching the king's headdress. The chair had been in the Akuwa family for generations, as long ago as when these eagles soared and carried bulls into the skies. Thousands bowed as he walked toward the royal stage where the queen waited for him. She looked radiant as ever in a blood-orange oval flat-topped headdress. At the base she had an assortment of little colorful beads fashioned into small purple, black and lilac jacaranda leafs. Normally she went extravagant, but today she opted for simple studded earrings. On her bodice, a sky-blue cloth wrapped over one shoulder exposing a queenly breast, heavyset with thick dark nipples.

In the middle was Tulu, a warrior renowned for his large muscular build and nimble toes some said could walk on water. He danced around several opponents in quick succession, barely breaking a sweat. The crowd roared in approval as he made quick work of his rivals on route to the final. There waiting for him was the formidable Tsavo herdsman En-Kai with his long, stretched earlobes. Whilst Tulu had used brute strength and speed to slay his opponents, En-Kai used his supreme stamina, hopping around like the grasshopper emblazoned on Tsavo shields. He would shimmy to the left, then duck right and flip over his opponents as they tried to grab him. When his challengers were spent, barely able to lift their legs, that was when he would pounce.

After a morning and a whole afternoon of wrestling, some a marvel to behold, others more one sided than the healthy throng would have liked, all that was left now was En-Kai and the formidable Tulu. The two men descended upon the center circle. Hippo Valley cheered as farmers, gold smiths, laborers, warriors and chiefs united in noise and celebration. The contestant's muscles rippled as they stared at each other, touching noses. King Farakaii rose and blessed the fight and then Tjingii struck the drum.

"So you are Tulu the Water Dancer," said En-Kai, as a ring of fire formed around them.

"And I believe you are En-Kai the Herdsman of Tsavo."

The towering wiry warrior nodded and fixed his gaze at Tulu, eyes as dark as his shiny skin. "It is a shame, I was hoping to get a chance to see those dance moves of yours, but sadly it looks like there is no water here."

"Likewise herdsman, I indeed too have been looking forward to this, though you will find that throwing me will not be as easy as herding cattle."

Now that the pleasantries were out of the way, the fight was on. Tulu crouched, and danced to the left, then shuffled back to where he began as he sized up his opponent. En-Kai prayed solemnly then slowly paced about, waiting for Tulu to attack. He shortly did, flinging himself forward, but En-Kai flipped over the water dancer, landing elegantly on one foot. The crowd raved as Chengetaii nodded his head in approval. *Finally,* he thought, *a proper fight.*

Prince Themba wanted to help spur his fellow tribesman to victory like everyone else, but something was holding him back. He and Tulu were two sides of the same spear. It was Tulu's duty to bring glory to the people, and his, justice. Soon he would have his moment in the sun. *Destiny awaits, soon my name will be on every woman's lips and my spear work the envy of every warrior!* He looked down at his sweaty palms. He tried to keep them steady, but he couldn't. They were shaking like he was trapped in a cold bath. His heart beat faster and harder, in thick solid thuds.

"Tulu," the crowd shouted, "Tulu, dance for me, dance for me, Tulu," they sang.

He held his chest and could feel cold sweat slide down its crack. He began creeping backward slowly. His necklace, a mixture of gold and precious stones felt heavy on his broad shoulders. Even carrying it was too much trouble for him. It felt like a barrel of *umqombothi. How have I grown so weak?* For the first time since he audaciously took it upon himself to exact the will of the ancestors, he began to realize that he could actually die, that very day. *It can only go one way.* He tried to convince himself. *This Muchita is a mere peasant and I, a son of a king.* Doubt engulfed his chest despite himself, like salt taking the form of a jar.

He took a couple of steps backward, crushing someone's foot. The girl shrieked in pain, but Themba did not care. "Out of my way," he snarled as he shoved her to the side into a group of people. They all went tumbling down, but they were too fixated on the battle to care. Now his face was covered in sweat. He felt a hand on his slick shoulder.

"Are you okay, Themba?" It was Takunda who was also covered in a thin sheet of sweat, but this one as a result of his fervent support.

"Get away from me."

"You're drenched. Do you have a fever?"

"What did I say? Like I commanded, be gone with you."

"Suit yourself, but you are missing a great fight."

Thinking became hard, he felt like he was drowning. He turned and started walking. He thought he felt tiny microscopic raindrops fall on his shoulders. He prayed it would rain, but as it turned out, it was just his imagination. There were no raindrops. The moon was in clear view, and the only clouds in sight had long passed, sailing away toward the Piripiri mountain scope. His spear slowly slipped from his hands. He started jogging and then running, faster and faster until he disappeared into the darkness.

CHAPTER 18

Now that Maghedzi had fallen in line with the Sangoma's vision, he had to convince the king's mysterious protégé, the Desert Snake too. He had asked around about him, but the foreign man's mystique remained. When someone did divulge, it was hard to discern what was real and what was not.

"His own father," one man exclaimed, as he shook his fermented milk. "His own sire sold his mother to merchants. Can you believe that?"

"No, you have it all wrong. The Desert Snake is actually Maghedzi's bastard. It has been a while, but those of you old enough should remember how he would go away for years on end. Strange that man is. He tried to cross the salt water, but was halted by a mermaid. He fell in love with her, and that boy is the fruition of his lust." The gossipers were united in their disgust, but the Sangoma found that tale hard to believe. He had no choice but to find out himself.

The next day, after an excursion, waiting outside his hut was the Desert Snake atop his giant zebra and by his side, that shotel of his. He reached out his hand. There was something alluring about it, something the Sangoma could not deny. He was up curled behind him in a matter of moments.

They had been riding for a good while when the spirit-medium finally summoned enough courage to ask where they were going.

"For a little ride. That's all."

"And for what purpose is this ride? I am very busy, with our lord's work."

The Snake-man laughed hard. "Indeed, you have been busy. However, I'm sure you have heard what they say about the curious."

"Yes, foreigner, I am well versed in our proverbs and wise words, but please do continue."

"The antelope which sniffs too long by the river is food for the crocodile."

The Desert Snake's words stung, but all the Sangoma could do was tighten his grip around the northerner as he sunk his heels into the zebra and upped the speed as they cruised across the valley, the Desert Snakes white robes snapping in the wind as they made haste.

It was a wonder to see Maghedzi's extensive work. He had inherited a clan on the verge of ruin and transformed Pyyros into a powerhouse again, rivaling cities like Hippo Valley, the Lion's Den, Snake Pit and the Eagle's Nest. They passed the Iziubindi farm, home to one of Maghedzi's lieutenants, the Chipongozi farm and Rusha, which were all along the river Nhunundudu. It seemed like they had been riding for eternity, passing kraal after kraal with a variety of cows and bulls, some a pitch black, others white and brown. Some of the villages they passed had been autonomous during the Sangoma's first stint in Pyyros, but now they had bent their knee to Maghedzi and laid down their spears. Most of the chiefs had managed to keep their heads, but where they resisted, he had added their skulls to the mound in his hut and installed his relatives as patrons. Small kids playing would stop their activities and watch mouth agape as the Desert Snake's zebra made its strides. Others would duck behind rocks, or trees lest be spotted by the man some called soulless, who was not bound by his ancestors for they were buried in a faraway land. They passed by several quarries, and iron ore deposits where slaves, criminals and workmen barely covered in loincloths wiped the sweat from their foreheads and continued striking the hard rock to bring forth copper, silver or gold. The Sangoma could see in many of their eyes that death was more desirable than slaving away in the dirt pits, but where death was better, it was not worse than being sent onto the slopes of Mount Pyyros to collect the black rock or worse, being exiled into the Forest of Abominations.

After the mines, farms and villages were no more, but acres of bare land and bush, they flew into a forest and cut through until they reached a cave entrance. The Desert Snake hopped off his zebra and helped the Sangoma down. He took out a fruit for the zebra and whispered in its ear. When its yips had subsided, he waved, "This way," but the witchdoctor was apprehensive. "I do not intend to kill you. I prefer blood spilled on the sands." They navigated down the dark passageway until they reached a small opening. When they emerged, they were on top of the world, on a cliff. The witchdoctor crept up to the edge and peered down to the treetops. His stomach began to turn, so he crawled back. The Desert Snake sat himself by the edge, and began polishing his blade.

This is boring, the witchdoctor thought. He found himself a good stone, far from the edge, and began whistling.

"You have been asking about me. Why is that?"

The Sangoma scratched his mask, startled by the Desert Snake's frankness. "I only ask because you are here for a great purpose. Why else would the ancestors have sent us a man from the north? You have been chosen."

"That is the same dung you told Maghedzi."

"Yes, but the ancestors work through many vessels. You and I are but small pieces in a greater plan. I gather you are not a man of faith?"

"Have they told you how they found me?"

"I have heard some stories."

The Desert Snake laid his sword down, reached into his bag and pulled out a flame-shaped *mbira* Maghedzi had given him when he first arrived. It sat in a wooden calabash carved with images of Gyiku'o and the story of the Piripiri's creation. He still remembered the king's words. "You will never be a Piripiri, but our customs you must learn nonetheless."

He plucked a string with his right thumb to produce a dull buzzing sound. He wasn't pleased so tuned it to a higher pitch and listened again. He hummed a tune then plucked the outermost strings simultaneously, skipped four sequences inward and plucked twice again to begin the melody 'Gentle Rain Before the Storm'.

"I was just a small boy then, but I remember it all. There was a sudden drought in our village, a drought unlike any our people had recorded. We searched the land far and wide for water, but whenever we got to a spring or an oasis, there was nothing. We searched the roots of cacti and anything imaginable, but they were all bone dry." The sandman's eyes narrowed and grew darker as did the *mbira's* melody. He looked at the wizard as if debating whether to continue or not. "Something strange began to happen. Men, women and children whom were once our neighbors, people we once traded with and intermarried for generations began to prey on our village. I remember looking down at a boy my age, lying with his neck opened with teeth marks over his little body, no bigger than mine. They had opened his throat and taken his legs."

"Cannibals?"

The Desert Snake shook his head. "How can they be cannibals? These were not people, not in the same sense. Fortunately we escaped and fled south, crossing the great divide. However, all we found was death."

The Sangoma had long thought the great divide impossible to cross. It was too large and treacherous. No man could withstand its heat and poisonous animals. On the other hand, he thought, he had thrived in the Forest of Abominations, where no man had – not for countless generations.

"We travelled for days with just a skin of water to divide between my parents, sisters and me. Father had some goods to barter, so when we finally bumped into a band of travellers, he approached them. It was the first time I saw those great zebras. They weren't like the camels my people used to ride."

"Camels?" The Sangoma scratched his mask thoughtfully. "Is it a creature your people ride?" The foreigner nodded his head soberly. The mystic wanted to hear more, but that he could do later.

"The great zebras circled us. I didn't understand what my father was saying. He could speak a little of your tongue as he was a merchant. Just as he reached into his bag, an arrow flew into his thigh and then his shoulder. Next they grabbed my mother and sisters and . . ." He couldn't say the words, but the metal threads illustrated his pain. "My sisters hadn't even bled yet, but they didn't care. I remember my father begging them to have him instead, but they communicated they already did. When they were done, they slit the women's throats and put a dagger through my father's eye. Suddenly a man appeared, dispersing the assailants. The man looked at me as I sat in my family's pool of blood. I thought he was going to kill me, but instead he gave me his hand, lifted me up and told me I was safe. He took me back with him, despite my protests. I wanted to lie there and die with my family. The man clothed me and fed me until I became healthy. He showed me kindness, even more so than my father ever did."

"Maghedzi?"

The Desert Snake nodded.

"Do you know who did this to your family?"

The foreigner laid his instrument on the stone in front of him, ending his harrowing tune, snapped his teeth shut and between gritted teeth he muttered, "Farakaii."

CHAPTER 19

Tulu had triumphed against all odds in what village folk were calling the battle of a generation. It had been weeks since, but it was still the talk of the town – as was Prince Simba's trial with Muchita. How swift the heir's movements were, the storytellers told it. They had even made a song about it. Simba had his spear in Muchita's stomach not long after Tjingii's drum thundered. At his foot was a red heap of colon, aorta and spleen. Muchita's head came off soon thereafter. Simba paraded it, lifting it into the sky so all could see and bask in the warm and sticky blood dripping from the dismembered neck. Themba had told everyone he had been attacked by a group of foreign looking vagabonds that night. He knew it a lie and so did everyone at court, but it was better that than admit he had grown craven.

A bang on the door greeted him as he snoozed, too feeble to face the world outside. "Wake up Themba. It's father, he wants you."

Father, he gasped. The king had not granted Themba an audience since his audacious challenge against Muchita.

"I'll be out right away." He washed his face with the wooden bucket he kept, and carefully selected his garb. He hadn't seen his father in a while, and first impressions were always important.

The room was dimly lit as he walked in. Comrade Chengetaii's grim face greeted him, as did General Moyo, Shato and the ancient, Sekuru Rwizi. In the middle was King Farakaii getting his morning grooming, servants rubbing oil up and down his back. "Good morning son," the king said, lifting his arms so the maids could access his side.

"My lord," Themba replied, falling on his face.

"Are you not my son?"

"Yes, your excellency."

"And my faithful servant?"

"In both lives, in the physical and spiritual realm."

The king seemed pleased with the answer. "You have disappointed me. That is the worst feeling a father can feel from a son."

"I will do anything to make it up, father," Themba pleaded, raising his face momentarily from the stone hard floor.

"Rise." The king laid his hands on Themba's shoulders, now his height and smiled. "There is one thing you can do to make things right. I need you to go to Pyyros."

Confusion flickered in Themba's eyes. "Pyyros? What for? Do you mean to see me dead father? Have I disappointed you that much?"

The king chuckled. "I do not mean for you to die, I mean for you to be wed. There is no shortage of dislike between our tribes, but I mean to heal the wounds that our ancestors opened. I mean for the kingdoms to be united, and what better way than securing a betrothal between you and his only daughter from his first wife, Princess Nia."

Themba wanted to object, but Chief Treasurer Mutasa cut in, "You would be wise to accept Prince Themba. All men shall envy you. Her mother? Queen Zandile? You might have heard of her?"

Themba had. There were plenty a song dedicated to the queen's ample breasts, orbicular behind and fiery eyes. After some moments of deliberations, realizing his opportunity, he accepted. "When do I go?"

"At the end of the moon."

"Thank you, father. I shall not fail you. I shall secure this betrothal, and when she comes of age, I shall pump numerous sons into her belly."

"Good boy, I am sure you will."

Themba grinned, and slid out of the hut.

A jacaranda leaf greeted him just inside the doorstep when he returned to his hut after a disappointing hunt. He had drifted alone into the deep bush to daydream about married life, following a stream until he reached a waterfall, three or four meters in length. He took out his skin of water and chucked down its contents as he admired the view. Though most of the land was now a yellowish brown, here everything was lush and green, as if the oncoming dry had forgotten its existence. A bush rumbled, prompting him to remove his bow, but upon closer inspection, it was a girl relieving herself, whistling merrily as her water flowed into the stream. She was beautiful to behold, and so was the techni-colored skirt that sat around her ankles. She wore no headdress, but beads covered her throat and shoulders, leaving her stomach and breasts bare. Themba blended seamlessly, as his sandy-colored garments and golden animal hides did well to camouflage him; however, when ants began running up his legs into his loincloth he could not help but break his silence. Her eyes widened in shock when she realized he was watching from afar, half hidden behind a tree. Wild berries and fruits fell out of her woven basket as she ran as fast as she could to join her party, away from the bush watcher.

He lifted the lilac leaf, studied it, then cast it into the fire. He paced around his lodgings, sat down on a stool, only to stand up again. He grabbed his spear and a cloth and began to rub the hard metal until his reflection became clearer. He snatched his bow and began tightening its strings as heroes of the past invaded his thoughts. He cleared his throat and began humming the tune to the song, Torindo the Red Arrow.

Few warriors from Akuwa history, save perhaps Changamire, Goneso the Tall and in more recent times, Tulu and Comrade Chengetaii, were as feared or respected on the battlefield as the greatest archer of them all, Torindo. There was almost no range, nor enemy, man or beast, he could not hit, whether it was five hundred meters away, on land or in the sky. Torindo wielded a bow made from trees only found in the Forest of Abominations and blessed by a powerful sorcerer, Sabawonge, renowned for learning the secret of elevation. Sabawonge had the bow constructed specifically so that only Torindo would be mighty enough to draw it. With one pull of his string, Torindo was able to send arrows clean through elephants and armor-shelled rhinos.

When it was rigid and stiff, he sat bored until his stomach began to grumble. He grabbed his spear and headed toward the local inn, using a longer route, doing his best to avoid as many people as he could. He arrived in the midst of laughter dying down. "What's so funny? Did I miss something?" Themba could be princely when he would.

"Nothing important," Takunda replied, "Your brother was just telling us a story."

"Is that so?" He did not seem convinced but nonetheless he placed his spear on the table and waved for beer. "Bring me a bowl of boiled pumpkin too." He could not help but lick his lips as the wench slowly walked back to the kitchen. "So, what lies do you spew today, brother?"

"I was telling them about a faraway land that no Akuwa has seen. A land of albino men, giant in stature, all standing two meters in length."

"Giant albinos, what foolishness is this?" Themba spat out his beer, signal enough for Takunda and the rest to join in the laughter. "Sounds like a fairy tale to me."

Tjingii ignored the jibe. "They have golden hair which sits on their shoulders like the lion, eyes as blue as the sea and have giant boats that can cross the salt water."

"A lion? I see. Then they can be no challenge to the hippo." All at the table nodded their heads in approval. To the Akuwa, the hippopotamus was the fiercest creature of them all. "Another round of *doro*." Themba chucked down another piece of the pumpkin. "If they can travel across the salt water, then how come we have not seen any of these albinos?"

Tjingii knew his brother well. It was pointless and unwise following this stream, especially after he had been drinking.

Takunda changed the topic to something of Themba's tastes. "How did it go with that peasant girl?"

The prince grinned, revealing small creeks at the sides of his eyes. "What do you think, old friend?"

"So you did it then?" Themba did not want to divulge anything, but his smile said it all. "How was it Themba? You have to reveal it to your brothers. We want to hear all the details."

"You know a prince's word is solemn and I made a vow to her. But if you must know, when I was done with her, she was purring like a wild cat in heat." More laughter ensued, though Tjingii was not as amused as the others. "It was really easy," he continued. "She now thinks I love her. She thinks I'm going to make her my wife." He shook his head in disbelief.

"So I can go for it then?" Takunda grinned.

"We are like brothers, Takunda, what is yours is mine. But I warn you, you will be trying to fill out a footprint as large as a hippo's."

After Themba was done playing the comedian, he stood up and ordered another round for the boys and threw a few copper pieces on the table. The girl smiled as they made eye contact and looked down. "Thank you my prince," she said as she curtsied.

"Until we meet again, my sweet woman, very soon I hope." He winked, and she batted her eyes, grabbed the copper pieces on the table and walked away slowly as her skirt bounced about behind her. He considered following her, but unfortunately he was behind time.

"She wants you, Themba," Sipho sulked. "They all want you."

"Don't feel too down. I cannot help it that I am a beautiful man, with a rock hard stomach and biceps the size of pumpkins. Oh, I am prince too. We all have our talents, I suppose."

"When are you getting married? At this rate there will be no virgins left for us. What are we to do?" Sipho lamented.

"Sooner than you know. Father has big plans for me. I shall provide him his first grandson. That should please him and usher me back into his good grace. It's getting late, brethren. Don't get too drunk. We have an early hunt tomorrow and we have to be more successful than we were today."

All except Tjingii jumped from their table, bowed and clapped their hands together as Themba wrapped a blue cloth over his shoulders, grabbed his spear and walked out of the eatery. *Just one more thing to do before this wretched day ends.*

***

"I am so glad you came Themba. I didn't think you would show up, but here you are." Tsitsi's plumb breasts pressed hard on his chest. It produced a pleasant sensation, but alas the prince was well versed in a woman's wiles and pushed her away.

"What do you want? I am set to travel shortly and there is much preparation to be made." He turned to leave their sanctuary of lust and return to the sweet comfort of his luxury mat.

"Wait, Themba, I have something important to say." She coughed like a lion cub crying out for its mother's sweet teat.

He offered his cloth, but she insisted she was fine. "Well then at least allow me to escort you back home before you catch a chill." He brought forth his forearm, but she refused that too. "Well then what is it? Why are we here?" Themba paused and thought. "Wait…" he smiled.

"No Themba, this is serious. I tried to see you at court, but the guards laughed at me and called me a whore."

"Hmmm, I wonder why," the prince replied matter-of-factly.

"What's wrong with you? I thought you loved me. That's what you said under the jacaranda tree. You said I was the most beautiful girl in all of Hippo Valley and that you would tell your mother you would marry me. It was right after a heavy shower and the smell of the earth was fresh. The son peered through the cracks in the clouds, and all the wild flowers bloomed. You said I was your first as you were mine."

"I told you that?" Themba was shocked. Some mornings when he awoke, it felt like a thief had visited him in the night and stolen his memories.

He was even more shocked when she said, "I am pregnant. I am expecting your baby, a prince of Akuwa."

In the black of night, only the ancestors could see the look Themba bore. "I am happy for you, but this has nothing to do with me. I will give you some wise advice though, visit a doctor fast and get some help."

"What you are suggesting is evil – blasphemous. Themba, I love you. It is a son, a prince. I know it is. It is what you have always wanted."

"What do you know about my wants?"

"You told me . . . that's what you said that night."

He embraced her then suddenly grabbed her by the back of her neck, widening her eyes in shock. He leaned closer and ran his nose up and down her neck, inhaling her sweet vanilla scent. "Listen, peasant girl, and listen very carefully. That baby is not mine. I am the son of a king and you . . ." he looked at her, eyebrows bridged. "Don't try to fool me. This is the work of some brick layer."

Tsitsi began to sob. "Why are you being so mean to me? I let you...." Her sobs turned to torrential rains, but the prince was not moved. "It is yours. I don't care what you say. I will tell my mother tomorrow."

"You wouldn't dare."

"I would."

"You say you are a man. If that is so then do your duty. You are a coward, and everyone in Hippo Valley knows it."

"How dare you? I am no craven!"

"Yes, you are. We all know your brother fought in your stead at the Festival of Tusks. You can run away from Hippo Valley and travel to distant lands, but your shame will follow you wherever you go. You are not Farakaii's son!" If Themba had suspected she might be a witch, now he was certain. "I wish I had never met you. I wish I had met your brother instead. He is twice the man you are, even your bastard brother Xolani is more man than you will ever be."

"You can't speak to me like that. Remember whom you are talking to, peasant girl. Have you forgotten in that thick head of yours, I am your prince?"

Tsitsi was now wild with fury. "My head might be thick, but I do know that you are no prince."

Themba thrust. "I am my father's son, an Akuwa, through and through, the best of his brood, wench. Take it back." She tried, but the poor girl could not answer. "Take it back," Themba reiterated in case she had not heard him the first time. "Take it back," he whispered, this time feasting his nostrils on her sweet scent. Suddenly, the air turned sour.

He remembered his uncle Munyaradzi's haunting words: *Laborer or general, servant or queen, at the end, they all shit themselves.* Tsitsi hunched over his hand and fell before his feet. He pulled out the spear as blood trickled over his feet. The blade was drenched in blood from top to bottom. So was his fist. He looked down at her, her mouth still agape and knelt beside her. He ran his fingers over her lips. They were still perky, but not as warm as they once were. His touch didn't have the same sensation they once induced. He caressed the side of her face and moved his fingers down her neck.

There was a rumble in the thick vegetation. He looked up and flung his spear. Soon thereafter, out hobbled a young man, about his age, with his spear logged in his chest. Blood ran from the boy's mouth, splashing over his chest, until the sticky black substance covered his torso. The boy dropped to his knees, desperately trying to pull the heavy spear out of his chest. When he did, blood erupted and came raining down like a waterfall of death. When the drizzle had stopped, Themba used some leaves from the jacaranda to wipe the blood between his toes. No longer was the leaf purple, but now a maroon, red. He casually walked to the dying boy. He recognized him. He knew those black eyes. It was the boy Tariro, the young messenger. He wondered what the boy was looking at, as he lay there with his eyes open.

He raised his spear with both hands and prepared to end the boy's agony, but suddenly out from the bush, emerged a girl. When she looked down and saw Tariro, her eyes bulged and she began to scream. "Shut up, you will wake the spirits." She turned and ran, but Themba was soon on her heals as his blade cut through the unkempt vegetation, laughing sadistically. It wasn't long before he tackled her to the ground. She resisted, kicking and screaming and poked the prince in the eye. "Stop it. You're hurting me, you witch." Despite her efforts, she was no match for Themba's brawn. He gave her a feel of his knuckles, licked the blood off them and then gave her a slap. "What were you and the boy doing out here? You are a very naughty girl. I like naughty girls, but unfortunately, you saw me."

"You don't have to do this. Please, I swear to all the ancestors I will never tell anyone. I swear it! I swear it! I swear it!" the girl pleaded.

There was no turning back. He was already living in shame. "The village fool," he muttered. "Laughed at by inferior men." There was nothing he could do to restore his name. The only thing that kept people from publically humiliating him was his family name and it was safe to say he hadn't done anything to earn that. His eyes widened, excited as an unrivaled thrill washed over him. He liked the look of terror she bore as she struggled like a dung beetle turned upside on its back. "My sincerest apologies, I bare you no ill will." With that, warm blood sprinkled over his face.

***

Sibongile's eyes widened when she saw Themba's stained hands, and blood shot eye, immediately rising from her mat. She poured him a cold cup of water and watched as he drank. He drank as urgent as he did when he was younger, cradled in her arms. Then, she felt at peace as he would curl his little fingers around hers, look up at her and smile. She would have done anything to prolong the boy's teething years, but as the seasons changed, children grew, like seeds to trees, lava to pupa, pupa to bees. She called for a servant to prepare a bath. "We'll wash you up and see what we can do. Everything will be okay." She pulled him close and hugged him as his head tucked in between her cleavage. "Has anyone seen you like this?"

"No, I was careful. Mother," Themba hesitated, "I murdered them. I took their lives. I don't know what happened."

"You did no such thing. Someone else did that."

"No mother, it was I."

The queen slapped hard and held his head. "You are a prince and soon to travel to Pyyros. No one can ever know what happened, is that clear? It will ruin your chances of marriage and your father's proposed alliance with the Piripiri. I will take care of it. You shall go to Pyyros, wed and bed Maghedzi's whelp and continue like nothing happened."

How could he though? How could he forget Tsitsi's dying breath or the river of blood around Tariro's body? "Yes mother, I understand."

"Who were they?"

"Tsitsi, some daughter of a farmer or something. I can't remember."

"And the others?"

Themba looked down. "Tariro."

"The messenger boy, the one with the funny eye?"

"Yes, him."

Sibongile was sad to hear that. She was mildly fond of the boy and his black beady eyes. He could always be relied upon to deliver messages accurately and with purpose. "And the other?"

"I didn't recognize her."

"Okay, good. At least they're not from a noble family." Sibongile sighed in relief, though Themba did not understand how she took these revelations so lightly, like it was a problem that could be swept away. Sibongile's servant arrived with the bathwater. "Quickly, hide behind the drapes." Themba did as he was told and in came the servant with two buckets of hot water, fresh from the logs.

"Will you need more help mother?"

"No, that will be all. Do not disturb me." The servant bowed and exited the room. "Take off your clothes." Themba was a little apprehensive, but his mother's stern eye had him naked with his hands covering his man parts. "No need to be shy child. I cleaned your feces when you were a baby. There is nothing there a mother has not seen." That did not ease Themba's spirits, but nevertheless, he did as he was told. Though the twins had come out hand in hand, Themba was hers, but Simba, belonged to the clan.

Themba was sorry to see his loincloth burn in the cinders as he bathed. He could always get a new one true, but it was never easy running down a cheetah. When he was done, though his flesh was clean, his soul was still soiled. He put on the new cloths his mother had provided, hugged her and turned to leave. "Remember Themba. Do not mention this to anyone. Not even your twin brother. You do not want your father hearing about this."

He nodded and grabbed his spear.

"What about the bodies?"

"I fled from the scene immediately and came to you." That was a lie. After he had slashed the petrified girl's neck from ear to ear, he took some time to study his work. It was a few minutes later when he finally got off the body and sat on a stone nearby, still trying to catch his breath. He then took a walk around the death scene and admired the carnage he had created, like an angry god unleashing tsetse flies on iniquitous villagers. *She was pregnant, with my baby. It was a son. I was a father and you, mother, you were a grandmother.* Themba could not find the courage to tell her that either.

"Are you sure?"

"Yes mother, I promise." He hated lying, but unfortunately it came often and easy enough. "What are you going to do with them?"

"Let us pray no one has already discovered them. It is late and as you said, you came here right away, so everything will be okay." She noticed the boy shaking. "Focus, this is very serious. Even though you are a prince, you could still face the death penalty and if the other tribes got wind of this . . ."

"Yes, mother, I know."

"Then act that way. One more question. The girl . . . can anyone link her to you?"

The prince looked at her confused.

"Don't be daft boy. Did anyone see you and her together, or know about you and her?"

Themba had to think for a second. *She never told. It was a secret. No one knew . . . she swore to it.* "No . . . I don't think so . . . Well, I told my friends about a girl I was seeing, but no names."

"What friends are these?" Themba was now feeling even more uncomfortable. He didn't like the idea of telling on his friends.

"Say it now, young man, or I will strike you." Her hand was up, cocked and ready.

"Takunda, Nthanda, Tinashe, Sipho."

She hit him on the side of his head with her knuckles. "You tell everyone about your conquests? Oh ancestors! What kind of child have I raised?" She shook her head in disbelief. "Anyone else?"

"Tjingii and Simba may suspect something."

"That's okay then, they are your brothers. You can trust them. Anyone else you think might have seen you two together? I'm guessing your father or his spies don't know either, otherwise I would have heard about it."

All at once it came flooding back. He had been drinking so much that night, he had forgotten . . . until now. "Xolani, he has seen us together."

Sibongile's eyes widened. "Xolani by Chipo?"

Themba nodded wearily. "He happened upon us in the bush." He couldn't look his mother in her eyes. "Me and Tsi . . . the girl, stole into the night. It was at the festival so everyone was merry and drunk. We thought we were alone until I heard something in the bush. It was Xolani. He was spying on us."

Sibongile's eyes narrowed.

CHAPTER 20

General Shato crept into the king's audience chamber, bowed and clapped his hands. As usual, Farakaii was getting his morning grooming, a servant, rubbing oil down the crack of his back and over his buttocks and legs as the morning fire raged in the middle of the dimly lit hut. Women sang quietly the morning hymns, the king's late father's widows, Queen Sibongile, Chipo to name a few. The king turned his head in acknowledgement of the general's presence, and turned his head back lifting his arms so the servants could oil his side. When they placed his headdress on his ever-greying head and fastened his leopard skin onto his shoulders, Ganizani the Amakazi handed him his spear. He sat himself on his stool, coughed horribly, and waved the singers away.

When they were gone, the general kept his head low and proceeded with his business: "Doma has been attacked by feline beasts." It was a village near the Shato homestead. "They say the whole village has been destroyed. The ones who survived fled into the bushes. A survivor described a stream of blood down the chief's walkway, and the hands and feet of the deceased placed in neat spiral circles."

"This sounds not dissimilar to the events that occurred at General Moyo's farm," said Comrade Chengetaii.

"Let me round up a small regiment of Tulu, Black Mamba, the Swinging Monkey, and myself. We will hunt these beasts down and slay them. You are also welcome to join us Comrade Chengetaii. I know your club has not tasted blood for a while. We will make sure these beasts do not trouble us anymore. The folk are beginning to lose confidence in the king's protection. Some are even saying the ancestors have sent these beasts on your account, *nkosi*."

Chengetaii thought it a bad idea. "*Mambo*, sending your best men away is a good invitation for those that seek to harm us . . . harm you."

"Then what do you suggest, commander?"

Chengetaii waited for the king to calm after a series of coughs to answer. "The rite of passage is soon. I think it would be worthwhile for the boys to spend some time in the bush. We will find where these beasts are coming from and eradicate them."

"Are you sure they are ready? The reports say these are not your typical beasts."

"I will have them ready."

Farakaii took some moments to deliberate, and then slammed his spear into the stone floor, creating a small cloud of dust. "So be it." He waved his hand. "Thank you for the information." The general curtsied and slid out. The king turned to Chengetaii. "Brother, as you can see, I have been in better health."

"Your wild coughs have not gone unnoticed, *nkosi*, or your lack of appetite." The king's breakfast had barely been touched. "You should let someone else perform your daily duties until you get better."

"Yes, brother. That is why I am sending you on a very important and dangerous errand. Not many have returned from this journey in the flesh."

"Danger is the life the ancestors blessed me with."

The king waved the commander closer and whispered in his ear.

***

The huts at the Stone Houses were now so miniature Comrade Chengetaii could fit them in between his closed fingers as he zipped through the savannah. He had been riding for a while when he heard thundering hooves in the distance and two manned zebras galloping toward him. He gritted his teeth, stopped his beast and waited for Prince Simba and Taonga Shato to arrive. "What in the ancestor's name are you doing here?"

"Greetings, uncle. We thought you would need some company."

"Who gave you that presumption?"

"The ancestors," Simba smiled.

"Your ancestors are mine, boy. Do not be cute with me."

"You are going to the oracles aren't you captain?"

Chengetaii did not answer, preferring to kick his zebra and continue on his way. Simba kicked his past the commander's, intruding on his path. "Can we come?"

The commander looked at the prince incredulously. "I cannot let you do that. The road is dangerous."

"Then you need us. You are a great warrior, but you cannot fight a group of bandits yourself, or worse, the beasts of the wild."

"I have travelled to places you see only in your dreams, overcome obstacles your puny brains cannot fathom. I do not need your help."

"Then what will you have us do? Turn back?"

Chengetaii was left with a tough decision. He could send them back, but it was getting late and when night came, so did the predators. Similarly, the path to the Sacred Hills was a precarious one with thick jungle, dangerous hills and bandits. "Fine," he finally grunted. "As long as you can keep up with my pace."

After riding for a little longer, they stopped to make a fire. Taonga killed a boar, sending his arrow into its side from an impossible distance. After Simba skinned it, it was roasting over the flames in no time.

Simba was the first to open his mouth as they ate, cleaning a bone of its meat. "A runner arrived at court, not long after you left, commander, carrying some interesting news. According to spies in Domboshawa, a girl . . . some Yemuraii, General Chinotimba's daughter rules and has brought darkness upon the village. According to reports, hundreds rot, impaled along the Domboshawa village walls, left to the vultures and flies."

"A woman you say?"

Simba nodded, seemingly suffering from the same repudiation afflicting the captain.

"What about the general's sons?"

"Son," Taonga corrected. "They say he took flight some time ago. General Chinotimba had five legitimate sons. Now he only has one. They say his male line is cursed. The fifth son has fled, unwilling to meet a similar fate as his brothers. They say this Yemuraii has employed the help of a powerful mystic."

"What else have I missed?"

Simba looked down and shook his head. "Sipho and Nthanda were found dead this morning. They were trampled tending cattle. When they were found, their faces were unrecognizable and bodies twisted."

The commander had trained the young men himself. They were capable enough, but lacked the mental strength of true Akuwa warriors. Chengetaii closed his eyes and performed a silent prayer, and continued to eat.

The next morning they continued up the winding hills until they reached the base of a mass of rock. Chengetaii dismounted his zebra, reached into his bag and pulled out a map. He surveyed it for a while, and then pressed his finger on their location. "From now on we're on foot. Here, help me up."

Simba dismounted, combined his hands and helped his companions up. There was a large gap before them. Chengetaii walked to the edge, knelt and looked down. His big toe hit a stone sending it falling for many moments until it disappeared into the wild flow of the Khumalo. He stood up, stepped backward and with a sudden burst of pace, leapt, landing on the other side with a couple of rolls. Simba followed suit, landing like a leopard, calm, without much fuss. Next up was Taonga who made his run and leapt, barely making the edge. He pulled himself over, but when he was almost up, the earth crumbled and broke under him. Simba grabbed him in time, and with the commander's aid, pulled him to safety. By the time Taonga was done dusting himself off and thanking the ancestors, Comrade Chengetaii was already on his way, leaping over another fissure.

They reached another mass of rock and squeezed through a slit, until a creek lay before them. Stones and pebbles decorated the area with luscious wild bushes, trees and birds soaring high above them. Snakes slithered and rodents ran to the safety of their borrows as the band made their way through. Without warning, an arrow zipped past Chengetaii, taking a chunk of his eyelashes as it cruised along, hitting an obelisk and splattering into splinters. Another arrow zipped past, sending Taonga down. More arrows flew their way, but Simba and Chengetaii managed to duck to safety. "Who is attacking us?" Horror broke from Simba's voice when he turned to find Taonga lying on the ground. He grabbed hold of his limp legs and dragged him behind the rock.

Chengetaii raised his head just enough to see the danger. "Outlaws," the captain cursed. Blood was coming out from

Taonga's mouth. His eyes were flickering as he desperately tried to breathe.

"Wake up Taonga, you're going to be alright." Simba pleaded, patting his oldest friend on his cheeks, hoping he would wake up.

"There is nothing we can do for him," said the commander.

"We will take him to the oracles, they will help him." Another hail of arrows zipped past.

"The oracles are prophets, not revivers. Your friend lives, but now in another realm." The commander took another peak at the attackers, turned back to Simba and slapped the prince on his cheek. "Wipe those tears off your face. Now is not the time for that. You'll take the two on the left, and I'll take care of the others."

The veteran vaulted from behind the rock and unleashed his spear. It took one of the bandit's head, sending him to the ground. He raced toward the second, leapt into the air and unveiled Dread, striking the bandit on the side of the head with lethal precision. When he landed, he swept the attacker off his feet with his leg and finished him off with an overhead assault on his face. Bone marrow and blood splashed over the captain's eyes. He wiped it off with one hand and used his other to pull out his spear from the corpse. Another assailant was soon on Chengetaii, but Simba's knife struck him in the chest, sending the bandit nose first at the commander's feet. Simba took from the stone and raced to the other, stabbing at the bandit, but the outlaw was no slouch, ducking out of the way and swiping Simba by the cheek. The attacker grinned and swiped again, but Simba had learned from his mistake, this time ducking low, punching him in the stomach and following through with his blade. The *masimbi* steel cut through until Chengetaii could see the tip of the spear on the other side. Simba tried to jerk it free, but it was stuck so put a foot on the bandit's stomach and pulled, creating a waterfall of blood.

Simba saw from the side of his eye another of the bandits brandish their axe. He thought he was a dead man, but a gust of wind appeared and a loud screech in the sky. The assailant looked up and as he did Koko with talons showing dug its nails into the attacker's face. He screamed and cursed as the eagle went in with his beak, taking chunks off his face. Soon the eagle was on the bandit's neck until the outlaw stopped kicking and went still.

Now there was one more. The outlaw leapt toward Simba, but with a slight genuflect the prince evaded the attack and swung his spear, which was blocked by the axe shaft. Its butt found the prince's chin, crushing against it, before an elbow between his eyes had him on his back. He grimaced, rolling sideways just in time as the axe rained down toward his head and snapped the rock in two. The prince used his leg to sweep the assailant to the ground, got up and regained his vision. He raised his spear to ear level, preparing to strike when he realized the soft features behind the cloth covering the lower part of her face. "Commander, it's a girl."

"So what? Kill her!"

Simba raised his spear again and threw. The *masimbi* steel cut through the rock and logged there. The girl stood with her hands covering her face. When she realized she was still alive, she parted her fingers and peeked, spreading her arms in submission. "I can't do it, commander. Look, she has yielded." Her axe was lying by her foot. "She is no longer a threat."

The girl spat at Simba, but the saliva landed far from the prince's feet. "Give me my axe, and you'll see what kind of threat I am."

"You see, Simba. Do as I have instructed."

"No, commander, you raised us to be true warriors, not executioners."

"This woman attacked you boy, are you mad? She even said it. Give her a rock, and she will strike you with it."

"Then we shall not give her one."

"Look." Chengetaii pointed at Taonga's slain body. "They did this to your friend."

"It was not her spear."

The commander shook his head, discombobulated. "What does it matter whose blade cut your friend?"

Simba was not moved. "She shall be my prisoner."

The girl charged toward the prince, but Simba dashed backward leaving his foot out and watched her sail to the ground. He knelt by her as she lay on the ground yelling profanities with an open gash on her knee. "That looks really bad. You'd be wise to accept your new circumstance."

"I would rather die than be your prisoner." Her eyes met with Simba's. Her face softened for a moment before the prince was wiping off a mixture of mucus and saliva from his face. The girl leapt to her feet and began to run. Comrade Chengetaii sighed, pulled out his sling and knelt to pick up a stone. He let the thong rotate above his head for a moment and released.

When the girl awoke her hands were bound and a blood-drenched cloth was wrapped around her head. The first face she saw was Simba's. "You are lucky to be alive. My uncle here is usually deadly with his sling. I guess the ancestors meant for you to be my prisoner." There was still hate in the girl's eyes, but her head throbbed, leaving her too weak to respond in any way. Simba offered his skin of water, but she refused. "At least tell me what your name is. Mine is Simba." The girl did not reply. "Very well then, you have no name. Girl works just fine."

After they buried Taonga and performed the prayers, they were on their way up the muddy slope, Simba hauling on a rope he had tied around the girl's neck, like a goat being led to the market. Every now and then she tried jerking back on the rope, but Simba responded with a tighter heave that threw her face flat in the earth, cursing as she brought herself back to her feet. The next day's travels were in silence. The group was covered in small cuts from wading through the bush and itchy skin from the poisonous plants. "Your mother is a whore," the girl would curse. "You probably have a small cock. Unbound me and show me you're truly a man, coward," she would hurl. "Curse your sons."

"I don't have any," Simba finally replied, with a wry smile pasted over his cut up face.

"A eunuch, you are?" she countered before Chengetaii turned around and delivered a savage backhand that echoed so wildly Simba was surprised it hadn't caused an avalanche of rock. That shut up the girl . . . for a while. Before long she was at it again until the commander stopped in his tracks, licked his finger and lifted it into the air. "I feel a presence." They followed the slowly flowing water until they were ankle deep in bones and rotten carcasses. Simba rummaged in his bag, produced a small cloth and covered his mouth. He knelt and unfastened a spear clasped by a fallen warrior. He dusted it off and looked for himself in the reflection. Though jagged, there was something alluring about it. He waited for the commander to look away, then slipped it into his satchel. He was sure the dead warrior would not need it in the afterlife.

"Careful, some cling onto their possessions even in death." The prince disregarded the veteran's words and fastened the leather sack. Chengetaii shook his head. *The boy will learn*, he thought, as he put his lips to his leather skin.

Suddenly Simba felt a chill. His arms were now a constellation of goose bumps as a mist gathered knee high. "Can you feel the cold?" The ground began to rumble and the bones began to rattle. The bones began to form, femur to tibia, humerus to ulna and radius until the ribs and spine formed and the empty skulls sat at the top. In one hand they carried metal shields and in the other, large savage spears, swords and axes.

Comrade Chengetaii looked at Simba wide eyed and gnashed his teeth. "I told you to leave the spear alone."

The girl with no name lifted her bound hands. "Untie me, please."

"No, you'll kill me remember?" replied Simba. "I like living."

"I like living too," she pleaded. "If you don't untie me, you don't have a prisoner, and I can fight, as you have seen, and you look like you'll need help."

Simba sized her up. Despite her petite frame, the girl had given him a good fight earlier. His *masimbi* steel cut through the rope with one smooth movement.

She twisted her wrists about, up and down, clockwise, and anti-clockwise. She coughed and looked at Simba.

"Oh, I suppose you want a weapon too." He reached into his bag and produced the girl's axe.

Her eyes animated as she juggled the weapon between her hands and re-accustomed herself to its weight and balance. "So, what are we waiting for? You're trying to get to the oracles right? This is the only way." The nameless girl was the first to walk up toward the army of the dead as thunder roared amongst the dark clouds.

CHAPTER 21

The elderly and the young swayed and shuffled their feet in neat elegant patterns. Others hopped like springboks, emphatically slamming their feet into the rusty brown earth. In no time there was a cloud of dust gathering around the congregation's exultant feet. The chosen girls were dressed in black gowns but when the ceremony was done, they would be given a red one, symbolizing their newfound purity. An elderly woman stood before a stone pulpit, whistled and raised her hands, waiting for the din to subside. She wore an illuminated red and yellow cloth over her head, covering her short white hair. She was as dark as a grape hanging on a vine. This grape though, was not juicy, nor nourishing. It was covered in wrinkles and dry. Her cheeks shone as the sun beat on her face, so it looked as though her eyes were closed. After she prayed for the rains and prosperity, she began, "These girls standing before us have come to be purified before the gods, ancestors and man. Behold them for one last time." They ripped off the black cloths that were covering the girls' nakedness. The crowd clapped and cheered. "These girls that have been presented to you are unclean." It took a while before the crowd finally calmed and the pandemonium had subsided before Mother Matariko continued. "These girls, like all before them, their mothers and their mothers' mothers, were all unholy. The most pious women to walk our holy lands, women like Mother Amonia, and Mother Neria, were also once unholy!" The priestess held her hand high in a tightly rolled fist. "Even I, who stand here before you, was once unwashed, was once foul . . . but no more. Like our fathers in our time, we shall not let these girls perish!" The crowd roared, echoing the priestess over and over again.

I have to stay strong, I have to stay strong, the girl repeated to herself. In the corner of her eye, her father sat in the front row. He bore a proud smile as he jested amongst his friends and associates who had travelled from neighboring villages to witness the momentous occasion.

"Let us not waste time, our precious girls' souls are in peril. Purifier, it is now up to you."

The Sangoma stepped forth and stood before the girls, slouched in an arc. When the drum rang, he began. Left, he darted, and then right, finishing off with an effortless back flip. It was amazing to see the agility the little priest possessed, and the coltish manner he twisted and turned, thrusting his stomach forward before he fell to the ground and shook violently. He came up the same way, panting and raving as his lithe arms glistened with sweat. He held his staff in one hand, flinging it high into the crisp sky. It seemed to have stayed up there for eternity before he caught it right before it landed. The crowd clapped in amazement. He waved it above his head with both hands, drowning himself in the orchestra of percussions, woodwind, string and drum. He glided left, bopped his head and then slid back to where he had begun. He bent over and laid the staff on the red soil, dancing before it. He extended his chest and thrust it into the air like he was balancing a ball on his chest. *Kara-ka!* The drum went. He went on all fours like a stray dog and began shaking and humping the earth. The crowd shrieked in ecstasy. When he returned to his feet, the insides of his palms were red with dust. He rubbed it on his mask, leaving smudges. The priest's hyena snarled as it stood poised with its mouth ajar, panting in the heat from the flames that burnt around the village square. Normally the girls would have been afraid of the hyena, such a vicious creature it was. Today was different. It wasn't the ugly animal they were afraid of, or its fearsome fangs. It was the small blade the little priest paraded high. He punched it into the air over and over again like he was fighting a flying dragon.

The Sangoma was not alone in this display. Even children, barely old enough to walk had now joined the festival of blood, as they joined the orgy of slick twists and turns. Women's jewelry clattered as men's spears united with the drums, rattles and shakers. All eyes were on the witchdoctor though, gyrating his hips and wriggling like his limbs were made of liquid. He performed another back flip, then another one, but this time kicked the air, stomping hard as his feet returned to the earth, sending the crowd wild with pleasure.

"This Sangoma," one man confessed to another, as he sipped his fermented milk merrily. "This Sangoma is something I tell you. A proper man of healing." The others nodded in approbation.

"Let's hope when my little Fari comes of age, he will be available, though I heard he is expensive."

"Look at him," The Sangoma was now doing swift cartwheels and rolling around in the dirt, like dung being transported by a beetle. "You pay for what you get."

"Indeed. I have been saving up for many seasons now. It is a father's duty to ensure his daughters' enter womanhood with dignity."

With that, two women emerged from the crowd and seized the girls on each side and directed them to the stone podiums they had prepared in the middle of the ceremonial square. The table had been decorated with statues and ornaments, dedications to all the fire gods. The Sangoma was now waving a torch slowly around his head, clock-wise and then anti-clockwise. He cast the torch to the floor igniting a ring of fire around the ceremonial ring.

I am the daughter of the fire. The girl convinced herself. *I have to be strong. I have to be a shining example and make my family proud.*

It was easier said than done, especially when the Sangoma put the rusty blade into the flame until it caught fire. He raised it like a torch and displayed it for the people to see. They roared in approval. Two priestesses came holding a calf with a rope tied around its neck, presenting it to the dancing priest. He circled the sacrifice, sizing it up, flicking his tongue by the calf's ear. He dipped the blade into the fire, reigniting the flame. The priestesses held the sacrifice down, exposing its neck. The witchdoctor adjusted his footing, tightened his grip and slashed. Blood came splattering out red and warm. She felt some splash on her feet too. The rest seemed to have squirted all over the priest's mask. The hyena charged, lapping up the spilled blood until a guard shooed it away with a large spear. It giggled and trotted away with blood dripping from its snout. The Sangoma put a cup to the dying calf's wound. When the cup was full, the priest lifted it over his head and let it fall over his cadaverous body. He shrieked and the crowd followed suit.

The girl had never seen anything so horrifying. She too must have fainted for a few moments because when she came to, she was on her back on the cold, hard stone table with the two women holding her tight by a her ankles. She wanted to scream but they had put a foul tasting cloth in her mouth. The Sangoma shuffled closer and closer as his eyes grew brighter, redder, and more vicious every time the drum was struck. She tried to move her hands, but they had been tied to the table. She couldn't hold it any longer. Tears poured down her cheeks. She cried out for her mother as the scorching blade crept closer. She could feel the heat on the inside of her thighs as the razor roamed. *What's he waiting for?* She felt a crippling answer from the razor's lick.

***

"Purification?" Queen Zandile challenged, as she returned to the present and gathered her thoughts. "These are customs from the past, not practiced by the Piripiri for generations." She thought of something, anything to make him change his mind, but nothing came from her lips. Her worst nightmare was coming to fruition. She should have known there was a price to pay for Alinafe's life. The Sangoma had said as much.

"It is the ancestors' will," the king reiterated. "They demand purity if we are to survive as a clan . . . if we are to prosper in the coming days. This shall ensure that our people are faultless." Maghedzi had an expressionless face, but the dark shade in the room did well to lessen his hideousness. "Nia shall be the first. Soon I shall call on our sons to spill their blood. Our daughters must do the same, and what blood do the ancestors cherish more than that of a princess?"

She had once loved another. When she was a little girl, every night she would set aflame a fire lily before she went to bed, asking the ancestors to marry her to a strong and handsome king. All the girls of her generation dreamt of Farakaii. He was heir to the Akuwa kingdom, a marvelous wrestler and had what the girls around the chiefdoms called buttocks made of *masimbi* steel.

She remembered fondly when a young Farakaii and his father, King Dakaraii, stopped by their village on their way to Pyyros. At the banquet, she had felt a carefree gentleness in his spirit, which was unlike other princes' whom carried themselves with entitlement and arrogance. He had smiled at her, and she took it as a sign he had chosen her. She prayed everyday it was true, and it was, as King Dakaraii had offered her father a handsome dowry. She and Sekai would giggle into the night and imagine the large walls of the Stone Houses and visualize the queen's compound with dozens of huts and sparkly stone pavements. Such childishness was extinguished when Maghedzi's father, offered twice as many cows. It was an offer her father could not refuse, despite giving his word. It was a small price losing his honor, she had overheard him say, for enough wealth to keep the Moto wealthy for thousands of generations.

"Besides, Zandile," Chief Lume argued, though she could see a glimmer of guilt in his eyes. "The Akuwa are not our people. They come from far away. They have different customs and ways of worship. Maghedzi is a good man. He will be good to you. You will be obedient and bear him many princes."

Zandile, who loved her father dearly, grudgingly did her duty. Over the years she had found some affection for Maghedzi, but now she could not abide. She was certain this was the work of the Sangoma. He had already taken her. She wasn't going to let him have Nia too.

"You will see it is a good thing," Maghedzi continued. "Look at all the good it did you."

"You can't. I won't let you."

"Can't?" Maghedzi chuckled, "I haven't heard that in a while, not since my father died. Can't is a word a wife should never use when talking to her husband, let alone a king." His nostrils flared once more. "I do not care to discuss this any further. The Sangoma has seen it. He is a man of great power. A man of great vision."

"How can you listen to that crazy little man? You speak of ancestors, Maghedzi, but did they not warn us not to suffer the testimony of false prophets? Have you forgotten his past crimes? The only thing to be gained here is his agenda."

"Oh quiet, woman, like you haven't been following your own agenda all these years. Have you forgotten who brought our son back from the black?"

The memory sent a shiver down her spine, the anguish and desperation she felt as healer after healer came and went. "What does his agenda matter anyway? His is mine." His mouth tightened. He placed his crown on his head and slowly put on his giant gold bracelet, with bright stones encrusted into it. "Look, Zandile." This time with a softer tone, but still rather harsh, he asked, "How many youth do we have at the shelter?"

Zandile was hands-on with the charities and social work within the kingdom. "Fifty-eight," she replied confidently.

"Fifty-eight, Zandile, fifty-eight bastards." The king looked like he had stumbled upon a half decomposed corpse nestling in the bush. "Remember that butcher's daughter, the one that committed suicide? If this foolish girl had been purified, she never would have been in such circumstance. Purification helps maintain chastity before marriage."

"Do you not care that she might die, your only daughter?"

"What gifts do gods accept that do not carry sacrifice? The Sangoma has proved himself a good healer – the best. He will make sure Nia goes to her future husband clean and obedient. It is my duty as a king."

There was nothing she could say to convince him to change course. She was resolved to take action. If she did nothing, her daughter would suffer the same horrors she suffered all those years ago. She still remembered the faceless priestess's cold, powerful hands snapping her from behind. She remembered the Sangoma's wild shriek as he slashed. The priestesses' iron grips hurt, leaving bruises that stayed for a week. However, nothing was worse than the bruise she would carry for the rest of her life.

By comparison, one could consider Zandile lucky. Various tribes had more grotesque practices. She had once heard of a woman mutilated so badly it looked like something else entirely, something out of nightmares. She heard tales of some tribes that after the cutting would sew the skin together, leaving a small hole so one could urinate. The husband could remove the string when he had use of her. She had also heard of some, who after cutting the flesh, cast it into a brazier and performed powerful witchcraft.

The queen crept up to Nia as she slept. She smiled, looking down at her little princess. *Look how innocent she is. She has never hurt a soul. How can they say that there is something wrong with my little girl? That she is dirty, that she is soiled?* She caressed her cheek softly, rubbing the dirt from her nose.

Nia opened her eyes, recognizing immediately that something was amiss.

"I have something to tell you, my sweet baby cub." She sniffled as tears started forming around her eye ducts. "I want you to know I tried everything I could. Your father," she stammered, "has brought back purification. You are to be the first."

"Purification?" she had to repeat. It took Nia a while to wrap her head around the thought. "When?"

"Upon the Flame Festival. Your father says the ancestors wish it so. He says men shed blood on the battlefields. Women must shed too."

"Then I don't like the ancestors," the girl declared, defiantly.

"Quiet girl, you do not want them to hear you. They are everywhere, even in this room."

"I can shed blood on the battle field too, just like my brothers. I can protect you and the people. I can fight, I've been practicing in secret." Nia covered her mouth, realizing she had divulged too much.

"Behind the servants' quarters, with your uncle Machupa's spear?"

"You knew?"

"A mother knows everything about her children, Nia. It is her duty." For the first time during that conversation, they both smiled.

"I can talk to him. Father has always had a soft spot for me. He would secretly give me tours of his chambers and take me to the Fire Shrine. He says that I am his princess and that he loves me."

Zandile was shocked Maghedzi would say something like that to anyone, even his daughter. She had thought such passion only reserved for the collection of spears and bows he had destroyed his late father's harem for – and his mound of skulls. "Your father is not the same man he once was. He has changed. That Sangoma has been whispering treacherous things into his ears and poisoned his soul. He will not change his mind until we remove the spell the mystic has cast."

"But mother, the Sangoma, he isn't that bad. He's not what you…"

"Hush now, child," Zandile interrupted. "Do not let him fool you. He is a wicked creature."

Nia did not want to believe that. He had saved her little brother, and they had shared a lovely afternoon together. She did not believe he would hurt her. "What are we going to do?"

"I will give you something your mother was never given. I am going to give you a choice."

"You were also purified? Mother, I had no idea, I'm so sorry."

"It is okay, sweet, sweet child. It was a long time ago." She grabbed Nia by the shoulders and looked straight at her with her pink, moist eyes. "Do you want to be purified?" Nia, still shorter than her mother, had to look up. She could see the trepidation in her eyes.

"No mother, I don't want to do it."

"Very well then, listen very carefully. There is only one way to save you." Zandile looked around to make sure no one was nearby eavesdropping.

CHAPTER 22

The girl with no name was the first to sprint toward the dead. Left and right she laid her axe about. Her first cut was low, which the skeleton deflected, but her next swipe hewed its arm off. Comrade Chengetaii was soon next to her, slamming his war club over a skeleton's skull, shattering it into pieces. He spun and slammed Dread into the skeleton's chest, then legs, until it was a pile of broken bones. He swung at another, and then another, but before Dread could taste the fourth, the girl with no name took it first, her axe dividing the skull in two. Chengetaii growled, "That was mine."

The girl smirked and commenced her avalanche of elegant whirlwind strikes. When Chengetaii turned to find Dread's next meal, miraculously the skeletons they had felled began to form once again. He shrieked in pain as something took a bite of his shin. He wriggled the skull free, sacrificing some of his flesh and sent his club down. It hopped out of the way before he gave it a good kick into the wall. Another lumbered clumsily toward him, slashing its sword across his face, leaving a deep cut on his cheek.

Simba was now on another, burying his spear into the walking dead's shield. He pulled back and went high, running his spear through its eye socket. As he struggled to free the spear, it backhanded the prince, sending him down. He got up just in time to dodge the skeleton's several jabs before its shield smashed into his face, sending him staggering back. He went in again, but the skeleton's sword met his spear shaft, cutting it into two. The skeleton raised its sword, ready to cut down the prince from shoulder to testis, but the girl with no name's axe flew past the prince and into the skeleton's face. The prince smiled, pulled out the axe and finished what the girl had started, smashing the skeleton's skull over and over again until there was just scattered bone.

Now a skeleton was slowly pacing toward the girl with no name. "You," hollered Simba, alerting the skeleton. Only its head turned. "You like hitting girls? Try me." The rest of its body turned leaving it invitingly vulnerable to the girl's axe, snapping its vertebrae. As its legs continued toward the prince, she lifted a large rock and set it down on the skeleton's cavity, over and over again.

Something took a hold of Simba's leg. He thought it a tree root, but he was wrong. Nails dug deep into his flesh. Then suddenly, more dead burst out from the earth. Simba kicked at it, but it made no difference. It took him to the ground and they wrestled in the dirt, punching and clawing at each other. He was eye to eye with the skeleton. It lashed its teeth, barely missing his nose. Its teeth slammed together with ferocious force. He managed to wrestle himself free, hurling the skeleton away, but as he did, more of the monsters rose from the earth, one by one. Some still had their clothes from their former lives, some were bone dry and others still had rotten flesh stuck sparingly on their bones.

The Amakazi captain was now surrounded from all sides. "Is that all you have?" he bellowed. If he was going to die that day, it wasn't without a fight. He grabbed one skeleton and flung it wench it came from. "Akuwa!" he bellowed, striking left and right randomly as they swarmed around him, grunting as the war club broke bone. "Akuwa," he screamed, saliva splashing over his lips. As the skeleton army swarmed around him, suddenly, Koko came screeching in, picking up a skeleton, soaring into the sky and letting it splatter into the earth. She did that a few times, giving Chengetaii a moment of respite.

It was now apparent they had no chance of defeating the creatures. Chengetaii had been in some perilous situations, but none quite like this. He remembered battling a pride of lions. He remembered winning a battle with twenty men against a hundred. But those foes could be killed. These could not.

"We will never win," said the prince. "They are respawning. I have a plan." Simba waved his arms wildly, gaining the creatures' attention. They all began marching toward him. He cursed and wailed as they followed him. He was now inching closer to the edge of a cliff.

When Chengetaii realized what his nephew was doing, it was too late to stop him. A swarm of walking dead separated them. He struck one down, and then another, but they were too many. "What are you doing boy? You're going to die!"

Simba smiled and performed the Akuwa salute. "Then so be it." As he said that, he jumped over the edge as skeleton after skeleton dragged their feet to the brink, following the prince over into the Khumalo.

Now there was one left. "This is for the prince, my nephew, Simba." Chengetaii swung Dread, hewing its skull clean off and kicked the skeleton over the cliff.

Chengetaii and the girl fell when there was no more danger, looking into the sky. Vultures ascended on the scene, but the commander rose and waved his club. "Not today. Be gone with you," he spat. The bird's feathers caused a light draft as they took off into the sky, cooling the commander. Sorrow gripped his heart. Simba had sacrificed himself so they could live. What was he to tell his brother, when he returned to the Stone Houses – if he ever returned.

"Isn't anyone going to help me up?" said a voice from beyond the cliff. Chengetaii crawled to the edge, and there hanging from a branch was Simba.

Chengetaii smiled for the first time in years.

After tending to their wounds, drinking some water and regaining their strength, the weary group looked up as they stood at the base of the hill. "This is as far as your journey goes," the commander informed.

"There is no way you are going up on your own uncle."

"What about your prisoner?"

Simba had not thought about that. She was bleeding from her gut, and the gash on her knee was now even worse.

"Don't worry about me. I can climb, watch." She felt the stone and found a pocket to place her fingers and tried to hurl herself up. She screeched in pain.

"Like I said, you're only going to get yourself killed." Chengetaii ripped off the pendent that was resting on his heaving chest. "If tomorrow ends and I have not returned, then I am dead. My weapons and leather skin are yours, but this . . ." He placed the pendent into Simba's palms. "Give this to your father. He will know what to do with it. That girl of yours, I have seen the way you look at her. I saw the same look your father had, one night, many years ago, well before you were born. Your father, however, was wise enough to not follow his desires, but those of the tribe."

With that the commander was gone, leaving Simba clutching the pendant. "He turned to his hostage and sighed. "So we wait."

***

Comrade Chengetaii was now thousands of feet above Hippo Valley, holding on to a crack on the great mass of rock. He shuffled along and hoisted his body to the side, clutching on another edge. He used one hand to feel above, felt it was sturdy and pulled himself up. He shuffled sideways, his stomach scraping against the hard rock and crumbles of rock falling onto his bald head and over his eyes. Suddenly the rock broke, but just in time he managed to hoist himself onto another ledge. His eyes followed the rock down, seeing a cloud engulf at the bottom of the hill. He let one of his hands free and wiped away his sweat, leaving his forehead light brown from the slag. He saw vultures, the king's of the sky, circling high above him, surely anticipating his impending demise. He gritted his teeth and continued up.

He was almost there. It was half a day since he left Simba, but it felt like he had been climbing for weeks. There was nothing but him and the wall, nothing but the howling wind and the grimness of his thoughts. He was renowned around the kingdoms and beyond as the bravest of men. There was nothing he feared, beast, spirit or man. He had once the feeling of trepidation, but rather than bravery, he was now a man who had no regard for his own life. He had wanted to end it with his own blade, but that was an abomination that his brother would never forgive, and worthy for his body to be cast into the Forest of Abominations, castrated and quartered after his eyes had been offered to the sparrows. First he sought comfort in *umqombothi,* but when that didn't work, he sought after death itself, entering battles without shield. He had swum in the Khumalo, in search of the nyaminyami, hoping it would take him under, but they had seized to exist.

He felt raindrops on his fingers as the final edge appeared above him. Every muscle on his body was aching. *Just one more push*, he willed himself as he gnashed his teeth, hurling himself over the edge. Nefarious laughter welcomed him as he crawled, echoing into the grisly sky and met eyes with a group of red-eyed beasts with spots as dark as their hearts. For what they lacked in their hindquarters, they more than made up for with their thick neck and forequarters. Despite that he did not flinch or move. He had to show them he was not afraid. The biggest one crawled forward, growling, as the rest circled him menacingly, licking their lips. It crept closer and closer as its eyes flared. The beast snapped its teeth in front of the warriors face. He could feel the force of the bite from the small gust of wind it created, and a detestable smell of rotten meat. Without warning, a whistle rang out. The rabid beasts giggled, turned and ran back to a dark figure as they wagged their bushy, black tails. The shadow, otherworldly, with eyes like a raging inferno and a head full of worms spoke. "You have done well to make it this far. You are Chengetaii. We have been following your journey and know why you are here. Do not be afraid. Follow me into the Spirit Temple so you can meet my sisters. They too have been expecting you."

Chengetaii emerged from the dark passageway after pushing away thick cobwebs to find the dark sister vanished into thin air. He gripped Dread tighter and navigated a little further until before him, by a raging fire, sat a woman and in her cradle, a baby lay with its lips firmly planted on her breast. The baby drank thirstily with its eyes closed and its fat fingers wrapped around a breast until the creamy milk flowed down the child's stomach. The woman raised her head and smiled. The infant let go of its mother's teat, turned and opened its eyes, a savannah yellow. The baby giggled, as sweetly as any new born, then opened its mouth, in it a row of razors, white and glistening.

"Chenge, I am so glad you came to us," the mother said. "Where have you been? I want you to meet someone." She rose with the only thing covering her, the thicket of hair by her nether parts and crimson beads that decorated her legs. She rubbed her nose on the baby's soft cheeks and grinned. "This is yours, Chengetaii. This is what we made." She set the boy on the floor and let it waddle around the room on its fore's, as its tail followed behind. "Aren't you going to come and say hello to your child?" It began to cry. "*Baba*," it cried, "*baba*."

"See, my strong warrior, it needs its father."

Cold chills ran down Chengetaii's spine. "I have no child. Who are you?" The baby's tail curled and whipped the dark stone floor.

The woman giggled. "Why Chengetaii, its me."

Thandi, it can't be!

She moved closer. "Look." She lifted her head and there around her neck were the rings of death and around them, hard-crusted blood.

"But you are….."

She finished the sentence for him. "Dead? My sweet Chenge, do you forget the words we said to each other that night you took my maidenhood? Did we not say death could never separate us?"

All he could do was stare with his mouth agape. It was her, Chengetaii fretted. How could it not be? They were alone in his hut, the night she came to him in the cover of dark. The night before she was to be married. He had not known what her words truly meant, but the next morning when he found her, it had become clear.

She looked just as she did that night, though now her breasts showed motherhood. She even had the moles on her thighs. Her hair was just the same, short and curly, and her lips, red and full. How he wanted to smell her.

"I told you that night, you were the only one I wanted to touch my body. The only one I wanted in me. Look what I did, Chengetaii. Look what I did for us." She touched her wounds and reached her hand out. Red smudges covered the tips of her fingers.

He pushed them away, barely able to contain tears that had lay dormant for a generation. "That is not what I wanted for you, *mudiwa*. I wanted us to be together forever but you . . . you . . ."

"I did what I had to. You told me you could not live to see another man have me. I did this for us . . . I did this for you."

Chengetaii could not mask the guilt that had throbbed in him all these years. He wanted to turn back the seasons, to a time he had never awoken bruised, on the brink of death in her care. To a time where he had never met her gaze, for she would still be alive. He shook his head. She was alive, she was right in front of him and he could feel the warmth that radiated from her shiny-bronzed body. His eyes wondered until he got to her nave. He tried to look away, but . . . he wanted her and the look on her face told him, she wanted him too.

She turned around and walked toward a dark passage, bending over to blow out the lamps that were spread across the floor. She had a tail, just like the child, but larger, and even more reptilian. "Follow me, Chengetaii, come with me so Farakaii may have a companion."

Farakaii? he gasped. He had told her what he wanted to call his first-born son, in honor of his king, his brother, his best friend.

"Like his mother, he is so lonely."

Chengetaii fought hard. He had fought his whole life. He had fought against his enemies and even those that were not. He was a soldier. It is what the creator had decreed. He had fought his affections when Zandile took his brother's favor. When he found Thandi, he could not fight her too. Dread fell from his grasp as he stepped forward.

"Don't be afraid, Chengetaii. We will finally be together. We will finally be as one, as we were that night."

The room was warm and perspiration had now covered his body, but somehow he still felt a chill in his bones. He passed the great flame that lit up the room and crept closer to the dark entrance as Thandi's finger beckoned him. When he got to the entrance, something held him back. "I can't. You are dead. I cut you down from the jacaranda myself and cradled you in my arms. I peered into your lifeless eyes and wept. I kissed you for the last time and closed your eyes. This . . ." Chengetaii shuddered. "You are the work of some sorcery."

Thandi gently held him by the wrist and directed his hand over her face. The shape of her nose, her lips, her cheekbones were just the same. She directed him down her neck, torso and nave until his fingers disappeared under her thick coarse hair . . . she was just as warm. The commander closed his eyes and felt his loincloth become heavy. He wanted to take it off right there and then, however, something held him back. He grabbed her by the hand forcefully and pulled it away. "Away from me. How come you are just the same as I left you, and I covered in the ash of time?"

"That does not matter my love. What matters is we can be finally be together. My father rests, as does my mother, my betrothed and those that contrived to keep us apart rest . . . they kept us apart all those years ago, only they never did . . . not truly." Tears began to flow down Chengetaii's cheeks. "Take me, take me now," she pleaded. He grabbed her by the waist and pulled her until they were chest to chest, letting his finger down the crack of her back. "Yes," she hollered. "Do it, do it, give me another child . . . give me your soul," she said, but this time with a darker voice. There was silence for some moments. "What are you doing, Chengetaii, my brave Akuwa warrior? Give me a child, Farakaii is lonely."

Before she could say anything, Chengetaii drew a line across her throat, and with that followed up with a thrust through her stomach. Thandi wailed and began to laugh, louder and louder until a bright light appeared and then, she was gone. The commander dropped to his knees, panting heavily, wiping the sweat from his forehead.

A voice sounded. "You are truly righteous Comrade Chengetaii of Amakazi. Only the strongest of men can turn down their heart's truest desires. You have passed the test of purity." Chengetaii found himself kneeling in the middle of a dimly lit hut and in front of him sat three figures. "What brings you all this way to see us?"

CHAPTER 23

Xolani crouched as he picked up the dusty club he had been trying to twist between his fingers like his uncle did so effortlessly. He had to master it before the rites of passage and time was running out. Matata hollered his name and proceeded to rotate his stick until a draft of wind emerged. "That's how you do it, bastard. See, it's easy." Khaya the Glut grunted like a pig, Korokoro the squirrel was on his stomach in laughter, whilst Thokozani, Gumisa and rest were holding their bellies, barely able to breath.

"Ignore them," whispered Batanai, with an encouraging smile. Xolani had, continuing his attempts. He was used to being condescended to, the price he had to pay, he guessed, for being born a bastard. "Here, give me that for a moment." Xolani surrendered the staff and watched as Batanai showed him the way, where to hold the stick and how to place his fingers for a more thorough rotation. Before long Xolani's fingers were aching and his jaw bruised from clumsily striking himself. But at least he had come a long way.

It had been a week now, and Comrade Chengetaii had not showed up for training and coincidentally, Simba hadn't been seen at the armory either. It brought great unease as the feeling of dread still lingered after the deaths of Sipho and Nthanda. "Death comes in threes," he had often heard the elders say.

"Where is your uncle?" Chipo had asked as they ate supper. It is irresponsible of Chengetaii to just wonder off. It is dangerous in the wild, especially now. We all saw what happened at the Moyo farm." Chipo shook her head in sorrow. "What they did to that boy, Korokoro, only the ancestors know why."

"It is not our place to question the ancestors, sister," Aunt Rabia answered. "All we can do is appease them."

Chipo nodded her head. "You were too young to remember Xolani, but the last time your uncle disappeared like this, he did not return for several years. The spark in his eyes he once had did not return with him."

"What happened whilst he was away?"

"No one knows. Chengetaii was a wonderful storyteller when we were younger. We used to sit and talk for hours on end, but when he returned his mouth was shut tighter than a clam. I remember asking myself, what has happened to my Chenge? I once asked Farakaii, but he told me to never ask him again."

"They say Prince Simba is also missing. Is that true, boy?"

Xolani nodded his head, as his mouth was full of pumpkin, greens and goat stew. "He usually comes and watches us training, offering help where he can, but I haven't seen him all week. I figured he was spending more time at court."

Chipo shook her head. "No, I don't think so. I have been at court a few times this week delivering your father his lunch, and I have not seen a trace of him there."

"Let us pray then, that they are safe." Those in the hut concurred in a unified murmur.

The next day at training, half of the cadets were away, skiving. Some took to drinking *doro*. Others could be seen hassling the young girls as they collected water at the well. Others, just sat around, told stories and laughed. Xolani kept to himself and honed his spear work to the amusement of others. Matata whistled toward Xolani, wiping away the thick residue of his beer from his lips. "Relax, bastard," he hollered. "The commander is not here. I am in charge."

Xolani ignored him, turned his head and flashed his teeth. "Hey everyone, its Simba, he's back."

Prince Themba had been at the armory, watching the cadets, as he made merry with his friends. He was the first to greet the heir: "You have been missing brother. I almost began to think the worst." They embraced. "And who is this," he asked as he set his blood eye upon the girl with no name. As it looked, his eyeball was taking its time to heal, despite several visits to several healers.

She had a loincloth that covered her private parts, but her muscular thighs were in full sight. A leather cloth covered her breasts revealing her rock hard stomach, and her arms, lithe, but muscular. Her hair was a bushy entanglement, eyes, a deep maroon, and lips, full. "She is my prisoner." Simba replied protectively.

"Then why is she not bound?"

"She promised she would not run."

Themba turned to the stranger and smiled thinly. "What is your name?"

"She hasn't said," Simba replied for her.

"And what tribe is she from?" There was nothing distinguishable on her, apart from her strapping physique, the scaly jewelry around her throat, wrists, and ankles.

"She hasn't said that either."

"And she is your prisoner?" Themba had a raised eyebrow. "She looks more like a guest."

Tired from the barrage of questions, Simba whistled and up came a couple of boys, the youngest of the bunch. "See to it that her wounds are looked to and that she is fed."

The boys nodded and led her away as Themba's blood eye watched her like a hawk. She didn't walk with the customary grace and elegance of the women the prince was accustomed to, but rather, purposefully sturdy strides. When she was clear out of sight, Themba turned back to his twin. "Coincidentally, you and Taonga disappeared as did Comrade Chengetaii. Were you with them?"

Simba did not reply, but his eyes said it all. He produced Taonga's bow, smeared in the dark reddish brown of his life's blood.

"I see." Themba looked down in sorrow. "He was a great friend, and soon to be a brother, by law."

"It's all my fault. I should have never asked him to join me, to follow Comrade Chengetaii."

Themba didn't want to ask the next question, but he did nonetheless. "And what of the commander?"

Simba took his time to answer, still not making eye contact. "He is on his way." It was a lie, but Simba desperately wanted to believe that. He quickly changed his demeanor to something more princely. "Why is everyone idling around when the rites of passage is just around the corner? Commander or no commander, practice commences. To your positions."

The next morning arrived and Comrade Chengetaii was still nowhere to be seen. The morning break came, then lunchtime, and finally sunset was upon them, and still there was no sign of the veteran warrior the next day or the next. Simba had to face the agonizing truth. His uncle was never coming back. He clutched the commander's pendant tightly as a tear broke down his cheek. Everyone stopped their activities – they knew what he was going to say. Some had already begun snuffling. "I'm sorry to have to say this, but our commander...."

"Is just behind us," Xolani cut in, as Comrade Chengetaii appeared by the training ground gates, in all his clenched glory.

Simba's eyes widened with bemusement, as did his mouth, exposing his chipped tooth. "Uncle, you're, you're alive."

"Of course I'm alive. By the looks of it, Simba managed to give you an even more thorough training session."

The young hippos laughed, relieved their fearsome commander had returned.

When Simba and Chengetaii had a quiet moment, the prince confided: "Uncle, I am so ashamed. I was afraid for you. I should have had faith that you would return."

"A warrior knows no fear. All he knows is duty and instruction."

The prince knew that. It had been drilled into him as long as he could remember, but it was harder to live by. "Uncle, did you meet the Sisters? What did you see up there?"

Chengetaii looked like he had aged considerably, the silver tuft of hair on his shiny head now a pale golden color. On his shoulders a constellation of sores, and his neck and arms, peeled skin. Koko screeched and elegantly landed on his master's shoulder, digging its claws into his flesh. He reached into his cloths and pulled out a peanut and held it out. "Nothing Simba, nothing at all."

***

Xolani put down his bag, looked around to make sure he was alone and began to hum by the riverbank. He was getting better at it, hitting the notes that had evaded him thus far. After a few moments, the water trembled, turned red, and out into the sky Aku emerged, swishing into the water and out again, noticeably larger than the last time Xolani visited him. "Hello, Xolani, have you brought me something?"

"Of course, you're so cranky and no fun when you are hungry." Xolani reached into his bag, pulled out a dead chicken he had plucked himself and threw it the water dragon's way. With one movement, Xolani could see the chicken squeezing down its long serpentine neck. Suddenly, the dragon began to cough, spewing out a thick liquid that landed on a large rock. It began to fizz and disintegrate, creating a trail of smoke. Xolani and Aku looked at each other in astonishment.

"I think I may be sick." Aku burped so loudly Xolani's loincloth flew back.

The bastard's eyes widened and a smile appeared on his face when he recalled his conversation with the wise Sekuru Rwizi. "Legends say that the nyaminyami could spit venomous liquid from its mouth. Your powers are developing. Try it again." Aku took a giant breath, opened his mouth and unleashed a thick ball of saliva that landed on a small bush turning it into ash. Xolani laughed in exaltation. The dragon went again, but this time failed. "Don't get carried away Aku. These things take time and practice." The dragon hissed as fumes sailed from its nostrils, and coiled itself atop a rock, scales, grey and azure, glistening from the sun's rays.

"I will be going away," Xolani announced. "To the rites of passage, an initiation ceremony that has a long tradition amongst my tribe. There I shall prove my worth as a warrior and the first stage in me becoming an Amakazi."

Aku lashed his tongue, and as he did, a violet leaf slowly fell and landed softly on Xolani's lap. He picked it up and smiled as he felt its texture. "Mom is so happy. It is all she has been talking about lately – and a wife for me. I wonder what she'll be like." The nyaminyami was not paying attention, preferring to hone his newfound powers, gleefully unleashing darts of deadly saliva.

"Anyway, it is time I go. When I return, you will be bigger, and maybe, I will be able to ride you." Xolani gathered his things, putting the five leaves the tree had shed into his sack.

The dragon slipped back into the river, turning the water red. "Good luck on your trip. Don't forget me."

Xolani could feel a tear struggling to escape from his ducts, but he fought it off and reluctantly rode off.

He arrived as a trail followed Prince Themba down the spiraling steps from the Stone Houses. "Ah, Xolani, there you are," Themba said. "Aren't you going to wish me well on my travels?"

"Where are you going?" Xolani hadn't heard.

Themba smiled ear to ear. "All you need to know is that things will be different when I return."

"Well, good luck."

Themba looked at Xolani suspiciously, wondering to himself why he would need luck. "Shall I bring you a gift, half brother?"

Xolani could not think of anything. "Make it a surprise."

"Very well then. I heard you made it to the rites of passage. You ought to be proud."

Xolani nodded humbly.

"I am sure you will do good. I slew thirteen beasts on my initiation. You'll be lucky to get half. Take care now." The prince winked, and continued down the steps with Chief-Treasurer Mutasa, his uncle Munyaradzi, their sworn spears and servants in tow.

Later in the night, Xolani tossed and turned. When he finally began to yawn, soon he was gazing into thick ashy clouds and within them, bright lights blazed, thundering with violet streaks. Waves raved as a colossus rapid charged his way. He dove in and found himself deep in the aquatic world amongst the reef, fishes of different kinds and a civilization of crystal palaces where water dragons and mermen lived in harmony. He passed through time, thousands of generations, and when time stopped he was a dragon king, and before him stood man in their numbers carrying spears. Arrows invaded the sky, covering the clouds, before they turned on him and fishermen wailed as they were dragged down to their deaths, cursing the water dragons. He could taste blood on his tongue as he snapped a merman between his teeth and spat venom, flinging his tail, splattering dozens at a time, meanwhile feeling the stings of flamed arrows and sharp spears.

He returned under the waves, another space, another time, but now his father appeared next to him, considerably younger, wearing heavy cow tails around his upper arms and under his knees. The tails were drenched in a substance, black and thick, but fire burnt at their edges, as did the bottom of his apron. Soon thereafter, a transfiguration occurred, replacing his father's head with the dragon king's. However, it was not the proud head of the great leviathan he saw. Instead of the polished dark royal blue color, this dragon's skin was dull. Its tongue stuck out from its dark pink mouth decorated by brown and red sores and in its gigantic mouth dwelled a horrible concert of rotten teeth, with its eyes twisted into tight knots. It wore a crown with poisonous barbs coiled around it with blood dripping from its tips.

The scene changed and Xolani was speeding through the aquatic, clutching at his mother's heels. He could feel the wetness of the underworld as he glided through the dark waters, his little heart pounding. They entered a dark cave and the dragon queen unveiled a shiny stone. She sang, and as she did, he could see mermen speeding their way, tridents in hand. The dragon queen spat, sending venom through the water. One merman disintegrated, then another, but they were too numerous. A bright light appeared. Xolani could feel the roughness of her tongue as she licked him one last time. As she did, a hail of tridents sped their way. The waters rumbled, and shook as they struck the dragon queen. "Quickly. Enter."

Xolani began to cry. "I can't leave you. I will never leave you." Xolani could see the steam rising from her nostrils before she shoved him in with the tip of her snout. The portal closed behind him. The last image he saw was that of the belligerent mer-king and in his mouth a human hand bearing an Akuwa bracelet. "Aku," Xolani screamed, rising from his mat, his heart pounding and forehead drenched in perspiration. Another sound rang out as he switched sides. *It must be Aunt Rabia.* His great aunt had been having problems with her bladder. *Or it might just be a broken tree branch.* The wind at this time of the year was fierce during the nights and could have easily carried with it loose branches. He laid his head again, but there was another rattle. He rose from his mat and looked around for his worthless spear. *Where is that thing?* The door creaked as it opened. He finally found the spear, fumbling it as he readied to defend himself.

"Hello, young man."

Was it death itself? If so, why had it not called him by name? Xolani had been taught there was no name death did not know. He was further surprised to learn that death had the smell of thick licorice.

"You will have to forgive me," the night creature whispered. "Put your spear down. You have nothing to fear. It is your father."

Never in eternity would Xolani have guessed this. His father had never visited him in his chambers, and why at this time in the middle of the night with the whole world asleep. "Mighty Hippo . . ." the boy apologized.

"Nonsense. Father," the king corrected, "I am your *baba* and you shall address me as such." As kings were entitled, Farakaii casually strolled around the compartment, taking sips of his pipe as mushroom clouds shot into the thatched roof. "I can imagine you are wondering why I have come to you, in the hour of the night wolf. I wanted to give you your father's blessing before your journey." The boy was still too stunned to return any words. "There are things you are too young to understand, but one day you will. Even though you may not see it now, the ancestors look favorably upon you. On the fourth day after your birth, the oracles made a fire from green leaves and your mother sat with you cradled in her arms as the leaves burned. When we sprinkled the remains from the fire around this very hut that you sleep in today, the earth trembled, like a hundred hippos dashing. Your destiny is great." Farakaii paused and rubbed his fingers over the miniature wooden statue of an ancient Akuwa warrior that stood in the corner. "This looks like the work of Mariga." The boy nodded. "Fine work indeed. I remember it. It belonged to me once upon a time." The king seemed to have gone into memory lane for a moment. He ended it with a frown. "Do you know that I had older brothers? One died at child birth, the other stupidity and the other…" He could barely say the word, "Treachery."

"I am sorry, father, I had no idea. Were they great men like you?"

The king nodded. "Greater. They never got a chance to fulfill their destinies. Never mind them. They are now resting with our ancestors. I am proud of the way you conducted yourself at the festival. You are a worthy Akuwa. Your uncle keeps me up to date regularly with your progress. He says you have great endurance, and obedient to your elders. However, you need to improve your technique and speed. He also worries about your focus. A warrior is always on the alert. Believe it or not, your father at your age was not too different in build to what you are." Xolani tried, but he could not fathom his father as small and slight as he was. "Your father was once called Little Farakaii, but that all changed when I slew Shapiro the Giant." There was a long pause, as though the king was forming his words. "I have kept you at a distance, but I hope that this will make it up." The king brought out a long object, covered in a cloth. Xolani's eyes widened when it was unpackaged, lighting the dark room. "It's called Night Slayer."

Xolani reached out and held it. It felt nothing like the spears he was used to, the ones that Comrade Chengetaii kept at the armory. "I don't know what to say father. Thank you?"

"It is your uncle you should thank. It is made from the best wood deep in the haunted woodlands of Domboshawa and *masimbi* steel. It was forged by the Sisters."

Xolani repeated the name and gasped. Legend had it the witches were conjoined with venomous vipers for hair, giant hyenas for pets and eyes that never slept.

"Your uncle went through a lot to get there and have it made." The gash on the commander's cheeks and several other scars were testament to this. "I would have gone myself, but my health fails me." The king coughed. "Its design is made through my specific instructions. It has magical properties which make it glow when you're near the supernatural."

Xolani juggled it from one hand to the other. "It is rather heavy, but it feels great and I am getting stronger by the day. Ask Uncle Chengetaii. He'll tell you. Ask anyone."

Farakaii began to chuckle lightly. "Slow down, Xolani, I believe you. However, this is no toy."

Xolani nodded, but it was clear his attention was elsewhere. He could not keep his hands or his eyes off the shiny new spear.

"You are mine own blood, no matter what anyone says. I want you to never forget that and remember that being my son comes with responsibilities. You shall live an honorable life and always strive to do the right thing, even if it is the hardest." The king's tone changed, and his eyebrows bridged in curiosity. "Do you have strange dreams you cannot make sense of? Answer it true."

Xolani was taken aback. He didn't want to appear craven in front of his father so looked down. "Sometimes."

"What kind of dreams, speak up?"

Xolani was unsure what to answer. He could not make sense of them himself. "I don't know. Sometimes I see very bad things. I saw a man murder three people, I think, maybe more. It was a blur. It was hazy, but I felt the panic of the victims and the blood lust of the assailant. I sometimes hear growling and mortal screams of terror. I can mostly only make out colors and shades. I saw . . ." he wanted to say *you father, twisted and beastly*, but he couldn't. "Sometimes in my dreams I feel like I'm flying."

The king stroked his beard in thought. "And what of that zebra of yours? How did you tame it? Is that not the creature no one was willing to ride? The one said to be possessed by malignant spirits?"

Xolani brushed that off with a chuckle. "That's what everyone says. But she's a good zebra.....Most times...."

".....She knows what you want her to do?" Farakaii finished, to Xolani's astonishment.

"If I may father, why do you ask? How did you . . ."

"Enough. We will discuss this and your dreams when you return from your passage." He made to leave, stopping just short of the exit. "May the ancestors guide you and your platoon." With that, the king was gone, but the sweet smell of licorice lingered, as did the warm feeling in Xolani's chest as he laid his head on his mat with Night Slayer cradled in his arms.

CHAPTER 24

Themba had been a nervous wreck on their voyage toward Pyyros though he exuded an air of confidence. He had heard so much about the capital of the Piripiri Kingdom. At Hippo Valley, all they had was Gwadza's and other small beer halls. There at King Maghedzi's court were inns that served fermented milk and porridges of different varieties as well as beverages made from sorghum, millet malt and deadly distilled spirits. Themba had promised his mother he wouldn't touch that, nor the fermented fruit mashes for he was on Akuwa business, but he knew in his heart, it was a promise he was unlikely to keep.

There was laughter as they marched along as banter was exchanged, not least from the chief treasurer, Mutasa, and his uncle, Munyaradzi, rehashing his tales of womanizing. Themba was usually in the midst of such, but during the course of their journey, he had been quiet and thoughtful. He had one mission and one mission only, securing the betrothal between Piripiri and Akuwa.

The Festival of Tusks was not something he or Hippo Valley could forget easily, sadly. They didn't care that Tsitsi the witch had cursed him with a craven's heart. All they did was laugh amongst their cups and calabashes. That was in the past. The witch, and her associates were now all dead. He had to stop worrying about that and focus on restoring his disgraced name. That was easier said than done, as cowardice was a powerful stench one carried until their burial, akin to a she-mere cat mating with a rival pack.

When they had settled and the fire Themba had made burned, the prince's mouth began salivating as the sweet aroma of the antelope he had felled tickled his nose. Despite that, Themba remained lugubrious.

"Why so glum, child?" inquired Treasurer Mutasa.

"What are you talking about? I'm perfectly fine." Themba lifted his cheeks, attempting a smile.

"That's what your mouth says, but your eyes tell another tale. To survive for as long as I have, one has to learn to look deep into the hearts of men."

"Is that so?"

Mutasa nodded.

"So what do you see in my heart?"

"I see a sad prince. I see a heart heavy with guilt. I see a heart suffocated."

"I have nothing to feel guilty about. You do not know anything about me, treasurer. You have courage, but remember I am your prince."

"A man who always has to remind people they are important, are usually not important at all. Remember that, my prince." He simulated a curtsy as he washed down the crispy burned chunk of antelope with water. "Prince you are indeed," he continued, "however, I am your elder, and you would be wise to listen to a thing or two. You might learn something." Themba seemed to discard what he had said. "Have you ever cared to visit the old Rwizi and have a chat with him?"

"What? Rwizi, the blind old man?" The prince had to laugh. "What business do I have sharing my *doro* with his likes? I am young and healthy. Besides he smells of pee and I can't hear a word he says."

"That's because you are not listening hard enough, young Themba. It is a problem with youth these days. Everything has to come easy."

"You know nothing, Mutasa. Soon all of you wise men will be dead, and your wisdom will mean nothing, but I will still be here. You might brush shoulders with us, and live in the Stone Houses, but you are not one of us. You do not have the blood of the hippo."

"You're right, but I do know how it feels to be deserving, but to know that no matter what one does, one will never be acknowledged, and it is because of small things, like birth, or where you're from. Do you know young man, how I got where I am?"

"Hard work and perseverance." Themba's face tightened like he had accidentally eaten a rotten fruit. "Yes, I know all that. You are sounding like my father now."

"Yes prince, hard work and perseverance, but do you truly understand the meaning? Since I was small, I was told I could never be something, that my life was destined as a peasant farmer or a bricklayer. When I was but three fists of age, they wanted me to marry a local girl from my village. I ran away. I felt a greater destiny than a brick layer's daughter."

The fire flared as Themba nibbled on a chunk of meat. Its blood channeled below his chin as he licked his greased fingers. He felt a little better now that his stomach was full. It also didn't hurt that he was beginning to feel the *umqombothi*. The prince and the treasurer's natter went deep into the night as Mutasa rehashed tales of the great drought. "I remember that period like it was yesterday. When the predators' natural game depleted, they turned to humans for nourishment. Entire villages perished through starvation and those that survived, fled in fear of being prey. Many flowed into Hippo Valley seeking refuge, and your father welcomed them all despite district chiefs' protests. At this point I had risen reasonably high, involved with the rationing of food."

"I suppose that's when you made your first fortune?" Themba cut in perceptively.

Mutasa smiled, revealing his golden tooth. The treasurer could see that the young man was proud of what he had said. "When people started showing up in their droves, even though I was new, I was not afraid to offer my opinion. When your father welcomed them all, I raised my voice, I thought it was foolish."

"You told him that?" Themba was astonished.

"Not in those words exactly. You see I am a man who specializes in beads. The beads, they spoke to me, as an aeromancer speaks to the spirits. Working with the reserves opens your eyes to many things. The consensus we had just undertaken the season before led me to believe it unwise providing food and shelter to all. We didn't have the resources for a long and prolonged drought, but you can blame my predecessor for that."

"Bodekaii Shamuyarira, my grandfather's cousin."

"You know your history I see. Bodekaii was a good man, but when I inherited his position the treasury was as good as empty. He lacked the qualities that suited his position. He only had that title because the Shamuyarira are powerful Akuwa allies. He never deserved it, I did. When Bodekaii died, they wanted to give his position to several more suitable appointments, men of great title, but I acted fast and took the position for myself."

"How did you do that?"

"I showed character, unlike my circumspect rivals. You see, your father and I differed on the subject of the refugees. Your father harbors notions of egalitarianism. He allowed them in despite my protests. Even though we disagreed on strategy, he recognized the need for brave men, who presented a different point of view. It wasn't that I was cruel or lacked empathy for the refugees. We were already on a tight budget, having just defeated the last rebels in the war over the Turkana farmlands. There was no consensus amongst the oracles how long the drought would last. Farakaii knew I meant well. He took more heed to that than the other chiefs who cited the refugees' strange ways and customs, and their penchant to criminality."

"But isn't that true? An Akuwa is worth ten and even thirty men from the lowly clans."

"I am from one of those lowly clans, young prince," replied Mutasa, bluntly.

"Oh, forgive me, I didn't mean to . . . It's just that you have always been so genial and calm, and obviously expert at what you do. You don't talk like the others. Most of your kind is usually roguish and simple."

All Mutasa could do was shake his head. "I remember the panic and hate that arose when a series of thefts and murders occurred. When seething chiefs and parents of the bereaved brought these issues to your father, demanding the refugees out, he told them such crimes existed prior to the foreigners' arrival. Your father believed instead of stigmatizing the refugees, we should learn from them, to make the Akuwa Kingdom great again. He cited their rich cultures, their men of knowledge – their strong and able he would incorporate into his regiments and agricultural plan. When he started talking this way, he was talking a language that I could understand."

"So that's the way you see the world, is it treasurer? A giant field of beads to be counted?"

Mutasa took out three oranges from his sack. "What do I have here?"

"Oranges, of course."

"Yes, but how many?" The treasurer juggled them about merrily.

Themba put out his index finger, then middle, and finally, ring finger.

"You want one?"

Themba had eaten too much meat, and needed some fruit to calm his stomach. Before he could grab it, Mutasa threw it into the night.

"What is this, old man?" the prince carped.

"How many oranges do I have now?"

The prince calmed himself and put up an index finger, and then middle.

Mutasa threw one of the oranges toward Themba, who caught it. "Now I have one. I divided my lot by two. How many do you have?"

Themba's middle finger flashed.

"Correct, and it will never be two, or three, or four, or a hundred. Such is the beauty of beads. They are never wrong."

"I guess they are more reliable than humans."

Mutasa discarded the orange peel and took a bite. "Now you're getting the bigger picture, young prince."

Themba smiled. "Tell me about cannibals. Is it true that people were eating other people's flesh?"

"Do not get me wrong, but if Bodekaii Shamuyarira had lived we may have seen it. Thankfully I got into the position in time to prevent such measures. For us in Hippo Valley, cannibalism remained stories."

"Oh, that's good." Themba was relieved. "I don't know what I would do if I found out that all the old people had most likely tasted human flesh. I would likely never sleep again." The treasurer and the prince laughed like old friends. Everyone was asleep now. All that was left was the sound of crickets, drums in the far distance and drunken snores.

"Sleep now my young prince and rest your troubled head. About the Festival of Tusks, forget that. You are still young." Mutasa winked and turned to sleep.

After tossing and turning, Themba looked on with envy as the others snored. He grabbed a skin of fermented milk, hoping to drink himself to sleep, but Tsitsi's lifeless eyes invaded his thoughts, as did the large gash he had left on Tariro's chest. *Why were you there?* he regretted, frustrated. *You shouldn't have been there.* Nor was the jugulated girl he had left with a twisted face and inert eyes. "I love you. It is a son, a prince," he remembered Tsitsi saying. He shook his head. He had to move on from that. Someone else did that. His mother had said so.

He grabbed his spear and threw a light cloth over his shoulders. He found himself by a gorge. He looked down between his legs as he sat on the edge. It was a mixture of hard rock and sediment. Everyone at the camp was asleep. He could just disappear forever and no one would ever know what happened. He stood up, wobbling, and tried to balance himself, but he slipped, knocking himself off his feet and over the cliff.

The prince exhaled as he hung from a ledge, and squinted as his body scraped the rough rock. Despite his cuts and blood that was now flowing from his side, he erupted into a hysteric laughter, which carried on until a sudden sorrow overwhelmed him. *I don't have a son. I've never had a son. I have nothing . . . but my spear.* His body was now getting heavy. Soon his muscles would tear and he would be lost forever. When the rainy season returned, the creek would be engulfed with water, and his body would be reunited with the hippo. He wanted to stop fighting. He wanted to let go. Mutasa's last words echoed into the night. He repeated the words and realized his life was worth living. With that, using his last ounce of strength, he pulled himself up and over the edge of the cliff. Once he had crawled far enough, exhausted, he looked up to find his uncle Munyaradzi sitting on a large stone, merrily whistling and nibbling on a mango. "Were you here the whole time? Why didn't you help me? What if I had…." The prince said the last words with such vulnerability.

"Died? You? Kill yourself? Don't be silly Themba. You overestimate yourself my boy," Munyaradzi laughed heartily as he helped his nephew up. "Cheer up. When we get to the next village, we shall find us some women."

CHAPTER 25

It was Queen Zandile's third skin of water, and it wasn't even noon yet. She felt unusually exhausted, even though she was well accustomed to the harshness of the season. Sleep had been proving onerous to attain, like a reservoir in the dry season, and when she finally did catch some sleep, she awoke with gritted teeth from head-splintering aches. She thought some rest in her chambers would do her some good – it was nice and cool there, with the clay walls, and heavy shade.

It was a chore in itself walking to her hut. She could not walk a few feet without someone troubling her with his or her burdens, or someone reminding her of her duties. More than often she would answer the questions with uninformative replies, a curt nod, or nothing at all. "Queen Zandile," Sekai, her oldest friend and confidant hollered. "I hope you have not forgotten Chief Mukonikoni and his house shall visit at the beginning of the next new moon." There was an awkward silence between the women. The name Mukonikoni reminded them of Neo, Zandile's brother, who was to marry the Mukonikoni chief's daughter, but had disappeared the day before his wedding. Zandile missed him terribly, and Sekai who had once loved him, longed for him too. "How much food are we to prepare?"

The Mukonikoni, a minor tribe, were strong allies to the Piripiri, and their chief, notoriously vain and ambitious. He would want to be treated better than he was. "Oh, greetings, Sekai. Thanks for reminding me. How large a party is he coming with?"

"The chief has five wives, and at least twenty children. They are all in attendance. Plus he is likely to come with a dozen warriors, and his close aids."

They were well stocked, and ready for any prolonged drought, but that didn't mean they could use their resources frivolously. "Ten goats, three cows and thirty chickens." Zandile decided.

"Very well your grace." Sekai turned to leave, but stopped midway. "Zandile, are you okay?" The heavy bags under the queen's eyes told it all, and eyes once so piercing did not have the same almond-colored glow. "Is there anything you want to talk about?"

Zandile tried to smile. "It's okay but thanks for asking." Before Sekai could inquire more, the queen was already on her way toward her hut. When she finally arrived, oddly enough, her door was half open. She opened it cautiously to a welcome, immediately transforming her eyes into spheres of scorn. "Don't move any closer, or I'll scream."

The Sangoma got up from the mat where he had made himself comfortable and walked slowly toward the queen as his eyes flashed bright red. "Calm down Zandile, I mean you no harm," he lisped as he stroked the miniature skulls that hung around his neck and studied her up and down. "A queen at last, as I prophesized. I saw it. Your father came to me before you bled, and he asked me, 'Will my daughter be a queen?' I told him it was the will of the ancestors." The mystic's pupils dilated, seemingly looking deep into her soul. "It is all you ever wanted, is it not?"

It was true. It is all she had dreamt of when she was a girl. However, she had dreamt to be queen to another. "How did you know I would return to my chambers alone?"

"I resurrected your son, did I not?"

She couldn't argue with that. "What do you want Sangoma?"

"I want what every man wants . . ."

Her mouth twisted in suspicion. She could feel his dark purple tongue flickering. She reached into her garments feeling for her dagger.

"I want to help you, my queen. I want to be of service to you. I came to visit you, to let you know that my first priority is the king and his household. There are evil spirits Zandile, threatening our very existence. We must be united for the dark times ahead." The Sangoma shuffled closer and when he was close enough, Zandile gave him a slap. "You can't do that," screeched the Sangoma in shock, rubbing his throbbing cheek. "I am a priest, a spirit talker, ordained by the gods and your husband."

Zandile was not impressed. She was on him, ripping the mask that covered the Sangoma's abominable face. With it, she began to beat him repeatedly, over and over again as the mage's plea for mercy fell on deaf ears. "Haven't you helped me enough?" she cursed and screamed. "When you had my life in your hands, as I lay on that cold hard stone table with those women with their hands gripped around my ankles, did I need your mercy?" The dagger sank, sending the Sangoma wailing to the ancestors as she drew a red vertical line from just under his eye down to his lower jaw. She hovered above the cowering priest and licked her lips. She could impale him straight through the heart, or she could slit his throat like a chicken. Better yet, she could stab him in the stomach, lie on her mat and enjoy a mango as she watched him bleed into eternity. *Why not?* She could say he stalked her back to her hut and tried to force himself upon her. She would tell Maghedzi she killed him to maintain his honor.

"Get up." she finally said. "Many years ago I made a solemn vow that I would kill you the moment I got a chance, but somehow, you saved my boy. So, I am giving you a chance to redeem yourself."

The Sangoma nodded his head frantically with his palms together. "Anything, your highness. How?"

"You shall not harm my Nia."

The Sangoma looked confused. "Why would I hurt Nia? She is a sweet girl. She gave me a gift. Look." He produced a dried up flower from the pouch hanging from his animal hide skirts. "See, me and Nia are very good friends."

"Don't lie to me, Sangoma, do you not mean to purify her?"

"Purify her? Of course! Are you not purified?" Out came another of the Sangoma's teeth. "So I gather, you don't want her to be purified?"

"Correct, and you will release my husband from his spell and get him to abandon the plans set for the Flame Festival."

"My queen, your husband, he is resolved. You know him well. If I do not perform the ceremony myself, he will just get someone else to do it, and quite frankly your highness, I am the best in town."

Zandile did, she knew the king as well as the back of her hand. When the king had set his mind on something, there was no turning back, rain, hail or sleet. "A map, can you get your hands on one?"

"What do you need one for?"

"Don't worry about that. Can you get one?"

"Yes of course, your grace," I will have one as soon as I . . ." Zandile's eyes darkened and the grip on her knife tightened. "I will have one for you by the moon's end."

She shooed him away like he was a wild dog trying to hump her leg. The Sangoma grabbed the broken pieces of his mask and scampered off.

She was now exhausted. She lay on the mat and exhaled. She felt good, even though the Sangoma had left behind that repugnant smell he carried, a mixture of death and feces. She closed her eyes to nap. She winced in pain. *There goes my back again. I must be getting old.*

***

At the end of the moon cycle, Zandile sat quietly outside her chambers on a short round wooden stool as young maids swept away the dust and twigs which had settled over the footpaths overnight. Young boys toiled around, watering the plants and the grass lawns and local sloths despite the early hours, enjoyed their beverages as they warmed themselves under their blankets. Despite the fresh aroma of the morning's breakfast, she could not bring herself to decent spirits. Not even the sight of her favorite flowers in bloom, the flame lily, could help her at least try to pretend to not be miserable, nor or a chat with the Desert Snake who had the uncanny ability of making her laugh.

Maghedzi now spent all his time high up on the mountain slopes praying. At the beginning of their marriage, he would sometimes ask her to join him, but as the years went by, he preferred to go alone. Recently it had grown worse. Some days he would go up there and not return for days on end. He might as well have. She was still revolted by his every touch. She had felt that way since that night, when he informed her of his plans for Nia.

Usually she would have helped with the morning chores and lent her sweet voice to the singing, but today, she did not have the might to participate. She had tossed and turned for the majority of the night and only managed to find sleep when the first sunrays appeared. Zandile, who was usually diligent and involved in the running of court, was not the same woman. Queen Zandile was a beacon of the community, a symbol of respectability and what a woman should be. The middle-aged woman with signs of child bearing that she bore on her stomach proudly was none of these things. This woman sitting on that stool was anything but. For this woman, waking up and facing the world was a chore.

She sat with her light almond-colored eyes fixated on the ground. To her delight, Maghedzi was preparing to leave with his regiment though it was hard to count how many they were amongst the obsidian rock spears, large shields and flamboyant headdresses. The usual Zandile would have been concerned and wondered where they were going or inquired about the food and water reserves she had presided over with diligence and a fist made of obsidian rock. When the treasurer had argued without provocation that there was still plenty in the reserves to survive two droughts, she nodded, to his surprise. He was used to her good-natured objections and sound advice.

She looked up to discover the Sangoma slithering up the queen's pathway. She was sure his tongue was flickering about like a boa constrictor navigating through a labyrinth of thick forestry. She could smell him as he approached, even though he was still a few good meters away. He stopped directly adjacent to her and stared at her with his red eyes flaring as flies hovered around him. "You seem troubled, child," he asked as he bopped his head and skipped about on his toes, hovering from side to side like a cobra caught under the spell of a flute.

"Look to your own troubles. Have you done as we agreed?" She did not bother to look up. She could smell him. She didn't need to see him as well.

"Your husband, he has the utmost faith in me and my capabilities, I just wish that you . . ."

"Oh, shut up. I have little time for your mad talk, or your prophecies. Simple question, have you done what we agreed?"

"Yes, as long as you keep your end of the agreement. The location is marked with black chalk. The rest is up to you. If it doesn't work out, which it probably won't, I was never involved." The Sangoma uneasily looked around. "Swear it. I put a lot on the line."

"I swear it by the ancestors."

"A vow before a spirit-medium is the most solemn of vows. You do understand that?"

The queen knew all too well, the perils of magic. "Yes, Sangoma, now be gone. Maghedzi is on his way. He cannot find us together, lest he suspects something." She was left astonished when the witchdoctor had vanished into the wind when she turned her head back.

"What's that smell?" Maghedzi grunted, doing all he could to shut his large nostrils. He seemed in an especially cantankerous mood.

The Desert Snake stood casually behind him. Usually Zandile found him pleasing to the eye. Few could resist his cocksure smile and deep mercurial eyes, however today she barely took notice. "Oh that? Cousin Yuse came by earlier with the baby. The poor thing had a bad stomach. It shat everywhere. Such a strong little boy, you should see his stool."

"Save us the lurid details." The king looked her up and down. "Have you no decency? Why are you not dressed? Are you not queen? If you are trying to turn this place into Hippo Valley, you are gravely mistaken. I would send you to change, but I do not have time. Preparations are ready. We leave right away." There was an awkward silence. "Do you not care where we are going, wife?"

"I hope it is to see your son . . . How many times have we discussed this husband? You need to bring him into the fold. Before you have lost him forever. I only say this for the love I bear for my king." It was a lie. Zandile knew that when the bastard came of age. His anger toward his father could engulf them all and Zandile was a hen that would do anything to protect her eggs. Seldom was a bushfire selective in its destruction, the elders would say. "But I pray you forgive me. A good wife does not ask questions of her husband."

Maghedzi wasn't sure if it was a jape. "Aye," he finally nodded, seemingly satisfied as his guard handed him his large, oblong shield with a large red flame emblazoned on it. She hadn't mentioned the boy in a long time, but whenever she did, it was never by name. He had forbid it. "We will deal with the matter of that boy when I return."

Princess Nia came jogging in, dusty as usual, with a small gash under her knee. "Where's father going, mother?"

Zandile grabbed the little princess, licked her thumb and tried to rub the dark smudge from her daughter's cheek. "You've been climbing trees again, haven't you? What did we agree about that? You shall surely be punished."

Maghedzi intervened swiftly, just before Nia had a chance to retort. "I tell your brothers, obedience is the greatest virtue of all. With it, we can overcome all. You might think we are strict but you will learn one day that it is the ultimate love. You had best found some upon my return."

"Can I go with you? Please. It's no fun here. I promise not to get in your way. I can fight too."

"Your place is here, with your mother," he replied stiffly. Now off you go."

That took some moments, as Nia was entranced by the artistry of her father's shield, made of tightly bent metal bands, layered with hide. His war sandals also beguiled her. The Piripiri were master foot-smiths, renowned across the kingdoms, and Maghedzi had the best in all the land, an inimitable pair, heavy soled reaching up to a little above his ankles. On the toe bar was a red-beaded flame and the parallel straps across his foot had little red leather threads flaring sideways like a chariot of fire. Nia sluggishly turned to leave.

"Where are your manners? Show your father the proper respect." Zandile scolded.

"My apologies, father. May the flame guide and protect you and your warriors. I pray you are successful." With that the princess skipped off as enthusiastically as she came.

"Take care of my children for me whilst I am away."

"Our children," Zandile corrected.

"If you like." He moved closer as to embrace her, but she would not have it, shrugging him away. "So be it," the king stammered. "My brother Machupa will be in charge while I am away." He paused. "Zandile are you listening?"

"Yes, husband . . ." She wasn't.

"I know he is not the best suited for governance, but he is my blood. If you need anything, go to him. Make sure the girl is ready for the Flame Festival when I return and let us hope that womb of yours is still working. I wouldn't want all those seeds I pumped into you to have been for naught."

Zandile crouched into a neat little squat, balancing herself effortlessly as she bounced up and down and clapped her hands. That seemed to satisfy the king, giving him a less hideous face. All he wanted from her was her submission. Anything contrary to that would drive him into one of his moods and she did not have the stomach for that right now. He turned, whistled and joined his men as his heavy crocodile skin loincloth bounced about him.

CHAPTER 26

They had been riding for a while when Prince Themba finally rose from his nap as he slumped atop his great zebra. He raised his head to find them passing through a row of haphazard huts that were but stacked sticks, with sparsely thatched roofs that did nothing against the elements. "Where are we?" he inquired.

"Welcome to the wonderful Village of Shambamuto," replied Chief Treasurer Mutasa, with a wry smile.

Curious eyes watched as women's wails decorated the afternoon sky. Themba took a sip of his skin and turned to ask his uncle what was going on.

"Sounds like a funeral. Come, we should pay our respects."

"Why? I don't know these people."

"You are the Akuwa king's son. It would mean a lot to the village folk."

"These people mean nothing to me." The prince wrinkled his nose and spat as he gazed upon an old cripple with a large rotting wound on his leg, with flies hovering around him and vultures circling in the sky. "A vile place by the looks of it, vile people."

"Oh shut up, Themba. I always told my brother when you were a little boy that you needed a few beatings here and there. I'd do it myself, but you'd run to your mother's teat like a newly born rodent."

"My father will hear of this."

"You mean your mother will hear of this." Munyaradzi chuckled. "Go ahead then. The road back to the Stone Houses is a long and treacherous one."

Themba looked for a rebuttal, but he found none. He knew he could not hope to return home by himself, not with bandits and thieves who would thank the ancestors for a gift like an Akuwa prince for ransom.

Munyaradzi softened his tone. "Look son, your father is my brother. You would do well to listen to me."

Themba grudgingly agreed. "We shan't stay long. My loins yearn for my future bride."

They followed the trail of grief and a monotone beat of a drum up a hill, passing by other graves, mounds of stones decorated with statues and artifacts. "Who's dead?" Themba was about to take another swipe of his *umqombothi* when Munyaradzi slapped it out of his hand. The liquid spread out over the red earth alarming the mourning crowd. There were some dissentient murmurs before they returned their attention to the dead.

"Have some respect. We are at a funeral, and by the looks of it, the funeral of a chief."

A priestess was concluding the burial ritual. "Watch over us, as you join the spirits," she pled. "Do not bring any trouble for the living, for we were your devoted subjects." The people of Shambamuto believed their ancestors were not truly dead, and through their mediums, they could plead for good favor. However, just as progenitors could bring blessings, they could also bring misfortune – especially a chief's spirit where there was a thin line between malevolence and benevolence.

An ox was led into the grave. Themba could just make out the chief's pale face before the priestess covered it with a leather flap and tied a knot. The priestess unveiled a blade and opened the ox's neck, spraying blood all over the dead chief's garments, herself, and various possessions the chief would need in the afterlife.

A young man stood at the foot of the grave, spear in hand, desperately trying to hold off what was sure to be a torrent of tears. He was of medium build, light brown skin, and shaggy hair over an orange shaped head. "That must be . . ." Themba was interrupted when the crowd shouted:

"Long live the new chief, long live Chief Kaliso." When the people were done hailing the new patriarch of the Village of Shambamuto, men began covering the chief's grave with their bare hands. It took a while before they were finished. After the burial, Prince Themba, Mutasa and Munyaradzi waited to receive an audience from the chief, as many at the funeral were eager to be the first to pay their respects to the new paramount.

When the subjects had finished paying their condolences, Chief Kaliso walked down to Prince Themba, an edge taller than the prince, but with a less air of gravitas. "You are from the Stone Houses. You must be Prince Themba." Before the prince could reply, in surprise, Kaliso continued. "Such fine animal skins. Only one of royalty can wear those. Besides, I remember you. You do not remember me, but I do you. It was many years ago when your father had a feast for all the village chiefs. I was in attendance with my father."

"Oh, yes, I remember you," Themba said, but he and everyone else knew it a lie. "You are, Chief . . ."

"Kaliso," was the reply. Mutasa and Munyaradzi bowed their heads and clapped their hands."

"Our condolences," Mutasa expressed. "It is a shame we come at such a time."

Kaliso genuflected, accepting the treasurer's kind words. "There shall be a feast for my father's passing at supper time. I trust you will join us."

Themba was about to answer when Mutasa cut in: "Yes, Chief Kaliso. We shall be there to celebrate Chief Kaya's life."

It was a small affair. Themba had been to several funeral feasts in his lifetime. He was used to hordes of people, mountains of meat and enough *doro* to fill an empty Lake Nhahara. Luckily enough, he had carried his own atop oxen and donkeys. He even contributed a few goats from his own stock. After they had eaten and their stomachs were full, Chief Kaliso rose. "Come my prince. Let me take you on a tour around my village."

Themba had to admit it was a miserable place. It seemed to him, the title of chief was easily bestowed. The village thoroughfare was small and filled with the sick and destitute. There was little sign of commerce, a few food stalls, butcheries, vegetable sellers and carpenters. Some huts were roofless, with charred frames and splintered wood. "What happened here?"

Kaliso looked down and sighed before he answered: "As you can see we are desperate people. We are dying likes fleas. It is no coincidence that a son of the mighty hippo came to visit us. You have been sent by the ancestors."

Themba thought the man wrong. His father had sent them to Pyyros, so he could woo Princess Nia and make her his wife, but nonetheless, he let Kaliso continue.

"Men from the hills come every moon and demand we give them our crops and animals. They are too many in number, so my father gave them what they wanted, hoping they would go away and never return. However, it was not enough. They wanted more and more until our reserves were dry. When they last came, father finally said enough was enough and refused to pay them. Their leader, Bolo, put a spear through his eye, burned our huts and took whatever they could. I was standing next to my father when it happened. His warm blood sprinkled over my face. I shall never forget."

"This is a very sad story you tell, Kaliso. My father, his enemies made an attempt on his life, but the ancestors were on his side." Kaliso did not reply. "This is all unfortunate, but what does that have to do with me?"

"I have seen all that steel you and your host are carrying. Some of them, carrying the mark of Amakazi." The dark-blue capes worn by the warriors and gold chains across their chests were legendary across the kingdoms. King Farakaii was not the type to send his son into Piripiri territory without men he could rely on to protect his seed. "Help us, Prince Themba. Help us vanquish these thugs so my people can live in peace and rebuild our broken community. We will be eternally grateful."

Themba thought for a second. His heart was yearning for his bride to be, and they were already behind schedule, but he was the blood of the hippo. *A king must be righteous*, his father's voice said. *A good king protects the weakest of his subjects, for they need him the most*. He hesitated, but in the end replied, "Very well, Kaliso. I shall help you in this endeavor. Let us return to the banquet. Tonight we celebrate your father's life. Tomorrow, we discuss how we shall avenge him."

The moon turned as they waited for the return of the reavers. During that period Themba set about preparing the villagers, but there was scarce metal they could use to make spears, axes and arrows, so he set women, children and the ailing to sharpen any sticks they could find into sharp arrows and fashion any wood they could into spears. Meanwhile he conducted combat drills. Themba cursed as he went around his cadets as they practiced bow and arrow. They were a miserable bunch. Themba understood why petty thugs could take what they wanted. In his thoughts, he thought they probably deserved what they got, but he had made a vow, and didn't want to break it. "You have never fired an arrow have you?" The prince frowned when he got to a young boy, Pikoro, a few years younger than he, like Xolani.

The boy shook his head. "No, my lord."

"Draw your bow," Themba commanded. "Raise your arms until the arrow is aligned with your eyes."

Pikoro did as he was told and released. It hit the board they had placed on the tree. The boy looked on in surprise.

"Again!"

Pikoro did, this time hitting the center of the board. Themba nodded in approval and moved along where he found one man striking his stick at a wooden dummy. "Not like that," Themba hollered in frustration. "How many times do I have to show you people, you do it like this." He snatched the stick from the villager's hand and began to strike the dummy in smooth horizontal strikes. "Like I said, it's all about the footwork." He skipped to the side and began hitting the dummy vertically. He gave back the stick and stepped to the side. The man looked at him confused. Themba shook his head. "What are you waiting for? Continue, as I showed." The man corrected his feet and began. "Yes," Themba said, now nodding his head in approval. "Like that. Legs apart, up, down, left right, yes, you are on your way."

A young girl approached him asking to be taught too. Themba looked down at her and smiled. He saw the future in her big innocent eyes. He picked her up and tapped her on the nose. "Go to your mother, young one, the hut is where you belong. There she will teach you how to cook and pound sorghum. We shall protect you." He set her down, produced a fruit, and shooed her away.

During the breaks, he and Chief Kaliso sat under a tree and ate their afternoon meals as they devised a plan to defeat the outlaws. "How many bandits are there?"

"Around thirty, and heavily armed."

"Thirty? That should be no problem. One Amakazi is as good as ten men, and a prince, twenty."

When night came, they would leisure in the chief's hut where the elders and nobility of the village told stories and mocked one another. Keba, a man in the village council's wife had just given birth, but rather than the joy which usually accompanied such news, he was left dumbfounded at what was now his eighth daughter – out of eight. Another man who had seven sons facetiously offered his help, to the chagrin of Keba, and hooting of the others. Themba also got to know the elder, Taonda, who served as Kaliso's advisor. Laughter filled the hut, as he and Mutasa exchanged wit. "You should pass by the village more often," the chief said, as he tasted the beer from Mutasa's keg.

"The best in all the land," Mutasa confessed. "First we shall deal with these outlaws, then I shall leave you one. I'm not too keen to let that scum taste this Turkana brew."

"And what weapon do you use, Mutasa?"

"My weapon is the tongue. I prefer to keep my cloths unsoiled by bloodstains. Can't stand it to be honest. What is your weapon sire?"

"I am too old to wield, but in my younger days, I wasn't too bad with the short sword. I killed a few in my time. You know, I even served in Themba's great-great grandfather's regiments, King Faso." The men in the hut nodded their heads in apparent surprise. "I was there when Imiyazi cut him down. What a sad day it was. He was a great man, your ancestor, and a great general." The old man's ramblings were interrupted by one of his daughters, who came in to refill the calabashes. "My daughter, she is my youngest," he winked. "She is yet to know a man."

Themba doubted that, sizing her up. She was attractive enough, he reflected. She had soft features, and a warm air about her. "What is your name, girl?"

"Tsitsi," she replied.

The prince's heart froze, but rather fractionally. "What a wonderful name." He studied her. "I once knew a girl called Tsitsi, but you are much more delightful. Unfortunately, my heart belongs to another. That is the purpose of my journey."

"She is a very lucky girl," Tsitsi replied.

"Yes, I believe she is."

Tsitsi bowed and slid out.

"Love," the old man said, with a sparkle in his eyes. "I remember what that felt like, but now all my wives are dead. It is only my daughters and I. All my sons are dead too. They grew tired of waiting for me to die."

"I've heard about you at court," Mutasa jested. "A hard headed one, they say. Even death doesn't know what to do with you." Laughter and the smell of licorice filled the room.

The next day as Themba cooled himself by a shed, pouring water over his head, he turned and saw something in the distance. "Reavers," he shouted. "They're coming!" From his estimation, they had five minutes to get ready. He ran around the village alerting everyone. "Girl," he shouted. "Bring my beer!" She frantically did as told, and fled into the bush. He took a large hurried gulp, threw the calabash onto the floor, and called out for Pikoro. The boy was in front of the prince in mere moments. "You remember the formations I taught you, right?"

The boy nodded his head, and turned to organize the other men. Themba arranged his group and hid in the bushes.

The leader of the outlaws, a large man, arrived at the front of the mob with a large war club. Themba knew he was Bolo. During his discussions with Kaliso, they had left no detail unexplored. He had crooked teeth and though Kaliso had described his feet as large, they were the largest Themba had seen, even more so than Tulu's. His beard was thick and uneven, as was his hair, and in his mouth he had a twig. Chief Kaliso was first to meet him with a basket filled with goods. "I see you have learned from your father's fatal mistake," Bolo grinned, as he commanded one of his bandits to collect the basket. "Have you got anything else? Gold? Silver? Livestock?" His war club was in full sight, a vulgar instrument, studded with a barrage of sharp objects.

Kaliso whistled and up came Pikoro with a skinny cow tied to a rope. You could count its ribs from its side and its pelvic bones protruding from its back.

"Is this the best you lot can do?" He shook his head. When the cow was in the bandit's care, suddenly Pikoro whistled. Bolo's eye's widened and promptly, one of the bandits fell, then another, and another, paving the floor with blood and the cries of men. A shriek erupted, and then out from the bushes came Themba and his men, spears and clubs in hand. Many of Bolo's men fell by the time they realized what was going on. "Surprise is the key in battle," Comrade Chengetaii had taught. Bolo fought valiantly, catching one and then another with his vulgar instrument, but nonetheless, one by one his men fell until he was surrounded, mouth agape in disbelief as his twig rested by that giant foot of his.

Themba appeared before him. Bolo was twice his size, but one could not know it by the trepidation the reaver bore. "Who are you?"

"I am Prince Themba of the Akuwa, and I sentence you to death. Kneel."

Bolo tried to resist, but Munyaradzi and Pikoro helped him down, giving him a good kick behind his knees. The outlaw begged and pleaded for his life as Themba brandished his spear.

Lilac and violet leaves fell in Themba's thoughts, paving the red earth with the leaves' colors, and Tsitsi's mischievous smile appeared before him. "It is a son, a prince," she said as the leaves fell onto her hair and nose.

He began to tremble and lowered his spear, sparking a smirk on Bolo's scabrous face, but that quickly evaporated when Themba turned and gestured toward Kaliso. "I believe the honor is yours."

Kaliso did not need to be asked twice. He stood in front of Bolo, spat on his face, and then raised his spear. "For Chief Kaya," he proclaimed before bringing down the blade through his shoulders and into his heart. It took the chief some considerable effort to detach Bolo's head from his neck, which he hoisted into the air and paraded for the good people of Shambamuto to see. "My people, now you can have peaceful sleep. Go to your homes, and tomorrow, we rebuild Shambamuto." The people cheered and scattered off, some pillaging the dead corpses for whatever they could.

Kaliso turned to Themba. "Thank you, my prince. Our people will never forget what you have done for us."

Themba nodded. "I hope you have learned your lesson here. Teach your people the way of the spear. It is the only way to survive, especially with the oncoming dry."

"We shall have a feast, in your name."

"You are very kind, Chief Kaliso, but it is time we go. My destiny awaits."

Pikoro ran and fell to his knees before the prince. "My lord, I offer my hand, body and soul to you. Please take me along so I can become a warrior."

Pikoro had shown himself to be capable, though he was not trained in the art of spear and had alacrity about him, a cheerful promptness and willingness Themba liked. He could do with loyal men around him now that Nthanda and Sipho were dead, but it was not his right. Themba looked at the chief, who smiled and nodded. With that, Themba and his entourage were on their way with much fanfare, whistles, clapping and song slowly fading behind them.

CHAPTER 27

Xolani was the envy of the squadron as the young hippos, led by Comrade Chengetaii, marched through the Hippo Valley countryside toward their rites of passage. Everyone wanted to see this great new spear, Night Slayer, King Farakaii had bestowed. He warned whoever wanted to see it to take good care, for its fangs were as sharp as the nyaminyami's and as treacherous as a viper's spite. "Be careful," Matata sneered sarcastically, snatching the spear from Xolani's grasp. "You are not the only one who is familiar with *masimbi* steal. My uncle has one just like yours and he lets me play with it all the time." The boy scratched the little hair he had on his chin as he observed the instrument, his man hairs considerable compared to his peers.

Khaya the Glut didn't believe him. "In your dreams, Matata, you've never even seen *masimbi* steel. I've been to your uncle's ranch. He doesn't have enough cows or crops to afford a decent spear, let alone one made of *masimbi* steel." The boy was the shortest of the bunch, but made up for it with his wide, stalky frame and brutish demeanor. He was easily the strongest of the bunch and regularly showed his supremacy after the boys had made a joke or two at his expense.

"You're right, Khaya, this story is as true as the one of you taking Rudo's maidenhood in the millet fields last week," Korokoro the Squirrel agreed. His friends called him that for his general uselessness in everything except climbing trees, and rather than around his arms and legs, he wore his bushy cow tails on his lower back, in homage to his namesake. "That never happened because she is in love with me."

The other boys didn't believe that either, not with his slender body, eyes seemingly too big for his head and incisors fit enough to gnaw through the trees he liked to climb. None-the-less Korokoro had to run for his life as Khaya sprang to his feet and chased the squirrel up the tree. All they could do was laugh, except Chengetaii who preferred to live in perpetual silence. He was typically solemn, but Xolani could see something had changed since he had returned from the Sacred Hills, as was his usual garb, now exchanged for a pitch black, long, hooded dashiki that flowed over his feet.

The spear was quite an instrument. It had a magnificently crafted ebony wood shaft, with small hippos carved in the dark wood from Domboshawa. Its head was wide and almost as long as half his arm, shaped like an avocado leaf and had serrations at its base with ivory four finger groves. Few men, let alone boys, could boast such a blade.

Village folk showered praise, whistled and clapped as they passed village after the next. They stopped by Domboshawa, home of the Timba, to replenish their supplies and rest their zebras. Xolani fancied their walls, made of great trees thatched closely together into an impenetrable barricade. They passed through the Crescent, Doma, Gokwe, a village that had birthed many of Hippo Valley's greatest warriors, most notably Changamire, Dingani the Bobcat, and most recently Tulu the Water Dancer. A melancholy overwhelmed Xolani when they passed the Moyo homestead rehashing the night of little Korokoro's death, but his spirits turned for the better when they passed through Mazowe, the home of the Chitemo clan, with its large statues and intricate irrigation systems. The simplicity of Mara, the home of the Tsavo herdsman was a sight to behold, with kraal after another dominating the lush green graze-lands, and the short boat ride to the island that housed the

Rwaivi was a good change of pace, giving them time to relax, as they glided to isle.

At one village, Matata was the first to whistle as they passed a group of young girls about their age, elegantly walking with large pots balanced on their heads. "The one carrying the oval pot with the red beads is mine," he proclaimed. They weren't far from his home village, so he vowed when he returned, he would consult his father and send an emissary.

That presented a problem because Batanai had claimed her too, slapping Matata cheekily on the back of the head, igniting a playful scuffle that ended when Khaya tried to join in. The girls giggled bashfully and the boys corrected their playfulness as soon as the commander noted their behavior. After the rites of passage, it would be time for them to be married, and the boys saw there was plenty they could choose from. Xolani though born out of wedlock did not have the same options afforded his peers. He was the son of a king. Like his half-sister Nonkuleko, he too was bound to the will of the throne.

When it got dark, Chengetaii commanded the boys to set up camp and prepare supper. When their stomachs were full and they were picking the meat from the gaps in their teeth, the boys asked the commander to tell them a story. They had asked him several times during their passage, but the answer was always the same.

"I have one," Matata volunteered.

"Sit down. No one wants to hear your romance stories. You will bore us to death and I promised Rudo I would return in one peace," snickered Korokoro, as Matata sat down in shame.

"Tell us the story about the Battle by the Hippo Basin," Thokozani pleaded as the rest joined in the petition. "Or perhaps Abuba can tell us a story." Everyone looked at the diffident boy at the back. Rumor had it he was only there because his father, an affluent merchant, had paid off a few of the council members to ensure his son was selected for the prestigious ritual many a boy had dreamt to be part of. Abuba clearly did not want to be there, but nonetheless, some of the boys made him suffer for it.

"Fine, I'll tell a story, but just this time," succumbed Chengetaii behind his hood. He wiped the *doro* from his mouth and set down the dagger he was sharpening. "Enough of the war stories, there is more to life than spear." A revolutionary thought to some amongst the crowd. He snapped his ashy fingers in-sighting silence. It seemed like he had even quietened nature itself, muting the crickets and the birds rummaging in the canopies. He began quietly, in a whisper. "Thousands of generations ago, in the days of the Stone Kings, there were two boys who lived in the same village. They quickly became best friends, sharing their meals from the same bowl and herding cattle together. They even took each other's appearances, both healthy and strong." Chengetaii's teeth snapped shut and flexed his jaw, donkey like, rippling in and out as he waited for silence. He raised his voice and amped the tempo. "When they became men, they built their houses opposite each other and prospered, fathering many children from many wives. Their success was well noted by their neighbor. During the planting season, whilst the friends rose early, the neighbor played *mbira.*"

"That sounds like Korokoro's uncle," said Khaya. "Have you seen him? Season after season he asks to borrow pumpkin from my father. Until next season he says." Laughter ensued, though Korokoro didn't find it as funny as others.

Comrade Chengetaii continued, "His family suffered greatly during the draught and as a result, turned to the ancestors and asked them, 'why?' But the ancestors remained silent. His heart became hard, as he grew envious of the prospering neighbors. Too proud to ask for help, he decided to teach them a lesson." Chengetaii paused and refreshed himself. His throat looked no different from a boa constrictor, thick and muscular as his Adam's apple danced up and down as the thick liquid washed down. "He commanded his wife to make him a robe. It was crimson red on one side and royal blue on the other. It was a magnificent garment to behold. The next day he woke early for the first time, even before the cock crowed and walked down the pathway between the two friends whilst they sat at their porches, sharpening their spears. Later in the day when the friends were drinking *doro* after a hard day's work, the taller one commented on what a lovely blue robe their neighbor was wearing earlier. The shorter one agreed. It was a marvelous robe and wondered where he had found the copper to afford it, knowing he had a meager harvest, but also casually corrected his friend on the color. 'Red, the robe was red,' one friend said. 'No,' the other replied, 'it was blue. I saw him with my own eyes. Even ask my wives. They will tell you the same.' The discussion turned into a quarrel and then into fists. They hurled cups and stools at each other, destroying the inn. Finally satisfied the neighbor returned and stood before the once inseparable friends in his beautiful garment in all its royal blue and crimson glory."

"Oh my," Matata said. "The lazy neighbor was quite the trickster." The rest of the boys looked at him cross, not appreciating his thoughtful insight and narration.

The commander grunted, and then continued. "When they realized what had happened they blamed the neighbor for causing a division between them. The neighbor laughed and told them to blame themselves." The young hippos were now scratching their heads, discombobulated, until Xolani's eyes livened. The commander pulled down his hood and flashed an accusing finger as the boys huddled together. "The neighbor told them it was their fault because they were both right and they were both wrong. 'None of you lied', he told them, 'but look at you, fighting like spurned lovers. You laugh at me amongst your crops and pity my meager yield, yet you fight amongst yourselves because you only wanted to see things from your own point of view.'"

The boys remained silent, still perplexed until their faces lit up with comprehension . . . except Khaya of course.

Tonight was Xolani and Batanai's turn at night watch. After a long day of activities and travelling, it was hard to keep one's eyes open. He called for Batanai hoping to pass time but no response came. *He's asleep.* Xolani couldn't believe it. He frowned and nudged him with the back of Night Slayer.

Batanai immediately awoke, wiping the drool from his mouth, apologizing. "Sorry for nodding off a little. It wasn't on purpose. I'll make it up to you. You take a short nap. I'll stand vigil and wake you up if anything happens."

That seemed too good to be true, but Xolani yawned. He was feeling tired, and the allure of the mat was indeed enticing. "Are you sure?"

Batanai smiled. "Go ahead, it's the least I can do."

"Okay then, but make sure to wake me if as much as a cricket sounds." Xolani laid his head, and soon enough he was snoring.

He had the sweetest of dreams. He was under the shade of a sprawling jacaranda tree taller and wider than any he had seen. Under it they ate fruit, him, his mother, his father, Nonkuleko and his half-brothers, a happy family, complete. Even Shiri and Aku the water dragon was there, smoke fuming from his nostrils and tail, long and coiled. He felt the knock on his chest the third time and hovering over him was Comrade Chengetaii, Dread, clasped tight under his knuckles. Xolani looked to his side and there was Batanai lying as still as an Amakazi, waiting in the king's shadow.

Xolani was about to chastise him for playing him a fool and cheating on their deal until he noticed a puddle of vomit and blood around the boy. In his hand was Xolani's extra skin of water he had kept in his sack for a rainy day. Chengetaii knelt, turned the body on its back, gave it one look, stood up and announced, "The boy is dead."

One by one the young hippos arrived, Korokoro and Khaya the Glut, first on the scene.

"Get him up, clean him and prepare him for burial," Chengetaii commanded.

The boys, dumbfounded, took some time before they did as tasked. Xolani remained in shock. "Captain, I . . ." the boy stuttered. "I don't know what happened."

Chengetaii did not reply, preferring to pick up the skin of water, emptying its contents onto a tuft of grass, fizzing and disintegrating it instantaneously. He put his nose near the mouthpiece and sniffed. "Spider's Rage," he muttered. Xolani, looked at his uncle, confused. "It's a deadly poison. Very rare. Only a person with wealth and influence can acquire such a toxin." Chengetaii drew the skin closer, and pulled a torch toward it to get a better look. "The skin has hippos engraved in it. Where did the boy get it?"

"It was mine. It was in my sack. He must have been thirsty as I slept and took a sip of it." It was dark, but Xolani could see worry appear in the commander's beads. It was unlike him, a veteran of a hundred battles.

"Then someone wants you dead."

"But, I haven't....done anything."

The commander contemplated for a while. "Say nothing to nobody. Not until we get to the bottom of it. Be careful what you eat, and most importantly, watch your back. Trust nobody. Even your friends.”

Xolani didn't have any, not really. Only Nonkuleko, Aku and Shiri. He couldn't think of any reason any of them wanted him dead. “Aye, uncle. I promise.”

“Good. Now off to sleep you go, if you can. We arise early tomorrow to burry the boy. Mourn, but be glad it was not you.”

CHAPTER 28

It had been a while since that fateful day, when Gamu squandered all he had at Gwadza's. His family had returned to him, but every time he caught Tanaka's supercilious gaze, he knew what she thought of him. She had threatened to leave, but he begged so hard his knees became bruised and covered in dirt. Besides, what could she do? The union between man and wife was a solemn vow. Only the husband could petition a divorce, and even in that event, her relatives would never allow it. The only option she had was proving impotency and Gamu had demonstrated his vigor, time and time again. He had been through so much despair in recent times he felt the ancestors owed him. "The ancestors owe you nothing," an oracle had told him.

"But I have done as they have asked, as you have taught. I have prayed every day, sometimes until my teeth crack and sacrificed the little I have, yet, it is still not enough. My wife despises me. She thinks I am less than a dung beetle." Since then, he had helped apprehend a fugitive of the Akuwa law, yet here he was. He didn't know what more he could do to succeed.

He grimly recollected his talks with Yago, as they sipped on cheap *umqombothi* in the shade of a large umbrella tree, after a hard day toiling in the sun, earning next to nothing. He felt his faith was being tested. "Be strong, the spirits listen," Yago had encouraged. It was the same drivel everyone gave him, from the oracle to his father-in-law. "Pray, fast and meditate solemnly and one day the ancestors will shower you with their blessings. I am certain of it." Gamu had taken the words to heart and persevered, but there was no fruit.

Luckily, the great hoax hadn't turned out a complete disaster after all. To their luck, they had arrived in Hippo Valley during the preparations for the Festival of Tusks. Gwadza, the beer monger, felt partly responsible for the predicament Gamu was in after the fracas at his establishment, so called upon a favor and got Gamu a position helping with the construction of the stage the king and queen sat upon at the festival.

Rather than being thankful, Gamu was sour throughout, barely saying more than was needed. *What man wouldn't be bitter?* he thought, as he went about his business grudgingly. He looked like a goblin with swollen eyes and lips, his wife had forsaken her filial duties and to make matters worse, the chief-carpenter was making the pulpit all wrong. He wanted to say something, but his swollen lips wouldn't allow.

Tanaka was faring much better, finding work at a food stall. It quickly became popular as she gave the food an exotic flavor. They didn't earn much, but at least it was something and they had been given some lodgings, even though it was not far from the latrine, and they shared it with a pregnant donkey that would relieve itself when it would.

When the festival was over, Gamu had reluctantly agreed to return to Tanaka's family in Dande, a day or two from Pyyros. Gamu was on the slow path toward his worst nightmare. He was going to be a laughingstock. He could see the young loiterers snickering as they returned in rags, no better than a pack of vagabonds with nothing to show but a few measly seeds stuck at the bottom of his sack.

All those years ago, Gamu suddenly rounded up his family, visited Tanaka's father, Nhoro, and informed him he and his family were moving away. "Where are you taking my daughter and grandchildren?"

"To Pyyros, father, we leave in earnest."

"Where did you get this notion? I've never heard you say anything about this. Leave, why? You have everything you need here. A small plot of land, yes, but with hard work your lands will increase. How long have you thought about this young man?"

"For a while now, I have prayed on it for many a moon and asked the ancestors to guide me. They have led me to this conclusion. I feel it in my heart. There is so much more to the world, so much more than this." Nhoro frowned. "I mean no disrespect, but this is best for my family."

"Best for your family? What nonsense is this? Boy, are you on *muti*?" Nhoro now looked flabbergasted, but managed to keep his composure after a bout of coughs. "Gamu, you have a good thing here. Let's be honest. You are an orphan. My daughter, she is softly bred. You can be anything you want here, a man of title. Perhaps one day you could be in the village council."

I don't want to be in the village council, he wanted to say. "With all due respect, father. You have been kind to me and mentored me on many occasions. Treated me like a son, but sometimes a man must make his own way." This went on for hours. It went as far as Nhoro forbidding it before the ancestors. It made Gamu ever more determined. He wasn't going to let another man, father-in-law or not, determine the destiny of his family.

They had begun the journey alone, stopping by a relative's for a few nights, but when Gamu got wind that Prince Themba was travelling along the same route, they joined his host, for it was safer travelling in large numbers. "How much longer, father? Are we there yet?"

"Not long at all, Kushinga. You have to be strong like your brother." Gamu hated lying to his children, but he found himself doing it all the time. With Kayalethu and Chiiko, he was easily caught in his lies, but Kushinga was sweet. He did not question his elders.

"I don't like these men. They look mean. Are they going to hurt us like they did the man at the festival?"

"No, they are our friends. If there is any danger on the road, they will protect us."

"Even from the tokoloshe?"

"Yes son, even from the tokoloshe." This smelled like the work of Chiiko. He would have a stern word with the boy, for the tokoloshe was nothing to joke about. "Look Kushinga, they have big spears like you will when you are older." Gamu had always envisioned one of his children as his apprentice and the other, a warrior. With Chiiko to take after him, it was then up to Kushinga to wield, which would take some doing, as the boy was of a sickly nature. When the boy had turned gravely ill, with good salt, he could have sought the help of healers in the mold of the masked oracle he had been hearing about amongst village folk, on one of their stops. The Sangoma they had referred to him as, whom had performed miracles surpassing the likes of the Oracle's of the Sacred Hills and the Green Leafed Nganga. Instead he had to rely on unscrupulous medicine men and false prophets. Kushinga nonetheless regained his health, but Gamu vowed that one-day he would have enough to protect his family. That day had failed to arrive much like the rains and now seemed even further away.

"What's going on now?" The envoy had stopped ahead. Gamu immediately dropped his tools, and offloaded his heavy satchel. Surprise flashed on Tanaka's face, but Gamu was already pushing his way through the thick crowd of leather and wooden shields. He emerged at the front of the garrison where Prince Themba, Chief-Treasurer Mutasa, and their lieutenants deliberated.

"The bridge was old to begin with. Looks like a storm finally destroyed it," said a man wearing flamboyant red colored cow tails around his arms and legs.

"The work of witchcraft I say," said another, this one wearing cow tails as well, but instead of the ostentatious red, wore his in their natural white with streaks of black.

The chief treasurer sighed. "I guess we have to turn back. It's going to take more time going through the Lion's Way, not to mention the new fees they've imposed around their routes."

"And more risk," Gamu cut in from nowhere.

Mutasa looked up. "And who might you be?" There was a flash of familiarity on the treasurer's face. "Wait, I know you. You are that foolish man who tried to steal Tulu's *umqombothi*."

Gamu looked down in shame as the men laughed. *I thought it was mine.* "The Lion's Way is too dangerous." Gamu had initially taken Muchita's advice as the work of a mind corrupted by *umqombothi* and *muti*, however, he had to admit, there was an unwavering honesty in his tone. "I met a man who claims to have witnessed a whole village in that area," he lied, marginally, "ravaged by a group of beasts, greater in stature and ferocity than lions. I'd say we avoid that route at all costs."

An Amakazi had raised his spear, ready to strike the big-mouthed peasant before Chief Treasurer Mutasa raised his hand. "No need for that. This one has a big mouth, but at least judging from the past, he is interesting. Go ahead, young man, what do you suggest then? We jump over the gap?"

The crowd laughed. Gamu found that funny too, affording himself a chuckle. Soon after his face was the epitome of dead-faced sincerity. "What if I told you I could fix the bridge?"

"What.....you?" Mutasa studied him up and down with displeasure. His clothes were no better than beggars at a dirty village market. Mutasa couldn't fathom why Gamu was wearing one cow tail around one of his legs. It was either on both, or none at all. "What do you know about bridges?" he sneered.

Gamu did not know anything about bridges, but he did know how to fix things. He knelt by the edge of the broken bridge and surveyed the carnage. "See there?" he pointed, "it's only the middle that is destroyed. The foundations are still intact." He stood up and turned to the treasurer. "We passed a thick forest, about a day ago."

"Yes, by Lake Dombo. What of it?"

"We will need wood, lots of it. The trees there looked long and strong enough to bear the pressure."

"Yes, dark wood."

"With your permission, I would like to take about seven of your men. That should be enough to cut down the large trees, and carry them back, with the general's permission, of course."

Themba who had been listening in silence until now decided. "I shall go. This mission will be fruitless without me. Plus, I have always wanted to visit this Domboshawa. The general will never deny his prince."

"The general is old and has become pricklier as the years have gone by," Mutasa warned. "He takes everything as an insult, even complimenting him on his health. I do not think this is something for you, Themba."

"Do not worry, treasurer. I know how to deal with these types."

Mutasa was apprehensive but ceded nonetheless. "If you say so, my prince." He bowed and turned to the woodman smiling, pulling him closer until Gamu could smell his breath, a mixture of old orange, pineapple and licorice. "You better not be wasting our time, or else."

CHAPTER 29

"I'm bored Nia, I'm tired of hunting locust. Can't we do something else, like perhaps knit, or sing some songs?"

"I'm horrible at knitting, you know that, Yuse," the princess replied.

"I can teach you. It's real easy. You'll see."

"I don't want to," Nia sulked. A thought came to her. "I know what we can do. I know a secret ruin, with great wonders, and perhaps, even some treasure."

Yuse looked apprehensive. "Hmmm, I don't know about that. That sounds really dangerous. My mother will be very angry if she heard I did that."

"But no one has to know. It's so much fun. I've been down there before, with Wafula." She forgot that was meant to be a secret.

Yuse's eyes animated. "Nia and Wafula, by the fire tree," she began to sing, "Bought her some cows, now they're a fam-mi-ly." Nia's face turned red with anger. "Go and ask your Wafula to go down with you. I am going to play with someone who is not crazy."

Before Yuse could skip off, Zodwa, another one of her cousins' voice called out as she approached. "Nia, Yuse, look what my mother made me, isn't it the prettiest dress."

Yuse's eyes widened with amazement. She turned to the princess. "Aren't you coming?"

"No, it's okay, I feel tired. I think I'll go home and rest."

"Very well, Nia, do as you will, hope you have fun with that Wafula of yours. I don't get what you see in him. His mother is a peasant." With that, Yuse skipped off briskly to praise the wonderful detail and stitching of Zodwa's new dress.

What was she going to do now? She looked at the sun and saw there were a few more hours of light. She took a walk around the palace until she got to the game grounds. She found a group of people deliberating in the middle, all holding wooden sticks with curved heads at the bottom that looked like a viper. Prince Atakachi stood in the middle as one of the participants got carried off. "What do we do now? We are now too few," one of the boys moaned.

"What about me?" All heads turned to find Princess Nia with her hand up, unsure if she had done the right thing. The boys looked at her apprehensively and then began to laugh. She wasn't deterred. "You can't continue unless you have one more player right? Why not me? I promise I'm good."

They all looked at Atakachi as he flipped the ball up and down on his palms. He looked around to make sure the queen was not in the vicinity, or any other high official or chief. "Very well, but only this time. I warn you sister, this is a dangerous game. Many have lost an eye, and some even their lives."

Dzogo getting stretchered off with blood flowing from the side of his head said as much. Despite that, she was undeterred. "I promise, I will be careful."

"You better. I don't want mother giving me grief for this." He tossed her a stick.

She smiled as she caressed it like she did uncle Machupa's spear she 'borrowed' next to every day.

"You are the goal tender," Atakachi smiled.

She wanted to protest but at least she was playing. The drum rang, and the game was on. Atakachi got things proceeding, sweeping the maroon and brown ball, about the size of an apple to one of his teammates. He controlled it effortlessly, and then smacked it forward toward the dashing Zebe whom grimaced when Idris, the stalky son of the palace stone-smith, intercepted it. Now it was the other team's turn to attack. Nia surveyed the game from her goal post as they began their attack, passing the ball amongst each other in quick short triangular passes. Before she knew it, Gozo was sprinting toward her with the ball at his feet. He pulled back his stick, a pulchritudinous instrument made of hardwood with red cloth wrapped around the handle and smacked it hard toward Nia. Time seemed to have slowed as the heavy ball made its way toward her face. She wanted to duck out of the way, but that was no way to impress her brother, or the other children. She held strong and took the ball on the side of her chin.

When she came to, several faces stood above her, talking and laughing. "Is she dead?"

"I don't think so, she seems to be moving." Atakachi held out a hand. "How many fingers?"

Nia quickly sat up and rubbed her jaw. "Did I-I. . ." she stuttered, still dizzy from the hit. "Did I save it?"

"You kept the ball out. Fantastic save, sister, but they still managed to score." That was not pleasing news to Nia. Atakachi gave her his hand and helped her up. "I can't let you play anymore. You're hurt. Mother will kill me for this. It's time you do whatever you spend your time doing. Leave."

She was loath to go. This was the most fun she had experienced since her misadventure with Wafula deep in the Fire Caves. She had been avoiding him since that night. She didn't know what to say to him. She was not ready to tell him the truth. *He must hate me. Everyone hates me.* She pondered for a moment. *I hate them too, their dresses, their knitting and their cute little songs.* She had to go and apologize. He had forgiven her in the past for her rudeness and selfish behavior. Perhaps he could find it in his heart to forgive her now as well. She dusted off her cheeks and knees and lurched off to Wafula's hut, cursing at Atakachi. swith a tightly rolled fist.

When she arrived, there was Wafula with his mother and a man with all their belongings atop donkeys and oxen. They met eyes. Wafula smiled. *Oh good, he doesn't hate me.* She tried to smile back, but it came out awkward. He ran toward her. "Hey, Nia, long time no see."

"It has hasn't it?" He seemed to have grown a few inches since she last saw him. They were now equal of height.

"I'm sorry . . ."

"It's okay, Nia, you don't have to. I was very angry at first, but after a while, I figured that you wouldn't abandon me unless there was a really good reason." He smiled. "I have some good news and some bad news. What should I start with?"

"The good."

"My mother, she has found a husband."

"Oh, congratulations! I am so happy for you."

"Thank you. He is a really nice man. His wife died without bearing any children, so he says that I will inherit his farm when he dies. It's not the biggest farm, but it's better than what we have now." She was genuinely happy for Wafula, but her heart was in dread for the bad news. His smile evaporated and was replaced by a somber melancholy. "The bad news is that we have to move far away." Nia's heart sunk. She hadn't expected this. She was expecting him to tell her that he had broken his bow, or lost one of his kites to a tree.

"You're moving away?" The boy nodded apologetically. "When?"

"Now." This was worse than that night her mother informed her of her impending purification. She wanted to ask him why he hadn't told her, but it was her own doing. She had after all been avoiding him. She wanted to cry, but she couldn't . . . not in front of him.

"That's great Wafula," she tried to smile. "It is for the best."

The boy reached into his sack and revealed two daggers wrapped in a cloth. "I want you to have one. They are twin daggers, so I can have one and you the other." She didn't know what to say. She had never owned her own weapon. All she knew was her uncle Machupa's spear. "Please take care of it, as I will mine. Whenever you cut something, you can remember me." She wanted to raise it into the sun, but Wafula reminded her where they were. If her mother saw it, she would take it away from her. "My father left them for me before he died. I only need one."

"Thank you, Wafula. You are the best friend I have ever had."

"Son," Wafula's stepfather called out, "it's time to go."

Wafula smiled. "He calls me son, can you believe that? He wants me to call him father."

"That's great, Wafula. Do you promise to visit me?"

The boy looked down. He couldn't answer that question and she knew it. "I have to go now. I have to be a good son and obedient."

"I understand."

"Goodbye, Princess Nia of the Piripiri tribe. Perhaps one day I will have a thousand cows and be able to afford your dowry."

Nia smiled. It was a handsome thought. "Perhaps." Wafula turned and ran off to his new family, leaving the girl where she stood. He jumped onto the back of the donkey that was waiting and waved. She waved back until he disappeared past the gate and only then, a torrent of tears swept over her face.

CHAPTER 30

Gamu and Themba were ushered into a large conical thatched hut made of wattle and daub. It was an unnerving room, lined with the skulls of ancient beasts, but it was at least better than the stoned pathway toward the audience chamber, lined with impaled corpses hanging fifteen feet up in the air. Some of them were children, not older than Chiiko and their twisted faces told the story of their gruesome ends. They sat themselves in the center circle as they clapped their hands in reverence of the great General Chinotimba. "Who are you? Why are you here?" an old and frail voice croaked.

"These men are from the Stone Houses. It is Prince Themba of Akuwa and a man who calls himself Gamu the woodman," replied a feminine voice. The lord of Domboshawa nodded sheepishly. "I have to apologize, the general is very old. His hearing is poor, but otherwise he is healthier than he has been in a long time. His newest bride is expecting."

Peculiarly, Themba found himself more startled by the woman's behavior, rather than the fact that the general despite his age was still productive.

"Are you having trouble speaking, esteemed guests?" she smiled.

"No, girl, tell the general we seek his assistance." Themba waved his hand and up came Pikoro, the prince's newly acquired lackey, carrying a few rocks of silver. "It is not much, but under the circumstances, it is the best we could do."

The woman put an ear closer to the toothless old man with skin so loose it hung off his bones, like lamb left simmering for hours in a large metal cauldron. "The general says in his youth, a prince would rather come before him naked than present such niggardly gifts."

Themba sprang to his feet immediately unclothing himself, exposing his private parts and buttocks to the guards posted behind him. He smiled, pleased with his form, seemingly comfortable in his nakedness.

Gamu felt a little ashamed, maybe because, unlike the prince, he was skin and bone, and that beauty of youth was slowly disappearing from his once healthy and prominent body.

"Might I remind you?" Themba said.

"Yes, yes, we know who you are. I believe I have presented you already." The woman seemed unfazed by the prince's nakedness.

Gamu found it strange, even otherworldly. He had never encountered a woman so bold. "Prince, please sit," Gamu begged, as he pulled on the prince's lynx loincloth that was now sitting around his knees. It took some doing, but Themba eventually sat down. "Let me talk, before you ruin this," he whispered. "Prince Themba of the Akuwa hasn't been feeling well, and we have been travelling for many a day. If I may ask, the prince wants to know whom we are speaking to."

"I apologize for my manners. You will find that us people of Domboshawa are not as refined as those from the Stone Houses. I am Yemuraii, the general's daughter. Welcome to Domboshawa." Gamu bowed, but the prince plainly nodded his head. "We trust that your entourage is comfortable and has been fed."

"Yes, your grace," Gamu replied, not failing to notice her shiny bald head lined with a red beaded headband with a large black stone that seemed to radiate, just as much as her large smile.

"And who might you be woodman? You look out of place, in the company of such men. You have no spear, so you are no warrior, and you lack any jewelry of worth, so you are no man of title. We are curious, what is your business?"

"I was travelling behind the prince, and his entourage."

"And why is that?"

"Well . . ." Gamu scratched his neck. "It is safer travelling in groups, especially with children and pregnant women."

"So I gather you have wives."

"Wife," corrected Gamu. "I have just one."

"I see." She looked genuinely shocked. She had painted her lips a dark maroon so it made her look fiendish. The piercings that trailed over her left eye and under her right accentuated this, as did the gap between her front two incisors. She moved her ear toward the general, clad in his full battle attire. "The general says he likes you. He says he can see you are a good man, with a heart filled with power, wisdom and courage . . . but not so much the other one." Themba's nose flared, and his blood eye brightened. "Calm down prince. My father is quite the joker. He means no ill will." She waited for the prince to calm before she continued. "Do you know that my father once killed thirty Piripiri warriors all by himself at the . . ."

"No offence, lady, but it is a hot day, our heads throb, and so do our feet. Save us the war stories," the prince rudely interrupted.

If it bothered Yemuraii, she didn't show it. "A straightforward man, I see." She studied the young prince as she flicked her long nose, her close-set eyes keen and unnerving. "It is true what the village folk say." When she was done praising prince Themba's manly sensibilities, her face changed to the concerned look she had earlier. "So, what is your business?"

Gamu raised his voice first. "We were travelling along the Pyyros way when we discovered the bridge had been destroyed, blocking the route."

Yemuraii studied Gamu silently, only stopping to whisper something into her father's ear. "That's unfortunate but please, what does this have to do with the general?"

Themba whispered something in Gamu's ear. "Prince Themba would rather speak directly to your father . . . or brother perhaps?" Gamu relayed.

"What's wrong with me? I thought we were having a marvelous time."

"Nothing is wrong with you . . . your grace." Themba whispered something else in Gamu's ear. "The prince says you are beautiful and virtuous of spirit, but we are pressed for time and seek audience with someone of authority."

Yemuraii put her ear to the old general and nodded.

"My father says you can take anything up with me. I am his ears and mouthpiece."

The prince wanted to protest but Gamu spoke first. "Your grace, we need wood."

"Wood? Why do you need that? Have you run out of spears? Are you going to ask us next for steel?"

"No, like I explained your grace, the bridge is broken, and we intend to fix it."

"Why not just go the other way, isn't that easier? Surely that bridge isn't the only way to Pyyros."

"We thought if we repaired the bridge, we would save us many days, and as you know, it is dangerous times."

"Yes, I am aware. Our chief-oracle, the most talented mystic if I may, says the spirits are displeased, they say it is uncertain times, the ushering in of change. What do you think about that Gamu, the woodman, are you afraid of change?"

Gamu wanted to tell her that he yearned for it. That he welcomed it with open arms for the world he was in was anything but pleasant. He was saved when the general began shaking horribly, gurgling. A girl came running with a metal bucket and cloth and held it in front of the general. He gurgled again, and then removed his entrails into the bucket. It was creamy white, with dashes of blood, which turned it into a light pink at the bottom of the pail.

"Father has been having a bad stomach the last couple of days," Yemuraii apologized. "It is hard getting a decent food taster these days. We have a new one now, the old one you might have met on the pathway." She smiled courteously. The unlucky taster could have been any one of the twisted, half decomposed heads that decorated the pathway up to the general's audience chamber. "As we were discussing, I assume you have come here seeking permission to cut my father's sacred trees?"

"That's correct, Mother of?"

"I am not married. I am a maiden." The day was filled with surprises. "Does that displease you, Gamu the woodman?"

"Oh not at all, I was just surprised a woman as pretty . . ." Gamu had to look down at his toes. "A woman as pleasant as you has not been taken by a wise and handsome chief."

"Perhaps I haven't found the right wise and handsome chief," Yemuraii replied, smiling. Gamu could tell Themba was now becoming even more agitated.

"What is this? Can we get to why we are here? What does your father want? We do not have all the time in the world," Themba barked.

"Hmmm, that's a good question. What does my father want?" She leaned to the general and set her ear to his mumbling mouthpiece.

"This is preposterous," Themba shouted. "You're a girl. I could have my father's warriors reign on this shit hole, Domboshawa, in a fortnight and take whatever we want." He looked Yemuraii up and down and hard at her breast and said with a calm asperity, "Even you."

"I advise you to change your tone, prince," she warned. Gamu tugged at his cloths, urging him to calm.

"She's not speaking for her father, she's speaking for herself. Look at him, he's a mute, he's as good as dead."

"That doesn't matter now. What matters is what they think about this." Several guards stood as still as the night around the room with their sharp spears well in view. Though the room was lightly lit, they stood out in their pasty-white painted bodies, which created a ghostly spectacle about them, like cadaverous specimens – walking dead.

"Perhaps you're right."

"Yes I am," Gamu assured. He turned to Yemuraii. "Your grace, we apologize."

"Very well, I will forget the insult. We do not want people at the Stone Houses to say the people of Domboshawa are humorless. Here in Domboshawa we respect all forms of life equally, man, woman and child, even those trees you intend to cut down." She stroked her father's bald head, smiling. "Fifty cows."

"Fifty cows? That's absurd." The prince spat out the *doro* he was drinking. "What are you people? Bandits? This is wood we are talking about, just a few trees," the prince exclaimed.

"Lake Dombo is almost dry. All our game is slowly migrating south. Our people are poor and starving. We do not have those large granite walls to protect us when the drought sweeps us all. Fifty cows, take it or leave it. Furthermore, father is looking for a new bride. Perhaps an Akuwa or a Shumba, or even possibly, an exotic Uche, and they come at an exorbitant price. Either way, this issue does not concern us."

"But I'm your prince. What if I command you to let me?"

"You have no right. My father, who was slaying giants long before your grandfather set his tongue on your great grandmother's teats, is viceroy of Domboshawa and rules as he likes."

She was right. She had all the pieces. The prince had to humble himself and accept being on the bad end of a deal. What else could they do but open the coffers. Gamu had to get his family back to Dande. He had to start earning again and get things straight with Tanaka and be something she could be proud of. Besides, fifty cows was indeed a lot, but he saw the lavish outfits Mutasa wore and the abundance of bananas and oranges he had in baskets atop the donkeys. Between the prince and the treasurer, Gamu knew they could easily afford it. "Yes. We accept the deal." Gamu announced resolutely.

"What?" Themba shouted incensed.

"Quiet, Themba, trust me. Do you not long for your bride? We are already delayed. What if she receives another suitor? A Shumba? Or perhaps an Uche?"

"You two," she giggled, "you two behave like quarrelling siblings. Have you settled your dispute, boys?"

The prince had grown pale. "Yes," Themba announced, finally. "I have come to the conclusion that you are right. Fifty cows is a very fair price indeed. After all, you have fed us well and been so hospitable."

"You are as kind as you are wise, my prince." Yemuraii curtsied, but rather than meet Themba's blood eye, she and Gamu locked eyes, but just momentarily. Gamu turned away fast, as moisture began to build around his neck. "My father insists you stay the night. It is too late to start cutting down the trees and I'm sure you have heard about the beasts, if you can call them that, that have been abducting villagers."

"We accept the invitation," said the prince.

"Wonderful," she smiled. "We shall throw a banquet in your name, Prince Themba." She turned to Gamu.

Why is she looking at me that way?

"I expect you at the banquet as well. You will dine with us?"

"I can't, I do not have the clothes. I look no more decent than a mere shepherd."

"Nonsense, woodman. Here in Domboshawa, we judge a man by his character, not his cattle." And there, despite the prince's obvious disagreement, it had been decided for Gamu.

***

Prince Themba, Gamu and their party made their way back to Chief Treasurer Mutasa and the rest of the envoy with enough wood to temporarily repair the broken bridge. Yemuraii Chinotimba tormented the young prince's thoughts during the trek through the Domboshawa woods and across the savannah. Though Themba considered her haughty and rude, there was something about her that stirred him in the deepest and darkest parts of his soul. "But my heart belongs to Princess Nia," he would fantasize in his thoughts.

"For just one night," Yemuraii would lament, as she rubbed that long nose over his cheek. "Let me love you for one night, please!" He tried to think of something else, something to get those eyes out of his mind.

At the banquet the night before, he had found Yemuraii's petulance irksome, but as the night wore on, as she sat amongst her maids, he could see her in her full glory between the large flames that separated them. He had tried to make eye contact, but it never came. At one point Themba stood up to dance and shuffled toward her and began to kick forcefully into the air, well over his head. His cow tails would fly into other's faces, disrupting their dance, but the prince did not care. Soon he had a dancer to his left, and another to his right, and before he knew it, a line of synchronized dancers stepped left and right, mimicking the prince's rhythmic pattern. Headdresses, an assortment of black and white feathers bopped around and cow tails swayed. Their spears were thrust up, then sideways, as feet thumped in neat arrangements. They repeated these movements, and the prince smiled maniacally from ear to ear as perspiration covered his face. His hips thrust forward, and then back in the direction of Yemuraii whom suddenly had to excuse herself to urinate. She said she had drunk too much *doro*. That sent Themba wild. He liked a woman that could handle the sour taste of the thick liquid. It meant she could handle him. He was convinced she was playing a game, one he was very much up for. Alas they had to leave, but he knew sooner or later, they would cross paths.

Meanwhile, Gamu's shoulders were sore from the heavy lifting, as were the other men's by the time they arrived at the foot of the collapsed bridge. Chief Treasurer Mutasa glided up to meet them, today in a new kenspeckle garment. He went easy on the gold, however his sandals were a marvel. They were clearly made by the Pyyros foot smiths, renowned as the best in the known world. Few men in the kingdom could boast such fine footwear. Rather than a loincloth, he opted for thin linen, with opaque dark shades wrapped around his waist, and a blanket with his family's totem sewn into it. "I trust you have found the material you need?"

"Yes, chief. We will need most of the men to be able to place the logs across the cliff and I'll also need men to help me hammer the horizontal planks of wood . . ."

"Slow down, young man." Mutasa held him by the shoulders and ushered him away. "I remember when I was once young, so eager, always running around like a busy bee. There is enough time for that later. You and the men must be famished. Your wife has made herself useful whilst you were away." He pointed toward her. Tanaka was hard at work stirring the pot as she whipped and whipped, making smooth soft pumpkin.

A tear fell down Gamu's left eye. He quickly wiped it off. "I guess we could do this after we eat. A rest would be best. One might collapse under such heat."

"I heard about how you handled yourself in Domboshawa."

Gamu was startled how fast news travelled. *Does he know?*

Mutasa smiled the most genial of smiles. "Without you there, this problem of ours would have been a lot more complicated."

"Oh, it wasn't anything like that. They exaggerate."

"Humble as you are resourceful it seems," the treasurer praised as he raised his cup. "This is one of Mariga the sculptor's works." It was made from dark wood and shaped like the head of an elephant. The elephant's trunk made for a good and sturdy handle. "Here, have a sip of some of my *umqombothi*."

"Really, it's okay, I can't." He peeked where Tanaka was from the corner of his eye.

"Of course you can. Take it." Gamu reached out hesitantly. "The wheat is from the rich Turkana farmlands."

Gamu had never had anything so expensive in his mouth. *Why not?*

Mutasa chuckled loud and merrily. "Let us sit down, eat, and you can tell me about how we are going to get across the gorge and after that, perhaps the future."

CHAPTER 31

Queen Zandile beckoned for Nia as the young princess played with her brother Alinafe a short distance away from her hut. Nia surprisingly more obsequious than usual dropped what she was doing and ran to her mother's call. "Remember what we spoke about a few moons back? I need to know that you are sure about this."

"I am just as brave as any man, mother. I promise. I am as brave as you."

The queen smiled, her heart filling up with warmth despite their precarious situation. "Listen closely. After dark, you and I will escape."

A chill breezed up Nia's spine. "So soon?"

"I am afraid so."

"What about father?"

"Never mind him. I will take care of him."

"But he will hurt you."

Zandile revealed a small dagger from her dress, startling the young princess. "No one will ever hurt me, or you. I promise you that." She tucked it away before anyone noticed. "Now go and play with your brothers, and remember, carry on as usual."

Nia was well into a misty dreamland of dark caves, secret pathways and steep stairs when her mother nudged her. It took a few more to get her out of her slumber and back to the grimness of leaving everything she knew, her family, her home . . . her life – for a short while, she had to convince herself. During the day she had tried to gain Atakachi's attention, but as always, he had little time for her. It was typical of him, but nonetheless, she had to admit she would miss him. She had looked up to him as long as she could remember, looking over the fence as he practiced spear and shield and made merry with the rest. Alinafe and Mukina were not the same, but in time they would change. They all did, *and sadly so will Wafula.*

"Wake up. "It's time to go."

The dogs howled as they crept outside the hut and a few steps into their escape, up came a night guard. "Your grace, what are you doing up in the hour of the jackal?"

"My daughter is not feeling well. She needs some air. Let us be and continue your duties. Thank you for the concern. You can be on your way now."

The watchman bowed and did as he was told, after looking at them suspiciously.

Outside the Pyre Fortress gates on a location marked on the map the Sangoma had provided, waited two zebras. To get there they needed to make it past the main gate, which was by no means an easy task. The guards were unlikely to allow them to walk out of the premises without a direct order from the king - That is why Zandile had a plan. She pulled down her dress a little lower revealing her bosoms, pressed them together and approached the three watchmen as the most senior held court. "You should have seen his eyes pop out of his face when my club connected," he chuckled. The watchmen's eyes seemed to do the same when Zandile emerged from the darkness in her typical regal beauty.

"Is this what you boys do out here? I thought you were protecting us from the evils of the night?"

The leader wiped the froth from his beard. "My queen, excuse us, we are very sorry."

"It's okay, your secret is safe with me. Sometimes a man has to have a little fun, no?" Zandile giggled. She set her almond eyes upon him. "I was just taking a walk. It was so hot in my bedchambers . . . and lonely. I couldn't sleep." She reached for the guard's calabash that balanced between his thighs, grabbed it and took a mouthful of the fermented milk. Cream beads dripped over her lips and down her chin, drop by drop as the guards looked on in amazement. "I get so sad when my husband goes off, god knows where." She stuck her tongue out and licked off the residue that had settled on her sultry lips.

"Your husband, the king, is protecting us from evil doer's, mother."

She discerned an imperceptible mound emerging from the top of his loincloth. "I am deeply distressed Masuku. That is your name, isn't it? Your leadership and diligence has not gone unnoticed." The head watchman nodded as sweat broke from the side of his head. She leaned over him and laid back the calabash where she took it. His hands shook as he tried to wipe the perspiration from his face. "Is there some way we can talk about this privately?" she whispered softly in his ear.

Masuku's eyes flashed as he shooed away the other watchmen and cleared a seat for her. As soon as they were alone, Masuku was on her, burying his face into the queen's luscious cups.

She pulled him away and put a sensual yet stern finger on his chest. "Slow down, warrior. We are in no hurry." The guard's hog-like grunts slowed into gradual, weighty gusts. She pulled him close by his animal skins and placed one hand on his chest. She could feel bawdy rings of hair around his fleshy nipples. She squinted as her other hand slid toward his nether regions. The man groaned as she felt a tuft of thick coarse hair at the bottom of his belly. Zandile looked around to make sure they were still alone. "I want to thank you," she whispered as she brushed her lips on his ear.

"Thank me for what, my dear lady?" Masuku answered, grunting softly.

"For letting us escape." Before Masuku could respond, Zandile sunk her blade into the burly man's throat. He tried to pull out the dagger, but soon enough he was slumped on top of her with all his weight. When his eyes had finally closed, she wrestled herself free, inserted her fingers into her mouth and produced a faint whistle. After a few moments, out crept Nia skipping past the courtyard, quick like a rodent darting across a smooth marble kitchen floor.

"Don't look," the queen commanded as Nia approached. Her attempts were futile. The young princess had already set her eyes upon the dead guard, and his punctured neck. Zandile picked up his weapons and handed them to Nia. "You might need these." Zandile had ignored it for most of her daughter's life, but deep down she had known all along that despite her efforts to make a proper princess of her, a blade and shield is all she had ever really wanted. "Do you have everything, sweet child?"

Nia shook her head and darted off, back into the palace. When she finally returned, mere moments later, she had Ginger the dog following happily behind her wagging its tail. "Now I do."

The queen smiled and nodded. "Then follow me."

Maghedzi had showered his queen with necklaces made from gold, silver and platinum. He had laced her fingers with the finest stones his wealth and influence could buy. He had gone to war in pursuit of these things and had grown bitter from the lack of appreciation. Perhaps other women would have been content, but not Zandile. She wanted more. Something Maghedzi could never give her. With that final thought, mother, daughter and the hound ran off into the night, hand in hand.

CHAPTER 32

The next day's mood had been dour following Batanai's death as the young hippos trekked through the woods during their rites of passage; however, soon enough, the usual suspects were at it again with the shenanigans and boyish chatter, unable to withhold their excitement at soiling their spears with beast blood and finally becoming men. Xolani knew better – they were all liars. They were probably just as afraid as he was. In the last rites of passage, two boys didn't make it home, and the one before that, four. When they got to a large empty space, Comrade Chengetaii whistled and unburdened his weight and commanded the boys to set up camp.

Xolani unrolled his mat, laid his head and prayed he wouldn't have that dream again. He did, but as he sped through the aquatic on his mother's tails, another scream rang, and then another. "Where is Matata?" Khaya shouted. "He was just here!"

And with that a frightening roar echoed into the night sky, shaking the earth. The whole camp was startled as they fumbled for their weapons. Abuba was still asleep with his thumb stuck in his mouth tucked under his blanket. Xolani shook his head and poked at him again, this time awaking the boy. With that, Xolani was on his way following the roars.

He could feel the cold wind brush his face as he dodged left and right, navigating through the thick forestation, jumping over a large root that stuck out horizontally over the earth. He thought to stop in his tracks and return to the comfort of the Stone Houses, behind the secure walls where no beast, natural or paranormal could get him. There his father with the help of Amakazi could protect them all, however, it was too late for that.

As he approached the end of the woodland, he unsheathed Night Slayer resting on his back and emerged from the canopy to find Comrade Chengetaii's black cloths flapping behind him with spear in hand. In front of him were beasts Xolani had only seen on cave paintings and in Tjingii's stories. They growled as their tails swished sharply from side to side, and Night Slayer thrummed and glowed a bright cyan blue. High above them perched on a large rock, was the king of this lurid pride licking its paws and by its side, Matata lay barely moving. It grabbed Matata with its mammoth sabers and shook the boy violently from side to side like a dancer enthusiastically shaking a *shekere* at a feast. Without notice, a one-eyed monster leapt into the air. Comrade Chengetaii was up to the task, rolling out of the way just before its tentacles took a large piece of his dashiki. He swung his spear around and stabbed, but the beast was too agile despite its girth. Its roar had Chengetaii's cloths flying backward like he was trapped in a cyclone. "Xolani, separate your team into three groups. Stage one, stage two and stage three."

Xolani was surprised. He had never led anything. "You heard him, young hippos, Thokozani you will lead group one." He flashed a finger the same way Chengetaii did, but with a fraction of his authority. "Korokoro, take group three and I will lead group two."

The creature sprang toward Chengetaii, paws flashing. The veteran performed a back flip out of the way and whilst mid-air struck it on its muzzle with the butt of his spear. It was a good strike, but all it seemed to do was irritate the creature even more. *That is good*, Chengetaii thought, pulling his hood backward for a better view, smiling sadistically at the prospect of a real battle. The beast scowled as it backed off, letting out a thunderous roar that shook the earth. "This diabolic creature thinks it can scare us with its loud noises," Chengetaii screamed. "Let us show them why we lost in the choir competition at the festival."

Xolani banged on his shield and began to sing. The rest of the team followed suit as they bashed their spear butts into the earth and battered their shields.

"Group one, to your positions," Chengetaii screamed. The beasts sprinted toward them as their claws tore the earth. "Hold it," Chengetaii commanded, "Hold it!"

All this waiting was not boding well with some of the members, particularly Kori, whose loincloth turned dark, and then with that tossed his weapons. The shield landed flat, creating a small cloud of dust where it sat. "We're all doomed," Kori cried. "They are indeed unnatural. This is the work of some evil spirit." With that, he fled.

The beasts were now a few moments away. The boys had been taught war strategy, but this was no ordinary battle. They had been taught how to anticipate a strike, parry it, exposing an enemy's chest. They had been made to run for endless hours barefoot and developed soles so thick they could walk over burning charcoal. They had been taught how to hold their breath under water for minutes on end. Xolani could remember vividly as Comrade Chengetaii held his head down as he struggled for breath, kicking and gurgling down water as his lungs engulfed. "Do not be afraid," the commander had said as he tried to snatch some air before the veteran's hands were upon him again. "We are of the hippo, and the liquid is where we belong." What he hadn't taught them was how to fight creatures thought a myth.

"Hold it," Chengetaii bellowed. The four beasts were now raining in from the sky, like comets zipping through a clear black night. It seemed like eternity to Xolani as they hovered above in the heavens with their broad nasal openings flaring.

Time had stopped. Nonkuleko's smile appeared before him. He smiled back as the image of his father appeared and all those strange questions he asked him about. He smiled as he saw himself, Night Slayer in hand, clutching onto Aku's horns as they glided over the Khumalo, wind brushing over his head.

Finally Chengetaii made the command. "Attack," he screamed, as saliva splashed over his lips. The first group of boys duly charged forward in a tight unit with their spears extended and shields neatly protecting their bodies. Gumisa went in first, piercing one of the female's flanks. It growled and swung its paw, connecting with the side of his head, sending Gumisa into a nearby tree.

Next the hairy beast turned to Thokozani and Abuba who stood side by side, complete contrasts, one a picturesque of fitness, the other as soft as fox's fur. The beast looked straight into the fatter ones eye's and roared. Abuba turned and looked at Gumisa's decapitated body and froze.

The hairy creature, all shaggy and grotesque sprang forth toward the inanimate Abuba. Thokozani managed to push him out of reach and stood firm on his lonesome. The creature couldn't turn down Thokozani's challenge. It tried to grab the boy, but he rolled under it and planted a dagger into its abdomen. It was a fine strike. Thokozani had muscular thick arms, which he gained being his father, the chief metal-smith's apprentice. He could feel the crackle as the dagger punctured its flesh and cut through bone until it lodged in the foul beast's breast, right between two ribs. He left it there, flipped up and unsheathed his spear.

Abuba remained inanimate, shaken by his close encounter with death, his tires of fat under his chin, wobbling like a fish on deck. "This is not what I anticipated," Abuba confessed, trembling. "I came here to kill a few lions and these are clearly something else.

There's so many of them. It's an army." Tears started pouring down his soft cheeks and rolled down the rings of flesh around his neck. It was true. No lion possessed such fangs, similar in size to the hippo's canines. "Look at its paws," the boy cried. "It killed Gumisa, with one blow!" He turned around and bolted the other direction leaving his brethren another man short.

"Abuba, come back. We need you," Xolani pleaded, but the coward had already disappeared into the vegetation.

"Let him go," Chengetaii snarled. "We are better off without him. His cowardice will get one of us killed."

Khaya the Glut now had his hands full as two atrocities attacked him simultaneously. He ducked and danced his way from one's bite and used his spear to parry away the other's strikes, but his leather shield could only do so much.

Thokozani was now on top of his beast, stabbing on its comb and ears. It flung him away, but he managed to land on his feet, repositioned his spear and sprang forward. He was greeted with a slap which he parried to the side and when the wounded animal was open, slid his spear into its chest. It landed on him, crushing him under its girth. Thokozani could feel its muscles pulsating as he felt his ribs almost break. One of the beasts saw Thokozani in his predicament and made its move.

Immediately he thought of Chipo – his betrothed. Strangely enough he had never set eyes on her, but he felt he knew her. She was described as short, with wide hips and a flat stomach. Her hair was plated into braids that looked like a fish skeleton and had cheekbones higher than the tallest trees. Sadly she faded, and his heart froze as her image disappeared like the last trails of smoke. He closed his eyes and cried out to his ancestors to intervene.

Just when the beast was a whisker away, a heavy spear came crashing through the creature's side sending its entrails and a fountain of blood all over his face. It could have pierced through three heavily armored rhinoceros. Such was its ferocity. He managed to finally slide out from under the beast, looked around to thank the commander, but he was already off, like a shadow cutting through a maze of meat.

"Group two, get ready," Chengetaii cried, as red beads dripped from the tips of his blood-drenched loincloth. When the commander made the signal, Xolani was the first out, ducking low as the filthiest of the beasts flew past above him. It whimpered as Xolani slashed at its tail, chopping it off by the brush. An arrow shot out, landing on one of the beast's forelegs. It grabbed it with its teeth, pulled it out and growled. Another arrow zipped by landing on the same leg. It hissed in pain, but Xolani had no mercy, despite what his uncle Batusai had revealed to him:

"Man is no different from a zebra, or a monkey, or even an ant . . . Only we are worse."

The words kept ringing in his head, but he slashed nonetheless and tried his best to survive. Now that the beast was limping, Xolani could do what he pleased. The stubborn creature took a swipe at him with its able limb, but Xolani ducked low, spun and planted half of Night Slayer into the soft part under its course golden beard. By now he did not mind the blood shower that followed as it sprinkled over his face and necklace. He slashed from left to right in the shape of a half moon, just the way Chengetaii had taught. Though he hated it, he felt a satisfaction when he felt the tear of muscle as the animal felt Night Slayer's serrations. He followed that up with a clean strike through the beast's foreleg like a knife through a well-cooked sweet potato. Its paw landed on Chengetaii's back as he stood off one beast with his shield and stabbed at another, catching it in the eye. It howled, springing back as it looked to its wounds. "Unleash the arrows!"

Chengetaii commanded. A hail of projectiles covered the night sky, landing on the grotesquery.

Chengetaii was now on the defensive, blocking a ferocious barrage of attacks with his shield. He shifted his body left, then right, then low, then high, and low again as he did well to meet the animals rapid combo. These shields were not made for such brutality. He could feel it depleting block after block. The beast retreated, growled baring its thick incisors and attacked again, which Chengetaii blocked, but this time the shield tore into shreds. He was exposed. Running was no option – Chengetaii had never run from a fight. He pondered on his options as the beast re-cocked its paw as it balanced on its hind legs.

From the heavens, Xolani emerged, leaping with all his might with Night Slayer in hand. The creature growled wildly, as he grabbed it tightly by its mane and with the other hand, stabbed it ferociously. Blood splashed in his eyes, but it did not matter. It seemed like he had been stabbing for eternity, but he had barely scratched the skull. It wasn't until the twelfth or thirteenth strike Xolani noticed any effect at all. Somehow it found some power from within, hurling him off. Xolani would have surely broken his back from the impact of such a fling, but he managed to cling on to the beast's long golden mane. It growled as Xolani regained his grip and held on tight on the back of the beast. He could feel its life slowly fade as its heart and the murmurs it made grew more tired and lazy after he planted Night Slayer into its bridge. The beast's final cry allowed Chengetaii to spring forth for the killer blow.

He held the spear in for a few seconds, twisting and turning the blade as he did all those years ago, when he lay with Thandi. That didn't matter now. She was long dead and was never coming back. She was part of a chapter he closed many years ago when he returned home. The only thing he could do now was earning his right to be with her in the afterlife. He squeezed tighter and gave it one last jerk then pulled out the spear as a stream of blood followed. Its stomach, colon and intestines fell out, revealing a bracelet as well as a half digested foot. With that, the stalky beast collapsed, landing face first with a thud, dead with its tongue sticking out.

Now that they had defeated the last of the beasts, Chengetaii felt a great sense of satisfaction, however, that all ended when he peered atop the rocks to find ten, *no*, thirty, fifty . . . *holy ancestors* – a hundred pairs of eyes catch aflame. The commander now realized the beasts had sent but a fraction of their forces and now they were threadbare, tired and injured. They had given their all. He considered giving the boys a speech of encouragement in the face of death, but what difference did it make? He rubbed his thumb up and down Dreads shaft and tightened his jaw. The creatures began to roar creating a thunderous effect, and then again, but the third time, it was evident they were roaring at something else. Amongst the roars, he caught the faint sound of drum in the distance, monotonous and growing louder and louder with every thump. The creatures roared again and did the unexpected. They turned and disappeared into the rocks.

Xolani looked around panting heavily as Night Slayer's thrum subsided, and its glow became fainter and fainter.

"They've grown craven," Korokoro announced. "We have won!"

"Have we," Xolani asked, as Night Slayer returned to its natural grey-azure. Sure they had survived the beasts' assault, however, one look around revealed they had won nothing. Even a blind man could see that, he wanted to say. He sighed and breezed past the triumphant Squirrel and tended to the wounded. He found Comrade Chengetaii praying, as he stood before a shivering Thabo with an open chest and half a leg. The commander brushed his fingers down his face then sunk a knife into the crown of his head. He cleaned the blade with his garments and walked up to Xolani, visibly shaken by his uncle's act of mercy. "You did well, young one. You handled yourself the right way, like a true Akuwa. Your father will be proud, when he hears of your efforts today. You know why I did that don't you?" The boy nodded. The veteran walked to another boy, in even worse shape than Thabo. He handed Xolani the dagger. "Here, it is your turn."

Xolani received the blade. He looked down at Sibonakaliso. He could see the boy was suffering. He had lost a lot of blood, most of it, but Xolani saw he did not want to die. "I can't uncle. I'm sorry, I can't." A tear rolled down his cheek as he dropped the dagger where he stood.

"Fine," Chengetaii snapped. He picked up the blade, knelt and sent Sibonakaliso to his ancestors. After he had finished praying for the boy's safe passage, the commander finally turned to Xolani. "Did you hear that?" The boy had. "It is as though the beasts were summoned by some malevolent being back to their lair." The commander contemplated for some moments, returning to the Sacred Hills as he sat before the Sisters in their gothic lair. Their lisps were an entanglement of contradictions and riddles. He picked up a necklace, wiped it down with his cloths, and then slipped it into his garments. He knew the young cadet's family would want it. "Xolani, you, Boreng, Korokoro and Khaya are going back to the Stone Houses. Tell your father what you have seen today. Tell him to send fifty of his best warriors."

"But uncle," Xolani protested. "I want to be here, I want to continue with you."

"You are the strongest riders. You will get there faster than anyone and time is of the essence." He opened his skin of water, stuck out his tongue and tried to get the few drops it had left. "Thokozani, do you have any extra water?" As the boy answered, an arrow flashed by Chengetaii and landed smack in the middle of Thokozani's forehead. *It's happening, the oracles words, they're coming to pass.* Chengetaii could hear the crack as the arrowhead pierced through the young hippo's skull, lodging itself in his cranium. His eyes bulged, and like the others, he was gone. Xolani caught the boy before he landed.

"What's happening?" Xolani cried.

Chengetaii ripped the arrow out of the dead boy's head and inspected it. It was unlike any he had seen in a long while. His next words began in a whisper and ended in a desperate cry. "Xolani, run. Everybody run. Run for your lives."

CHAPTER 33

Prince Simba bore a solemn countenance as he performed the royal visit of the Hippo Valley market square, complementing carpenters on their craft and ensuring veggie peddlers the rainy season would come soon. *At least one more*, he hoped. Many an oracle and aeromancer had predicted a great draught that would last a generation.

"Praise King Farakaii," a group shouted, as he passed one stall.

"May the king live for a thousand years," an old woman croaked.

"A hundred sons for the prince," a metal smith bawled.

"Ancestors bless the king," an old man spoke.

The prince waved and continued his royal business as two Amakazi followed behind him, their midnight-blue capes trailing behind them. Simba felt Taonga's presence beside him, advising him, or whispering a jape, but when the prince turned his head, it was the face of another. They had sparred together from as old as they could hold a stick, pretending they were Goromonzi the Nyaminyami Slayer and Ezeudo the Burning Spear.

"Look," Simba would yell, as he lit his stick aflame. "I am Ezeudo, look, look."

"And I am Goromonzi," Taonga would roar, plunging his stick into the giant granite statue of the water dragon that stood in the king's compound.

They had performed the warrior's ritual together when they were a fist of age, and shared a leather hide on their rite of passage. He was there when Taonga picked up his first bow, and could still remember the look on his face as he tickled the strings, pulled the bow back and unleashed his first arrow.

Nonkuleko, in the wake of Taonga's death had been inconsolable. "It is my fault," she had confided. "I did it to him."

She was wrong, Simba thought. In truth, it was his fault if anyone's. "It's a bad idea Simba," the prince remembered his friend saying, but he had managed to get him to follow along nonetheless.

"I prayed we would never be married. I even made a sacrifice!"

"Not so loud," Simba had warned her. "If anyone hears you speak like this, they'll take you for a witch." He had tried to convince her otherwise, but it was no use. The queen had thought it best she was sent to the Lion's Den. There she could regroup whilst they arranged another marriage for her.

Whenever he could, he would visit the girl with no name and enquire on her upkeep. The daughter of a king, she had proclaimed herself, so Simba made sure she had suitable quarters with a guard posted outside. It was a far cry from how she had described her home – a crystal palace with large open halls, but it would have to do. Sometimes he delivered her meals personally. She would leave the vegetables and meat, but never the fish. After a while all that was served was bronze bream, white steenbras and tilapia. When he had first come with a cup of milk, she had looked at it suspiciously, sniffing at it. Simba found great joy when she took her first sip, and her eyes widened in delight. "Milk," he told her.

"We do not have this where I come from, but we should," she smiled.

Sometimes he found himself behind time as their conversations went into the night. He had asked her where she was from, what clan she belonged to. "A tribe a hawk's eye away." Simba had asked her what she, and her group was doing in Hippo

Valley, if they were spies, but all she replied was. "We were hunting."

Simba had killed her betrothed on that day. She had mourned him every day, and at night, her sobs could be heard into the early hours of the morning. "What was he like?"

"He was sweet. He wasn't the tallest, or strongest, but he was brave, and kind, and his eyes . . ." She became melancholy. "He loved me."

Simba could say nothing. It was after all, his *masimbi* steel that had cut him down. *From now on,* Simba thought, *people should call me the Betrothal Slayer.* "Do you pray for them?"

"Ours is a proud tribe, with a rich illustrious history. We bow and look to no being. Dead or alive."

Their philosophizing on theology was interrupted by a heavy knock on the door. "Open up. Is that whore in there?"

Simba was on his feet in a snap, and spear tightly clasped in his hands. "Who asks?"

"A bereaved father, heavy of heart and a thirst for revenge."

Simba turned to the girl. "It's General Shato, Taonga's father . . . My friend, the one that your betrothed murdered?"

The girl was not surprised. She had been captive longer than she expected. "I cannot begrudge the man his vengeance. I am not scared of him."

"Well you should. Wait here." Simba closed the door behind him.

In front of him stood the general, and his clan members, a dozen or so, bearing torches and steel. He was calm as usual, and soft spoken, but the tone in his voice showed he meant what he said. "Deliver her to us, so that we may heal."

"Revenge has been carried out, general. The man who struck down Taonga met my spear. My prisoner here did not slay your son."

"In battle, one enemy's smeared spear smears all."

"I swore to her protection. Without her, Comrade Chengetaii and myself would be dead, your heir, the son of your king. I owe her my life, so you should too. I owe her a fair trial, before the king, elders and ancestors."

"Where is this trial? How long must a father wait for his justice? How long must our ancestors? For a moon I have not slept, my sleep disturbed by cries from beyond. 'Avenge your son' they say, 'avenge our Shato.'" He pointed his spear at the door. "You just want to fuck her. If that's what you desire, quench your lust and be done with it, but do not stand in the way of our justice."

The general and Simba stared each other down for a good moment before the grieving father succumbed to the prince's resolve, turned, and walked away with his clan in his trails. "Do not think this is the end of it."

When their torches had disappeared in the distance, Simba returned into the hut. "You can't stay here. You will be safe at the Lion's Den. I will personally keep guard of you tonight, and tomorrow before morning break, I will spirit you out."

The girl looked at Simba peculiarly, like she couldn't quite understand him. "Why are you doing this?"

"Because it is the right thing to do."

There was one mat in the chamber so Simba slept on the cold floor. There was one hide, so the girl could hear the prince shivering as he tried to sleep. "Get up and join me here, unless you want to freeze to death."

"I can't."

"Why not?"

"Well, you are a girl. We are not, you know? Married."

The girl laughed. "I won't tell anyone if you don't."

"I believe you, but the ancestors, they see all." With that the prince turned his body away from her and closed his eyes. Before long, the cold had seeped into his bones, and his side was bruised from the stone floor. When he turned back toward her, and found her lifting the hide with a welcome, it was too much to deny. "Just this once," he ceded, slipping into her warmth.

"You're so cold," she said as his body rubbed on hers. "Here, like this." She took an arm and helped it around her body. She was warm, and Simba could hear her soft breathing. She turned around and met his eyes, grabbed his hand and laid it on her breast. He could feel her nipple, and gasped a moment later when it grew between his fingers. He snatched his hand away. "What's wrong?"

"It's nothing, just want to sleep that's all."

She thought for a second then realized: "You've never been with a woman before have you?"

"Of course I have," the prince lied. Between the twins, the younger had been the more adventurous of the two.

"Then you know what to do with this." Simba closed his eyes and gasped, as did she when his finger entered her. The girl rose, as did the prince, but she pushed him onto his back, threw his loincloth to the side and mounted him. "As I said, prince, I won't tell anyone if you don't."

Simba rose first. It was still dark. "Wake up," he whispered. He exited the room and returned with a bag with provisions for their excursion. The girl smiled when she was reacquainted with her axe. He gave her a cloth to cover her head and shoulders and off they went. The Stone Houses was still asleep, and the Hippo Valley thoroughfare was quiet before day broke and commerce commenced.

It was an hour or two of silence as they rode. "Simba, what's that in the distance?" Before the prince could answer, an arrow appeared in the clouds before it landed by the girl's zebra's galloping feet. Another arrow flew past her head.

"General Shato's henchmen," Simba muttered, between gritted teeth. He realized it was quite naïve to think that they could escape completely undetected by the general's spies. Another arrow zipped past, but Simba realized they weren't aiming for him – only the girl. "I have a plan." The prince jumped off the zebra to the girl's surprise and waited in the bush. As the Shato men charged after the girl, his boomerang hit one's chest knocking him off his zebra. The prince came out from the bush and readied himself as the second henchman galloped his way. At the last moment, he produced his club and in one motion, sent the rider crashing onto the earth. He refastened the club onto his back and whistled. When the girl and his zebra returned, the men were pinioned to a tree, and their zebras sent back to the Stone Houses. "They shouldn't trouble us anymore." The prince hopped onto his beast, pulled the reigns, kicked and off they went toward the Lion's Den.

After a good ride, they were a good distance away from Hippo Valley. By the zebra's yips, Simba knew it was time to let them rest. He found a good location next to the Khumalo and hopped off his zebra. He tried to help the girl off, but she preferred to do it herself. He pulled out breakfast from his sack, dried fish, some fruits and sour milk. They were joking and laughing when suddenly the prince began to scream. "Army ants," he raved. "They're in my loincloth." He was only relieved when he jumped into the Khumalo. The girl could not stop laughing. "Aren't you going to join me? So I can shut your mouth."

"I don't know if that is a good idea."

"Why not?"

"I don't know. Something might be in there."

"Like what? The nyaminyami?" he jested. "There is nothing for you in here to fear." He dove in and returned to the surface after a few moments. "The creatures of the aquatic fear me. I am the blood of the hippo."

"Indeed you are." The girl with no name took off her loincloth and placed it on a stone nearby. Her body was a wonder to behold, her burnished bronze skin shining in the sun. One hand covered her private parts, the other her breasts as she felt the temperature with her toes.

"Spread your arms. I want to see all of it." She did as told and slipped into the water. They kissed and embraced as the current swept past them toward the great water where only the sparrows go. His hands cupped her breast and then spent some time on her stomach and the crack on her back.

She purred like a cat. "Miri'Ya. My name is Miri'Ya."

The prince repeated the name as his lips brushed her soft cheeks.

"I have not been completely honest with you. I was truthful about being the daughter of a king. I was also truthful about coming to Hippo Valley to hunt. However, I didn't tell you what we were hunting. In order for my father to consolidate his kingdom, there is one more thing he needs to do . . . find a certain something which holds the key to powers you cannot fathom." She ran her nose down his neck and sniffed. "I knew it the first time I saw you. I could smell you. You truly do have the blood of the hippo – powers."

"Powers to do what?" His hands moved down, below her waist. Suddenly he stopped, discombobulated.

"Why, the old powers, the powers of the river gods. Many years ago a child was spirited into the realm of man, the last hope of our enemies. The prophecies say that a prince, pure of heart, with the blood of the hippo will befriend that child, and under his guidance will the child will grow courageous and powerful and destroy us all. I cannot allow that to happen. Where is he, Simba?"

His hand slid under her waist as he untangled himself from her. It was smooth and left grime on the tip of his fingers that sent a chill through his spine. "What are you?"

"Do I have to answer that question for you, my prince?" Her mouth opened, revealing a row of razor sharp teeth.

She screeched and leapt forward.

THE END

About the Author

Born in Zimbabwe and raised internationally, the Stockholm-based writer suffered a series of artistic setbacks such as a failed school play directorial début, trying his hand at comic books, and writing short stories that mostly ended up in the dust bin. It all came together when he finally achieved a hundred or so pages, and from then, never looked back. Now he brings you 'Red Jacaranda Leaves', the first book in the series, 'The Rites of Passage'. To keep up with more of his success stories, follow him at:

http://www.curtissagwete.com

Tell-Tale Publishing would like to thank you for your purchase. If you would like to read more by this or other fine TT authors please visit us at:

http://www.tell-talepublishing.com